VINEYARDS Can Be *MURDER*

By: Tammy Wunsch

Copyright 2021©

Acknowledgements

I would like to thank my editors Elizabeth Upp, Gwen Sanchirico, and Susan Herrick. My work would not be as entertaining, engaging, and grammatically correct without their tireless efforts.

I would also like to thank all my wine-drinking friends, colleagues, and family who came out for the book signing of *Reunions Can Be Murder* at Hillyland Winery in Scotland, Connecticut. I look forward to seeing you again at the launch of this book, too!

If you have any suggestions for wines you would like to see in the next book, please send me a message via Facebook or an email to Tammy@TammyWunsch.com.

Check out the *About the Author* section at the end of the book for your free link to *The Holidays in Harmony.*

Author Note

The characters and locations in this novel are fictional and do not depict any persons either living or deceased. Any similarities are purely coincidental. While some events actually happened, the solutions presented are fictional and do not represent an actual hypothesis. Enjoy!

Table of Contents

Chapter One

"What was that noise?" Ricky demanded as I reached for my glass of chilled Milano Chardonnay. One of the best perks of working for Milano Importers is that I am entitled to three free bottles of wine from their warehouse every week. Milano Vineyards & Importers is owned by my friend Marco and the business is located on his family's local vineyard. I make sure I take my three bottles of wine every week, and at least two of them are usually Milano Vineyards wines to help promote the local economy (and protect my job). It's not a hardship – the wine is quite good.

I stopped with the glass half-raised to my mouth. "That was me. I'm not used to manual labor and every joint and muscle in my body aches." I grimaced. "Apparently, that noise was my body revolting from all the hard work."

I started working for Milano Importers three months ago. The company is an importer of high-quality wines, usually from newly discovered vineyards, and I am getting a whirlwind education in viticulture. Marco thought I had a good wine palate, but he also wanted to ensure that I was familiar with all aspects of the wine business. He put me to work at his family's vineyard, conveniently where the Milano Importers offices and warehouse are located.

Actually, Milano Vineyards & Importers was in the midst of a major upgrade and transformation. Marco ran the family vineyard, which helped make him relatable to small vineyard owners worldwide. He is expanding the current wine tasting room into a venue for large-scale events and adding a private wine tasting room.

It was all exciting, but as happens everywhere I suppose, there are construction delays.

I am still recovering from a vicious attack that occurred at my 20th high school reunion – and from earlier stab wounds from a hyped-up meth addict – so Marco started me in the Milano Vineyard tasting room. The original tasting room is about one-quarter of the size that it will be after the expansion, but still very functional and often very crowded. Massachusetts has its very own wine trail and Milano Vineyards is a popular spot on the trail...as I'm quickly learning. Its location high above Harmony harbor affords beautiful, sweeping views of the family's vineyards and the busy harbor below.

I thought that working in the tasting room would be a piece of cake – but I was sadly mistaken. My days consisted of standing on my feet for eight to ten hours at a time, walking up and down the stairs to the cellar for more cases of wine, cleaning tables, pouring wine tastings, and smiling at guests. I haven't smiled so much in my whole damn life. I am not a naturally outgoing person and it sometimes feels like torture to me to make small talk with random strangers. Of course, Marco thought this was hysterical and made me endure the tasting room for two whole months.

On the plus side, I've been learning a lot about customer service, wine tasting, and Milano Wines. Eventually, my job will include assisting Marco with sourcing new wines to import, as well as managing the tasting rooms and event space. Marco is currently in Peru meeting with the owners of some new, organic vineyards that he had heard about. He is hoping to be their exclusive U.S. distributor. That is the part of my new job that I am really looking forward to – traveling and evaluating small vineyards to determine if their wines fit in with the Milano Importers' wine catalog.

Marco hadn't been very clear on exactly what I would do and how much time I would spend on each facet of the position, but it had sounded interesting and worth pursuing. It certainly beat sitting at home, collecting disability, and waiting to die. All I knew was that it would include travel and wine and that sounded good to me. Did I mention wine?

I've also spent some time in the wine cellar and the wine caves. I frequently explored the wine cellar on my lunch break. It was interesting to walk through the old bottles and soak up the history. I loved wandering down through the tunnels into the vast caves, which maintained a constant underground temperature of 68 degrees. The caves were vast and the temperature was constant. I only went down the main tunnel when I was alone, though. It was very easy to get lost if you didn't know your way around. Marco told me that the tunnel network twisted down into Harmony and that the tunnels were originally used by bootleggers and pirates. I think he was just trying to impress me, though, but who knows? This area was a rich spot for pirates back in the 1600s so it may be true.

For the next week or two, I would also be working in the fields. Labor Day had just passed – it had been a busy weekend at the tasting room – and that meant that the grape harvest was fast approaching. The vineyard manager, Pierre Berger, has been

3

teaching me how to determine when the grapes are ready to harvest and it is fascinating. I never realized the science that goes into crafting a good bottle of wine.

I've also spent some time with Giovanni Brunello, Milano Vineyard's general manager, learning about the administrative aspects of running a vineyard. I met Giovanni at a wine tasting at my high school reunion and he's a lot of fun – when he isn't crunching numbers and wrangling employee schedules. Despite having lived in the United States for twenty years, his Italian accent is still quite heavy and I sometimes have a difficult time understanding him. I'm amazed at everything Giovanni has to manage, like permits, health inspections, labor laws, human resource issues, and a million other things. It seems overwhelming to me.

Hi! I'm Kat Snow and I'm the new Assistant Manager at Milano Vineyard & Importers. I've been called Kat for most of my life – I was Katrina for a brief period until Hurricane Katrina put an end to that – and I currently live in Harmony, Massachusetts. I served two tours in the army in the Military Police and then worked for the BPD, also known as the Boston Police Department. I worked my way up to Detective and was assigned to Homicide. I loved the job until a meth addict in Roxbury ambushed and stabbed me ten times, nearly killing me. Part of one lung had to be removed, but I've been making a steady recovery in physical therapy. I can now walk a whole mile without getting winded. I had a slight setback three months ago at my 20th high school reunion, but that's another story.

I moved back to Harmony after my mother passed and my friends and I refurbished her dilapidated cottage. I sold her dive bar, The Harbor Bar, to one of my high school friends, Chance Wolf. Well, friends might have been wishful thinking in high school, but we're friends now. He and his sister Hope have been converting The Harbor into a wine bar and coffee shop called Two Cups for more than four months now. They had finally been cleared to open and Chance was planning a soft opening for friends and family later in the week.

Between exhaustion from my new job and Chance's never-ending bar renovation, we haven't had many opportunities to hang out since our high school reunion. Despite the multiple murders and mayhem there, it had brought Chance into my life – and that had possibilities for becoming *something* – though nothing had happened yet.

On the other hand, there was also Marco to consider. He gave me a great new job, but he had also been flirty at the reunion. And now? Nothing. The reunion had been a traumatic weekend with death and destruction around every corner. I thought that high school was tough but let me tell you, reunions can be murder.

Chapter Two

Fortunately for me, my two best friends, Ricky and Syd, also lived in Harmony. Harmony, if you've never visited, is about an hour northeast of Boston. Syd and her husband Ty had been high school sweethearts. They are that rare couple that actually made that work. Syd is an artist and gifted with both creativity and an abundance of energy. In addition to creating her own watercolor paintings, she owns a gallery in downtown Harmony and runs a graphic design business. She and Ty came back to Harmony from Providence when Ty got hired as Chief of Police two years ago. Their three kids were amazing and I loved hanging out with them – when they have the time.

Ricky is a genius. I mean it. He is literally a genius – and every Asian stereotype you could fit into one person, plus more. He graduated from MIT, was headhunted by just about every tech company you've ever heard of, and now owns a digital gaming company that created a wildly successful MMORPG (Massive Multiplayer Online Role-Playing Game, for the uninformed) called *Call of the Wild*. He's still single, too, but he's gay so he's not a dating option. I've happily settled into the role of his gal pal – unless he wants to go out in drag. Then I stay home. My ego can't handle hanging with a guy who is prettier and more feminine than me.

Call of the Wild made Ricky tremendously wealthy and he purchased a beautiful three-bedroom condo in the refurbished marina on the harbor. Ricky, Syd, and I usually hang out on his balcony and drink wine. There are not many problems in this world that an ocean breeze can't fix. And wine. Wine fixes many problems, too. We couldn't hang out at Syd's house because she always has a few of her paintings in progress and it is difficult to find a place to sit. My house has a nice view of the harbor – but Ricky's was still better. We can actually hear the water lapping at the boats in the marina and there were always interesting people walking around.

I was looking forward to working in the vineyard even though I knew it was going to be very tough work. There would be a lot of bending, stretching, and lifting and I wasn't *really* sure if my body could handle it yet. I would give it the old college try, though – not that I ever went to college.

Marco had been very generous and patient with me, so I decided that if the vineyard needed help during the crush, which is how many vineyards refer to the harvest, then I would do my best to help out. I had learned a lot from Pierre about the various wines produced at Milano Vineyards and the Brix, which is a very important component in determining if wine is ready to be harvested. I'll describe more about Brix later, but basically it is the sugar content of grapes.

When I think about the calculations needed to determine the correct Brix and harvest time and temperatures, my head hurts. At least the headache kind of distracts me from my everyday aches and pains.

They say that misery loves company, so despite my aches, I went ahead and joined The Mercury with Ricky. The Mercury is a hot, trendy gym that Cal Jr., a former classmate, owns. Ricky had won a membership for two at our high school reunion. That was another good thing to come out of that weekend, but I didn't always feel that way after a strenuous workout with Cal Jr.

Ricky had coerced me into joining The Mercury with him and I regretted it almost every time we worked out. I did notice that my stamina was increasing – but I'd never admit that to Ricky or to Cal Jr. Ricky was assigned to Rajesh, a tall, well-built Indian guy who Cal Jr. had met through some Dollywood production he had consulted on. Rajesh was hot. I have to admit, I got a little tingly when I watched him flex.

Cal Jr. insisted that he had to be my trainer. I think I was supposed to be grateful, but I usually felt somewhere between irritated and creeped out. Cal Jr. had graduated with me and we had reconnected at our high school reunion. After high school, he became a celebrity trainer when he moved out to Los Angeles after apprenticing with one of the big-name trainers out there.

Cal Jr. was the son of my former high school's football coach. While Cal Sr. had aged to a giant mound of flabby muscle, Cal Jr. kept himself in peak physical condition. He had come back to Harmony two years ago and his prestigious gym already boasted a six-month waiting list to join. Word on the street is that he was going to franchise The Mercury – maybe then I would find a more sympathetic trainer. He was ruthless with my workout regimen and then would creepily ask me out as I stood there panting and sweating all over the place. I always felt dirty after a conversation – or a workout – with Cal Jr. I wanted to quit the gym, but I had promised Ricky and Marco that I would stick it out. I just hoped that Cal Jr. became tired of training me, and would move on to his next obsession.

Back to my work situation: I think I'm going to miss working in the tasting room, which is kind of strange because, I think I mentioned, I'm not a very social person. I've made friends with some of the staff there and that has been good for me. I needed to expand my social circle and get out more. Syd is my best friend, but she is married and frequently engaged in whatever it is that married couples do. I can sometimes count on Ricky, but he is a hot gay man with a sense of style and a flair for finding adventures – and adventurous paramours. I didn't always want to participate in his escapades.

We had just opened the tasting room for the day when a group of five women entered. I could tell just by looking at them that they were a bridal party, out for a day of fun, wine, and probably more wine. Usually, I was fine with these bridal party groups, depending on the age and maturity of the ladies. These ladies were in their late 20s and had a youthful exuberance that I vaguely remembered from my past. The bride was clearly marked with a sparkly sash that read "BRIDE." The other ladies with her were all wearing a shirt or dress in a fuchsia color, so I could guess the primary color of the wedding.

I had woken up on the wrong side of the bed this morning and I was still a little cranky. I was not in the mood to deal with a bunch of twenty-something women who were all excited about marriage and babies. I sent a silent prayer to the universe that they would go to Justina's station, but, as fate would have it, they found their way to mine. Justina tried not to smirk as she caught my eye, but I could tell she thought it was funny and silently vowed to get her back later.

"Hey!" yelled out one of the bridal party members as I made my way over to them. I pasted my fake smile on and mustered my energy. "Hi! How can I help you today?" I asked, as if I didn't know what they wanted. Many people love to tell you things that are really very obvious, and they seemed like that type of group.

"Hey!" the self-elected leader of the group shouted again, despite the fact that it wasn't very loud in the tasting room. "We're here for my friend Kim's wedding shower. We would like to have a tasting for six, but we'll just use the tasting notes at our table. No need to waste time on our party." I wasn't sure if I should be insulted or if she was being generous. "We are just playing at wine tasting anyway." She smiled and I resolved that she was being generous. "We'll decide what wines we like best and then get a few bottles." She pointed to a large picnic basket. "We brought some food for when we're drinking the bottles, is that OK?"

I instantly liked this girl. In fact, she was my new favorite customer. I wouldn't have to spend an hour with the bridal party, reviewing wine tasting etiquette and our wine list. Also, we always allowed people to bring in food because we didn't serve any yet, but it was always nice when people asked. Sometimes they even shared their food with us, which was even better. These women looked like they would share their food. My mood slightly improved.

"Absolutely," I said brightly and handed over the laminated sheet which had all the Milano wines listed along with a brief description. Of the ten wines we produced, customers could pick from a variety of tasting options - five wines for $10.00; seven wines for $12; or all ten wines for $15. I always tried to determine who was driving to ensure they maintained some degree of sobriety.

Each of the girls opted for the five-wine tasting, which was smart in a large group. You could always share tastings and try them all. I set up glasses for everybody and began pouring.

I saw Pierre enter through the patio door and stalk across the tasting room, trailed by Max. They appeared to be arguing as they reached the door to the cellar stairs. I could still hear hushed, angry voices as they descended.

Justina looked at me and cocked an eyebrow. I shrugged my shoulders and turned back to the bridal party. They all turned out to be nice ladies, which was a welcome change from many of the bridal parties I had served since working here. They finished their tasting, ordered three bottles of Milano Chardonnay – aged in French oak and very buttery – and went to sit at a large table by the open doors to the patio.

That table had the best view – you could see the harbor, the rolling hills, and the vineyard, making you feel as though you were in Italy. One of the ladies brought out the huge picnic basket and passed out plates and silverware. Then they brought out the food and my mouth started watering. It smelled delicious. Kim, the bride, brought over two plates that were overflowing with food, and Justina and I thanked her profusely.

I kept an eye on the bridal party as more people came in and I got busy serving tastings and answering questions. At one point, the friendly girl who was the spokesperson for the bridal party – I found out her name was Samantha – came over and ordered four more bottles of wine. She also brought over some heavenly chocolate lava cupcakes that were somehow still warm, but I digress. Samantha gushed about how delicious the wine was compared to some of the other wineries in Massachusetts and how she would definitely be ordering a few cases for her own wine cellar. I smiled politely and then asked who was driving. Samantha giggled a little. "I understand why you're asking," she said. "We actually hired a minivan to drive us around today so we didn't have to worry about someone being the designated driver." I nodded in approval and again thought more highly of these women as I saw Kim, the bride, bring out a plate of food and a bottle of water to their driver for the day.

As the day went on, the bridal party ladies left for another vineyard and we stayed busy. It was a beautiful day in northeastern Massachusetts and people were certainly out enjoying it. For the most part, everyone who came in was in a good mood and treated me well. I practiced my people skills and finally took my lunch break around three o'clock.

I walked over to the employee break room, opened the staff refrigerator, and pulled out my brown bag lunch. I looked at my boring ham sandwich and apple and thought back to that delicious plate of food I had devoured earlier. I wasn't really hungry, so I stuffed the bag back into the refrigerator. Tomorrow's lunch, I thought.

Chapter Three

I sank onto the sofa in the staff room and put my feet up. I swear I heard them sigh in relief. I smiled as I remembered last night's dinner. Chance had finally been able to take a break from the renovations and had tried out a few potential recipes for me that he wanted to serve at Two Cups. If all the food at Two Cups tasted that good, I would be eating there a lot.

He had prepared a mouth-watering dish of homemade orecchiette pasta with grilled chicken, broccoli florets, cranberries, goat cheese (from Taylor's Goat Farm outside of town), and sage cream. Massachusetts is famous for its cranberry bogs so they feature in a lot of local dishes. He had also baked some fresh focaccia bread. He paired the pasta with the 50 by 50 of Carneros Rosé of Pinot Noir. He informed me that the 50 by 50 brand was started by the bassist of Devo, which I thought was very interesting. For dessert, he whipped up a traditional chocolate mousse with homemade whipped cream and a fresh berry compote. He elected to stay with the 50 by 50 brand, so we sipped their Sonoma Coast Pinot Noir which was a medium-bodied, delicate balance of fruit, oak, and acidity.

I had no idea he was such a good cook. "When did you have time to learn how to cook? That was amazing!" I accidentally hiccupped a quiet little burp.

Chance grinned. "I'm glad you enjoyed the food." He was currently living in the apartment located above Two Cups. I had spent a fair amount of time up there when my mother owned the bar.

14

I remembered it more as a place for her to sleep off her alcoholic hazes before driving us home, but Chance had fixed it up nicely. There was a new bay window with a nice view of the harbor and he had configured the living area as an open loft space. "After college, but before law school, I took a year off and worked as a sous chef at the Boston Harbor Hotel. It was a lot of fun, but definitely made me decide I didn't want to be a chef." He looked out the window. "I then applied to law school and spent the next fifteen years either studying or practicing law." He shrugged. "Until I got bored with that."

"Are you planning to do the cooking at Two Cups?" I asked.

He shook his head. "No. I actually hired this guy I used to work with at the Boston Harbor Hotel. His name is Chops."

"Chops?"

"It's a nickname, obviously. His real name is Winston Chopin the Third. He came from money and went to a boarding school where everyone called him Winnie – you can see why he prefers Chops. He had his own restaurant for a while but hated dealing with all the administrative tasks and the Health Department. He tried catering, too, but didn't like having to always hustle for new clients. He jumped at the opportunity to come work for me." He laughed quietly.

"What?" I asked.

"He's a funny guy – I'll leave it at that. You'll like him." He looked at me. "He's coming tomorrow to help me finalize the menu and put the finishing touches on the kitchen. I think we will finally be ready to open next week, if the building inspector approves."

"If your menu is going to be anything like what you served me tonight, I'll be a frequent diner – well, as long as I continue working out."

"You are perfect as you are, Kat," he winked at me and my heart fluttered a little. "Don't let those gym-freaks convince you otherwise."

"Thanks," I said quietly, looking up at him from my stool at the island counter where we had dined. He rubbed my back gently then stopped abruptly, got up, and cleared the plates. He busied himself in the kitchen and refilled our wine glasses. When he finished loading the dishwasher, we wandered over to the couch that provided the best view through the bay window.

Everything with Chance was still in the friend zone and I wasn't sure where we were headed, if anywhere. Three months ago, at the reunion, both Chance and Marco has been very flirtatious with me. Syd decided that they were both interested in me romantically, however, nothing has come to pass with either of them besides a brief back rub or peck on the cheek. Not even a friendly hug. In fact, Marco was more likely to lightly punch my shoulder than hug me. I wonder if that's the modern-day equivalent of dipping my pigtails in an inkwell?

I sighed as thoughts of Marco flitted through my brain. I had been working at Milano Importers for three months now and spent a lot of time with Marco. We have done numerous wine tastings to refine my palate. He even had me build a wine aroma box as he wanted that to be an event we could offer when all the construction was finally complete. In that time, we had consumed *a lot* of wine. Nothing had happened with him either. I didn't know what to think, except I was pretty sure that neither of them was interested in me romantically.

I won't tell Syd, but I have to admit, that makes me a little sad.

Chapter Four

I finished my lunch break and passed Pierre in the hallway as I was heading back to my station. He looked distracted and I had to tap him on the shoulder to get his attention. He waved his hand at me and walked away instead of replying to my question about today's Brix levels. A moment later, Max came out from the backroom and trailed Pierre out to the vineyard. His face was red and he looked upset. I went behind the tasting room bar and sidled over to Justina.

"Any idea what that fight was about?" I inquired. Justina usually had the inside information on everything that happened at the vineyard.

Justina shook her head. "Those two are always fighting. I don't think that Max agrees with Pierre about when the grapes should be harvested."

"What?" I almost screeched. "Max is an intern who is just learning the business. How dare he question Pierre with his lifetime of experience?"

Justina nodded. "I know, but Max does have a lot of experience, too. His grandfather owns a small vineyard in Germany and Max spent time there during school breaks. Plus, he's getting his degree in viticulture. He thinks he knows more than Pierre because Pierre doesn't have a degree."

I shook my head at Max's arrogance. Pierre was originally from France but had lived here for almost thirty years. He had probably forgotten more about wine than I would ever learn. He used all the calculations as proof, but he also used his gut to guide him in the grape-picking, decision-making process.

I sputtered, "First of all, the countries' winemaking strategies are completely different. Each vineyard is unique, from the terroir, the location where the grapes are grown, the winemaker, and many other factors. Brix is just one of many considerations." I threw my hands up in the air for emphasis.

Justina just chuckled. "God, now *you're* starting to sound like Marco." She walked back to her station as a group approached. I cleaned and stocked my station to get ready for the evening rush. We usually got pretty busy after five when people got off work and wanted to end the day with wine. For me, that's every day. There is a pretty even split between people coming in for tastings, people buying wine to drink at the vineyard, and people buying wine to stock up for the week ahead.

The time flew by and suddenly it was eight o'clock and I was getting ready to go home. Justina had just finished cleaning her station and wiping the tables on the patio while I finished up at the tasting room tables. She walked over and asked, "Any plans tonight?"

I smiled. "Yeah, Syd, Amelia, Sunny, Ricky, and I are getting together at Ricky's for dinner. He's supposed to cook, but I'm sure he'll just pick something up. He loses track of time when he's programming new levels for *Call of the Wild II*. The release date is coming up and he's a perfectionist. I haven't even made it to level 10 in *Call of the Wild I*, yet, but Ty's kids have mastered level

24." I shrugged. "Tonight should be fun. I haven't seen any of them in two weeks."

Justina smiled conspiratorially at me, "We didn't get to chat much earlier. Do you have any gossip for me?"

Justina and I are usually on the same shifts so we shared a lot about our personal lives. She was aware of the time I spent with both Marco and Chance – and aware that nothing had happened with either of them. When you work closely with people, especially in a service environment, you tend to forge a close, even if temporary, relationship. Justina and I had gone out for drinks a few times and she is a lot of fun. She is only 30 years old though and, while an eight-year difference isn't much for adults, it sometimes feels as wide as the Grand Canyon. I often felt like her dowdier, less fun, way older sister.

I shook my head. "Nope, nothing to report. Last night was just dinner and wine."

"What is up with that man? And Marco, too?" Justina slouched into a chair.

Again, I threw my hands up in the air. That was becoming a habit I didn't particularly like. "I don't know. Both of them can be a little flirty, but when it comes to taking it to the next level, they both turn away or find something else to do. Chance started washing dishes rather than take a step forward with our relationship. Frankly, I'm beginning to think I'm not as attractive as I once thought I was."

Justine laughed out loud. "You're plenty cute, Kat," she said. "Men are just clueless sometimes. I think I am going to snoop around and see what I can find out."

"No," I practically screamed. "I don't want anyone to know how frustrated I am with the both of them."

Justina nodded. "Don't you worry, Kat. I can be discreet."

I started to argue then clamped my mouth shut. I knew that the more I protested, the more adamant she would become about her little mission. Maybe if I stopped arguing, she would just forget.

We walked out of the employee entrance together and over to our cars. We were the last people to leave the vineyard and I was exhausted.

Marco's grandfather had built dormitory housing and Milano Vineyard hired interns every summer from overseas to come to learn the wine business and help with the harvest. The interns earned a stipend as well as free room and board. They also spent a summer near the ocean and close to Boston. The internship program was a smart way to promote the Milano brand and forge ties with potential future winemakers.

I looked toward the intern dorm before I got in my car. The six interns were seated around the fire pit drinking, laughing, and having a good time. I saw that Giovanni was with them and looked around for Pierre. As vineyard manager, he spent a lot of time with the interns and liked to show that he could be one of them. Actually, he *had* been one of them 35 years earlier, when Marco's grandfather started the exchange program. I didn't see him around the fire, though.

I drove down the vineyard's long driveway toward Route 1A and saw Pierre sitting on the side deck of his house. As the vineyard manager, he was given use of the carriage house on the vineyard. He had hosted a small dinner party a few weeks ago and invited me along with Marco, Justina, and Justina's boyfriend, Claude. The food was wonderful and I got to see the inside of the historic house, which had been built in the 1800s as an actual carriage house. When I was younger, Syd and I used to go to open houses and pretend we were "in the market," so I had a lot of experience evaluating original versus phony historic features.

The carriage house was a two-story structure that had once been used to store Marco's great-grandparents' actual carriages. It had been converted into a cozy home, perfect for one or two people. The craftsmanship that had been put into the home was exquisite. Even the staircase leading to the second floor was adorned with a beautiful bronze finial in the shape of an eagle. I remarked on its beauty and Pierre told me it was a family heirloom that he had brought over from France. I remember thinking how beautiful it was, even if it was a little out of place in a converted carriage house in Harmony.

The house was decorated very nicely with lots of museum-quality prints that were framed and illuminated carefully to showcase the art. There was an eclectic mix of prints from both Impressionist and Baroque painters, which seemed an odd assortment of styles to me. Not that I'd ever be able to afford an original period painting, nor probably even one of these nicely framed prints; I just preferred museums with strictly classical collections as opposed to modern art. Syd says it's because I have an old soul.

Pierre's art collection was rounded out with a lifetime of wine memorabilia, such as grape harvesting tools, tiles from different vineyards, and a variety of pricey – empty – wine bottles that I assume he had personally consumed. His choice of art seemed out of character, as I had heard him openly disparage even French Old Masters as being overrated when some of the interns were discussing visiting Boston museums. I remember him saying that spending money on art was wasteful – when people should instead be purchasing exquisite wine. He called museums cultural thieves whose collections were ripped from their native homelands. Pierre could be quite passionate about his beliefs at times.

He was also a superb cook and made a beef bourguignon that was out of this world. He paired it with one of the Milano Cabernet Sauvignons and the five of us had a great evening. Claude was originally from France and he and Pierre had some type of debate in French that was spoken so quickly, I didn't even try to use my high school French lessons to decipher it.

As I drove by that evening, I saw Pierre scowling and he didn't acknowledge my wave. I wondered what had gotten him so upset.

Chapter Five

I went home and showered quickly to wash off the wine that somehow managed to get everywhere on my body when I worked in the tasting room. Plus, I had spent some time out in the vineyard during the heat of the day and I was a little sweaty.

After pulling myself together, I dashed over to Ricky's house. I walked through the door, looked out to the balcony, and saw that everyone else had already arrived. Damn! I hated being last and getting stuck with the rickety chair.

Sunny had recovered from her near-fatal attack she suffered at the reunion. She was back to work at Sunny Side Up, the bakery and tearoom she owned on Market Street. I know her staff had used her recipes while she was recuperating, but the pastries just tasted better when she made them herself. I was glad to see her – that meant fresh pastries for dessert!

Amelia looked very upbeat this evening. She was still grieving the loss of her husband, but had thrown herself wholeheartedly into her real estate business. There wasn't a bus bench or billboard in town that didn't have her face plastered across it. We all grieve in different ways and Amelia had obviously decided to move forward with hard work.

They all gave me dirty looks and Syd pointed at her watch. Okay, I was a little late, but just my standard ten minutes. I glanced at the wall clock as I walked by. Whoops! Better make that twenty minutes late today. I put the wine I had brought into Ricky's wine fridge. Now that I worked at a vineyard, I had made all my friends

25

buy proper wine fridges so our wine would always be served at the correct temperature. I was becoming a wine snob but I was not about to apologize for wanting my wine the way it was supposed to be served.

Ricky started unpacking four large bags of food which seemed like enough to feed a small army. I slid onto the creaky chair on the balcony and reached for the glass of wine that Syd had generously poured for me when I walked in the door. She may be annoyed that I was tardy, but she always took care of my wine needs. I must have made an audible sigh of contentment as I sank down on the chair, balancing myself so as not to topple over – I had seen it happen on this very balcony. Ricky laughed and then he looked at me quizzically. "Are you more sore from working out at The Mercury or from your job at the vineyard?" I took a large gulp of wine and thought it was good that Marco wasn't here to chastise my wine etiquette.

"Both!" I quipped and everyone chuckled.

I noticed that Ricky had turned the bags so I couldn't see the name of the restaurant where the food had come from. Amelia was helping him by quickly distributing the containers around the table. The obfuscation was obviously intentional – Ricky never could be coy and Amelia was trying too hard not to look guilty. Of course, this subterfuge only triggered my detective senses, and I leaned in, on the hunt for the truth. "That smells delicious. Where did you get the food from, Ricky?" I asked, with a sarcastic lilt to my voice. I had my suspicions as to where he had purchased the food.

Ricky wouldn't make eye contact with me. I surveyed the labeled packages of gruyère macaroni and cheese, roasted brown butter sage chicken, sautéed brussels sprouts, and honey-glazed carrots. Ricky continued to look anywhere but at me. Finally, he stammered, "Kat, I know I promised, or said, that I wouldn't give her my business, but I was running late today, too." He risked a glance in my direction and quickly looked away again, "I was rushing through Harmony Court, you know, where all the food trucks park?"

"I love it there," Amelia interjected. "I take clients there all the time. The tables in the Court are nicely spread out and there's a fantastic view of the harbor. The food variety is incredible and there are usually some buskers during the day for entertainment. The bands that play on the weekend nights are top-notch, too."

Sunny nodded. "I've been thinking of setting up a small kiosk at the Court. There are currently no dessert offerings and I think it would be a great way to attract more business."

Ricky sighed and realized he couldn't put it off any longer. "Yeah, well, I ran into Mindy."

I knew it was coming, still, when he uttered *that name*, my eyebrows arched so high that I think they hit my hairline. "Mindy?" I screeched. "Mindy?" I repeated at an even higher octave.

Mindy Vanderbilt has been, and always will be, my arch-nemesis, if a normal human being can make that claim. She had been horrible to me throughout high school and, now that I moved back to Harmony, has continued to be horrible to me. The things she said

27

to me at our high school reunion a few months ago still rang in my ears. How could somebody still be a mean high school girl after 20 years?

I glanced at Amelia. She and I had definitely not been friends in high school. In fact, she and Mindy had been in the same clique. Amelia had rediscovered religion, or at least spirituality, and we had bonded at the reunion due to some traumatic events. Now, a few short months later, I count her as a very close friend.

Ricky still wouldn't meet my eyes. He sighed dejectedly. "Well, Mindy has set up a little kiosk at the Court. There weren't a lot of choices because most of the day food trucks had already sold out and left. None of the night food trucks had shown up yet."

I looked at him with confusion. "What do you mean day food trucks and night food trucks? The same trucks aren't there all the time?"

Amelia shook her head. "No. I was at the Town Council meeting when the Court was accepting applications from vendors. There were far too many applications to fit them all in that space, so we split the vendors into day and night shifts. It has worked out great and everyone seems to be making good money and happy with the compromise."

Ricky sighed theatrically, "Right. So, she wanted to go home and I got these four full bags of food for only $25." He inhaled the food aromas. "Say what you will about Mindy, she does make good food."

I inhaled and grudgingly agreed, however, I silently vowed not to enjoy a single bite. Tonight, we were starting with the Milano Pinot Grigio that perfectly complemented the brown butter sage chicken. Nothing makes me happier than hanging out with my friends. Or, should I say, hanging out and drinking wine with my friends?

We laughed and talked in that way you can only do with people you've known most of your life. Syd and I had grown up next to each other and Ricky was a natural addition when we met him in high school. Even when we grew up and moved away, getting an email, a text, or Snapchat from either of them always made me smile and could break my bleakest mood.

At one a.m., Syd and I packed up – yes, I took some leftovers – and walked down to our cars. Amelia and Sunny had left at midnight. We chatted about our plans for the weekend. Weekends were the busiest time for the tasting room, so I usually ended up working both Saturday and Sunday.

I mentioned earlier that Syd owns a gallery. It's located in the part of the harbor that used to be run down – not too far from where my mother's bar was located. It's now a chic neighborhood with cute shops, cafés, and a new wine bar. Syd also worked most weekends because that's when the tourists poured into our little town. She mentioned that Ty was barbecuing on Sunday evening before the kids went back to school and invited me to join them. I agreed because, if I haven't already mentioned it, I don't really like to cook for myself. Syd smiled and asked if I could bring some wine. "Sure," I replied. "Red or white?"

"Some of each, please. Ty bought a new grill and he wants to barbecue a variety of different meats. So far, he has decided to cook a brisket, chicken wings, and a few steaks. I'm trying to decide what to serve with all that meat. Any suggestions?

"I don't need anything other than all that meat," I exclaimed and began to salivate.

"Cal Jr. doesn't have you on some stupid diet, does he?" she inquired suspiciously.

I hastily shook my head. "No, but *I* would like to lose five or ten pounds and cutting back on carbs always helps me do that."

Syd shook her head. "You're incredible just as you are, Kat. If Marco and Chance don't see that, well, they can both jump off the harbor pier." She stamped her foot for emphasis.

"This doesn't have anything to do with Marco or Chance. I think my side would feel better if I weighed a little less."

Syd looked at me disbelievingly. "Do *I* need to have a chat with Chance and Marco?

"Absolutely not!" I shouted and then looked around to see if anyone had heard. After all, it was after midnight and voices carried over the water. I could see Two Cups across the harbor and slightly to the left from Ricky's condo. The lights were on in the upstairs apartment so Chance must have finished working for the night. I wondered if he was cooking dinner for someone else tonight. "Look," I explained in what I hoped was a convincing tone. "It's

30

fine if neither of them is interested in me romantically. I'm not even sure I'm ready for a relationship."

Syd shook her head. "I call B.S. Guys can be such jerks. They were so flirty with you at the reunion and now, nothing. I don't get it."

I chuckled. "Me neither, Syd. You're lucky you found Ty back in high school. Guys change as they get older. They're hard to read, or maybe I just have less patience for the conflicting signals."

Syd nodded knowingly. "I'm thankful every day that I never really had to endure the dating scene. I hate watching you go through it, Kat."

"It's not dating if you're just hanging with friends and employers," I shrugged and Syd just sighed.

We hugged and then each of us got in our cars and drove away.

Chapter Six

The next morning, I drove slowly up the long, winding driveway to work. I shuddered as I thought – not for the first time that morning – that the last bottle of wine we had consumed last night had not been such a good idea. As I passed Pierre's carriage house, I saw the door was ajar and I thought that was a little odd. Pierre was usually the first person out in the vineyard, checking the grapes every day, but maybe he had run home for some reason.

Sundays usually started a little slower – I think other people were like me and didn't need to start drinking early in the morning. It was eleven o'clock when I arrived for my shift. The only thing that made me smile a little was seeing that Justina was in even worse shape than me. Do we have any hope for the future when these twenty-somethings can't even hold their liquor? Justina was serving a wine tasting to a mother and daughter and the rest of the tasting room was empty.

It was an overcast day so it could go one of two ways. If it stayed overcast, we were likely to be busy because people didn't trust the weather and usually canceled their outdoor plans, leaving them to plan an indoor activity. Wine tasting was great on a cloudy day. If it actually rained, we were generally slow, as people don't usually think of going to a vineyard in the rain.

I had my first wine tasting customers come in around 11:30. They were a couple who were on their honeymoon and touring New England. It was good for me because they only wanted to talk to each other and enjoy some wine. They finished their tasting, ordered a bottle of wine, and headed over to a table in the corner. I noticed they had a picnic lunch from Mindy's catering, so I knew they'd be there for a while.

A few more people trickled in, but it stayed slow until two o'clock when the skies opened up and the deluge started. Most of the people in the tasting room packed up and headed for the door. Justina and I started cleaning and prepared to close. We probably wouldn't get any more customers for the rest of the afternoon. The workers and interns from the vineyard also started trickling in. There wasn't much they could do in a rainstorm – especially a deluge like this.

I knew that Pierre worried about the grapes when it rained so heavily because we were so close to harvest. The smallest change could affect a grape's Brix and harvest time, and Pierre liked everything to be predictable. I expected to see him walk through the door with that grave look of concern I had grown accustomed to, but he never showed.

I called Max over when I saw him trudge through the tasting room doors. Max was a second-year intern with Milano Vineyards so he was the *de facto* head intern. He was enrolled in the MBA in Wine, Sustainability & Sales program at the University of Applied Sciences in Ludwigshafen am Rhein in Germany. "Where's Pierre?" I asked Max.

Max shrugged his shoulders nonchalantly, trying to hide his irritation. "I haven't seen or heard from him all day." He turned away abruptly and continued into the back room before I could ask a follow-up question.

I thought it was peculiar that Pierre had not been in contact with anyone at the vineyard today and then I recalled that his front door had been ajar when I drove by this morning. Justina and I were basically done for the day, but Marco liked us to stay until the official closing time in case some people came late. I made a snap decision.

"Justina," I called out. "I'm going to check on Pierre. He hasn't been in today and Max said he hasn't heard from him."

Justina cocked an eyebrow. "That's odd." She looked around the tasting room. "I'll finish cleaning in here. Let me know if Pierre needs anything and I'll stop in on my way home."

I nodded and grabbed my keys. Of course, I got completely soaked on my dash to my car through the deluge. I drove down the sloping, vineyard driveway to Pierre's house and pulled right up to the front door. His car was parked in the driveway and the front door was still slightly open.

I stepped cautiously through the door and was assailed by a strikingly pungent odor. It smelled like burnt garlic, smoke, and something else I couldn't quite put my finger on that danced at the edge of my memory. I called out Pierre's name as I ventured deeper into his house. I didn't hear a response so I made my way into the living room. As I mentioned before, Pierre's house is nicely decorated with lots of museum-quality prints. I stopped about five feet into the room and looked around with concern. The room had

34

been ransacked and was completely trashed. Couch cushions were torn open and chairs were knocked over, the upholstery in tatters. Most of the artwork had been torn off the walls. Most of the prints had been ripped and some were basically shredded. Instantly, that evasive scent came to me in what must have been a suppressed memory from my days in homicide. It was blood.

I stood rooted to the spot for a moment, torn as to whether I should look for what I thought would most likely be Pierre's body or whether I should just call Ty, Syd's husband and Chief of Police. Perhaps Pierre is merely injured, I thought wistfully. Be prepared, I admonished myself, as I drew my pistol from my concealed holster behind my back. As a former cop, I was almost always armed. I continued my cautious route through the house. I got to the kitchen and saw that whatever Pierre had been cooking was completely burnt in the pans. The food was unrecognizable, but strangely enough, the burners were turned off.

Having found no evidence of Pierre in either the living room, dining room, half bath, or kitchen, I warily approached the staircase. I hadn't been up there when I visited, and I *really* did not want to invade Pierre's privacy, but maybe Pierre was hurt and needed assistance.

As I climbed the stairway, I noticed that something was missing, though I couldn't put my finger on it. I reached the top of the stairs and headed down the small hallway toward the back of the house. I peeked into two bedrooms on either side of the hallway and saw that they were torn apart like the living room. Mattresses and

35

box springs were slashed open and lying on the floor. Dresser drawers were thrown around the room.

There was still no sign of Pierre, however, so I bravely continued. I made my way to the last door and stood there, dreading what I *knew* I would find on the other side. This was the only room I hadn't checked yet, and the blood smell was stronger here than anywhere else I had been in the house.

Standing outside the door, I became aware of a loud buzzing noise. Damn! I knew what that meant. I took a deep breath and gingerly opened the bathroom door. I used a tissue to open the door in case there was evidence that needed to be collected later. When the door opened, the buzzing sound was so loud that it was almost intolerable.

Even though I used to be a homicide detective, nothing could have prepared me for what I saw in that bathroom. Pierre was lying in a literal bloodbath, although the blood was not only contained within the bathtub. Every wall, ceiling, and floor tile surface appeared to be covered in blood. Oh yeah, that buzzing noise? It was the sound of about a million flies fluttering throughout the bathroom and covering Pierre's face. I managed not to scream as the flies made a beeline for me and I quickly took two steps backward and closed the door, again using the tissue. I walked quickly outside and took deep gulps of fresh air, my body shuddering. My lung capacity was still diminished so I made some very unfeminine chirping noises as I tried to vanquish that smell from my nostrils.

The rain was still pouring down, but I didn't care. It could've been hailing pitchforks and that would've been preferable to staying in that house with Pierre's dead body. I called Ty directly – after all, he was my best friend's husband – and reported what I had found. I knew that he would get quicker results calling the dispatcher and medical examiner than me.

I walked slowly to my car and got in to wait for the chaos to begin.

Chapter Seven

As expected, the area around Pierre's house was soon a chaotic mess. Ty and at least ten of his officers raced up the vineyard driveway with lights flashing and sirens blaring. They also brought a sense of nervous anticipation which I thought was misplaced until I remembered being a homicide cop. You get a certain excited feeling when you roll up to a crime scene. At least, the rain had slowed down.

Ty knocked on my window and I lowered it slowly. "Are you OK, Kat?" he asked with concern.

I nodded numbly. This scenario was becoming far too commonplace in my life. Why do *I* always have to find the dead body, I wondered bleakly. I'm not a homicide cop anymore. I shouldn't have to deal with dead bodies.

Ty leaned in and rested his hand on my shoulder. "Sit tight, Kat, and I will get to you as soon as possible."

Ty turned around and began giving directions to his officers. He sent four of them around the house to search for signs of foul play or any possible evidence. I knew that all the evidence would probably have washed away in that monsoon we had earlier today, but they still had to search. Ty, Officer Therman, and Officer Jablonski – I had met them at my high school reunion – entered the house cautiously with their hands poised on their service pistols.

I could hear Ty and his team clearing each room as they made their way through the house and then it became eerily quiet. I assumed that they had just opened the door to the bathroom. The forensics team pulled up behind me and began to unpack their gear. Ty and Officer Therman came outside and I noticed them taking deep breaths of fresh air. I assumed Ty had left Officer Jablonsky to stand guard over the crime scene, not that anyone could possibly get past all the police officers at the scene.

Ty walked over to the **forensics van** and spoke with Officer Jackson, who was in charge of the forensics lab. Before anyone went any further, they had to wait until the medical examiner arrived. I had heard from Syd that Dr. Nilsson, the district's medical examiner, was not known for haste, especially on a Sunday. Dr. Nilsson finally arrived at Pierre's house about ten minutes later, still dressed in plaid golf pants and cleats.

I could tell that Ty was furious, but he was doing his best to remain cordial. Apparently, your case could be prioritized downward quickly if you annoyed Dr. Nilsson. Ty quickly briefed Dr. Nilsson as they walked into the house. They stayed inside for about half an hour. Meanwhile, nature was starting to call rather loudly and I wondered how much longer I would have to sit in my car and wait. Dr. Nilsson emerged and the forensics team was finally able to enter the house. I knew that they would photograph everything from every angle throughout the house and collect many of the flies that were in the bathroom before the morgue attendants were allowed to remove the body.

Ty walked over to my car shaking his head. He removed his hat, took the bottle of water I offered him, and let out a long sigh. "Kat, I'm so sorry that this is taking so long, but you know how it is. We're going to be another hour or two but I don't want to make you sit in your car any longer. Can you give your initial statement to Officer Freely and then I'll follow up with you later tonight with any questions?

"Of course, Ty. Anything I can do to help."

He smiled at me and leaned against my car. All I could think was that I would do anything to get home and take a shower. I felt like I was covered in both wine and the oily stench of blood.

I noted the time and that the tasting room had just formally closed for the day. I had texted Justina that there had been an incident at Pierre's and I watched the vineyard staff creep by Pierre's house as they left for the day. Most of the staff were interns who lived at the vineyard, so it was just curiosity that had them driving down the drive. There was an officer directing traffic, such as it was, but I had managed to catch Justina's eye as she drove by. I made the universal sign to call her later and she nodded and continued down the driveway.

Officer Freely got into my car and turned on a digital recorder. She asked me some identification questions after recording the time and date, and then asked me to tell how I had come to find Pierre.

I took a moment to collect my thoughts then started to recount my story from my morning arrival when I had driven by and noticed his door ajar. I went on to tell how none of the vineyard staff had seen him and that I decided to check on him around three o'clock.

At this point, Officer Freely interrupted to ask me why I came to investigate. I explained that I was an employee as well as good friends with Marco Milano, the vineyard owner, and that Pierre was one of his valued employees. I also explained that Marco was out of town and Pierre had not missed a day of work in the three months that I had been working there, so I was concerned about him. Officer Freely nodded at me to continue my story.

When I finished, she had me sign an official form and got out of my car. Ironically, the rain had completely cleared up and it had turned into a beautiful evening.

I drove home and immediately jumped into a scalding hot shower. After I put on my pajamas, I collapsed onto the couch with a glass of Milano Pinot Grigio – I could not stomach the thought of red wine right now.

I thought for a moment and then picked up my phone and called Marco. I took a large sip of wine as I tried to remember the time difference between Massachusetts and Peru. I gave up my calculations as soon as he answered the phone.

"Kat," he roared into the phone. "What's up? I'm coming home tomorrow. Couldn't you wait to speak with me?" he roared with laughter.

I smiled. Marco always had that effect on me, even when he was obnoxious.

"Marco," I began, "I don't know how to say this – " I paused.

Marco's tone instantly became more serious. "What's wrong, Kat? Is there something wrong at the vineyard? Are you okay?"

I took a deep breath. "I'm fine. The vineyard is fine. I...I have some bad news."

Marco, ever the joker, interjected, "What? Are you quitting already? Couldn't hack it, Snow?"

I pulled the phone away from my ear and stared at it for a second. Why would he think I was quitting? "Why would you think I'm quitting, Marco? Have I given you a reason to think that I don't like this job?"

He sighed. "No. I just don't think I want to know what the bad news is. Go ahead. Shoot."

I took another deep breath and let it out noisily. "Pierre was found dead in his house earlier today."

I could hear Marco's sharp intake of breath from 3,500 miles away. "Dead? How did he die? Did he have a heart attack or something? Was he out in the vineyard?"

I shook my head and then realized Marco couldn't see me as our call was only audio. "No," I said. "Not unless a heart attack produces copious amounts of blood that then covers his entire bathroom.

"Ew, Kat. That's not a pretty picture. Wait! What were you doing in his bathroom?" I heard a woman's voice in the background. It was a slight murmur but then everything was muffled when Marco covered the phone's speaker.

42

I felt my face turn beet red and my chest tightened. I was irrationally angry and instantly jealous that he was presumably with another woman – not that I had any reason to be. I also felt a little sad that I now wouldn't get to explore my feelings for Marco. I felt very confused with my emotions in such turmoil. I should really be more concerned about Pierre's death than Marco's love life, but I guess you can't help how you feel.

Marco came back on the phone and I tried to quash my volatile emotions. "Never mind. Fill me in on the details later." I could hear him poking at his laptop. "OK, if I rush, I can take the 10:15 flight tonight from Lima. I should be in tomorrow evening around 5:30. If I send you my flight details, can you arrange for me to be picked up at Logan? I knew I should have replaced my assistant when she moved to California."

"Of course, Marco," I murmured.

"Thanks, Kat. I trust I can count on you to continue to be my eyes and ears at the vineyard until I get back." He sighed and was quiet for a moment. "You spent quite a bit of time with Pierre these past few months, right?"

"Yes," I said slowly.

"Good." I could almost hear him nod. "I'll need you to test the Brix tomorrow and decide if we're ready to harvest or wait a few days. Was it tested today?"

I stuttered while trying to formulate a reply. Deciding whether or not to harvest was one of the most important decisions

43

made at a vineyard. "I don't know if it was tested today," I said falteringly. "You want *me* to decide whether the grapes are ready?"

I could hear Marco moving around wherever he was staying and I pictured him throwing clothes haphazardly into his luggage. "I don't need you to *guess*, Kat. I *need* you to be certain. You know everything that goes into deciding if it's time to harvest or not."

I sat up a little straighter and took a big sip of wine. "As long as it's only until you come back, Marco. I can do it."

"Good. Giovanni's there, too, if you need any help with anything. He'll be able to answer any questions you might have until I get back."

"OK," I said. "Enjoy the rest of your trip."

He scoffed loudly. "Really? Do you think I'm going to enjoy any more of this trip knowing that one of my long-term employees, and friends, has been killed?"

I shook my head and again realized Marco couldn't see me. "I'm sorry," I said. "That was thoughtless of me. What I meant to say was 'safe travels.'"

Marco sighed again. "I know, Kat. I don't mean to take it out on you, but you're handy." I smiled as I knew he was grinning impishly.

We said our goodbyes and hung up. I knew I wouldn't sleep well tonight.

Chapter Eight

As soon as I got off the phone with Marco, I started a group FaceTime chat with Syd and Ricky. I was sure that Ty had already told Syd about Pierre. He wasn't supposed to talk about his cases, but I expected that he would give her a quick overview, especially since I was involved.

Syd already knew and Ricky was stunned when I told them the news. Then, Ricky made a curious face. "How come you always find the dead body?

I tried to smile, but it barely registered. "I don't know," I yelped, and to my chagrin, a few actual tears dripped from my eyes.

"What is your problem, Ricky?" yelled Syd as she shook her head. "We are coming right over with dinner. I know you probably haven't eaten yet and you're telling yourself you don't need to eat, but I see you've got wine, so you need to eat." Ricky was about to beg off, but even virtually, Syd could stare anyone down at a thousand yards.

Ricky said he would pick up a couple of pizzas on the way over and asked about the beverage situation. I glanced over at my wine fridge – another perk of working for Milano Importers – and saw that I had more than enough wine for tonight. Fortunately, I was always fully stocked now.

Thirty minutes later, Ricky and Syd were on my doorstep. I had decided to put on clothes as Miss Manners would not think it was acceptable to entertain anyone, even your best friends, in pajamas. They came in and Syd immediately gave me a huge hug.

45

"I don't know why I am so upset about this," I lamented. "I didn't know Pierre that well and, hell, I used to be a homicide detective. The sight of a dead body shouldn't bother me this much."

Ricky looked thoughtful. "You know, maybe you're still dealing with the grief of not being a cop anymore."

I looked at him questioningly and Syd gave him a sharp kick. She was about to admonish Ricky when I put my hand on her arm. "Let him speak. I'm interested in where he's going with this."

We were now sitting in the living room with the pizza boxes open, a wine glass in everyone's hand, and soft music playing in the background. Ricky picked up a piece of pizza that was dripping with extra cheese and slowly brought it to his mouth, trying to navigate the path without losing any cheese. "Well," he began, "Being a cop – both in the army and for the BPD – was a huge part of your life. It was how you identified yourself for nearly twenty years. Having that taken away from you, *involuntarily*, must have left a huge gap that you've needed to fill for well over a year now. You tried filling the space with renovating this beautiful cottage," he smirked as he and Syd had contributed quite a bit of planning and labor to the renovation, "And then, you were reminded of your time as a detective a few months ago at the reunion when you kept finding the dead bodies there, too."

I nodded thinking about everything he was saying. "Go on," I encouraged.

Ricky chewed for a second and I could almost see him arranging his thoughts. "Well, Kat, I think that everything that happened at the reunion triggered some form of emotional feedback for you. Emotional turmoil that both Syd and I," he glanced quickly at Syd and then back at me, "think you haven't dealt with properly yet."

I lowered my slice of pizza to the plate and looked back and forth between them. "What?" I demanded in a slightly offended tone.

Syd rushed on breathlessly. "It's not that we talk about you, Kat. Well, it's not like we talk about you all the time. But, you know how it is with three friends. Whenever one isn't there, the third person naturally comes up in conversation. And," she was quick to add, "We do not talk about you maliciously." She leaned in and squeezed my arm. "We care about you, Kat, and we just want the best for you."

I sat back, the pizza temporarily forgotten on my plate, and took a long, slow sip of wine. I had never really thought about it before, but what they said made sense.

Syd leaned over and grabbed her purse. "I have a card for a doctor who might be able to help," she rooted through her cavernous bag. "Here," she held up a business card triumphantly.

I sat and looked at the card for a moment, then reached out and took it from her. At that second, my doorbell rang. Syd, Ricky, and I looked at each other quizzically. I certainly was not expecting anyone else. I got up and walked to my front door. When I looked through the peephole, I was surprised to see Chance standing there. I put the card into my back pocket and opened the door.

Chance stood there holding a bottle of wine and smiled at me hesitantly. "I heard about what happened today and thought you could use a friend." He looked into the living room at Syd and Ricky and murmured, "I guess you already have your friends here."

"Nonsense, come in. You're part of the gang."

He still looked hesitant. "Are you sure? I don't want to intrude…"

"Absolutely!" shouted Syd from the living room. Chance grinned and walked over to the chair in the corner. He set the wine bottle down and asked where the wine glasses were.

"I'll grab you one, Chance," Ricky volunteered. He popped out of his spot on the love seat and crossed to my wine cabinet. Ricky pulled out a glass and walked over to the coffee table which still held the pizza and our second bottle of wine. "Do you want to help us finish this first? It is from the Milano Vineyards."

Chance chuckled. "Sure, Marco makes a decent wine." Then he looked at me with concern and cleared his throat. "I heard that Pierre was found murdered today in his house – and that you found him." He looked at me intently. "What is it with you and dead bodies?"

I knew he was joking, but the comment still stung a little anyway. Why *did* I keep finding all the dead bodies? And why did people have to keep making an issue about it?

I shook my head. "I don't know," I said miserably. "I was concerned when Pierre didn't show up for work today and just went to check on him. I had seen his door open when I went to work and then he never showed up at the vineyard."

Chance looked embarrassed. "I'm sorry," he said. "I didn't mean that like it came out. I'm sure it must have been horrible for you. Do the police have any suspects?"

"I don't think so," I shook my head, but then looked at Syd questioningly.

Syd shook her head. "Ty didn't mention anything to me about any suspects. He said there were a lot of clues, and that it was *really* messy, but nothing concrete so far."

Chance looked around at the three of us and then zeroed in on me. "I think you said you spent some time with Pierre at the vineyard. Did he ever mention any enemies or problems?"

I shook my head slowly. "Not that I recall. His biggest argument seemed to be with Giovanni over whether France or Italy produced better wine."

"France," exclaimed Syd while Ricky chirped, "Italy."

We all chuckled.

"It's a stupid argument," I sighed. "Both countries produce amazing wine." I thought quietly for a moment. "They really only seemed to be half-serious when arguing about wine. I wasn't sure if perhaps the wine argument was a cover for some other issue."

Syd looked at me sharply. "Really? You never mentioned anything about an underlying reason before. Did you tell Ty?"

"No, I'm just thinking it through in my head right now." I shrugged. "I never paid much heed to their bickering." I leaned back

49

and thought for a bit more. "They didn't spend a lot of time together anyway because Pierre was out in the vineyard most of the day and Giovanni was inside with all the administrative tasks."

Ricky popped up again and grabbed the wine bottle. He refilled all of our glasses and emptied the bottle. He raised his glass. "I know this is something we'll talk more about in the coming week, but can we change the topic for now? I think Kat needs a distraction."

Syd smiled. "Sounds good to me." She looked at Chance. "What can you tell us about the renovation? When is the big opening?"

Chance settled deeper into the chair. "Well, this is preliminary and I'm not supposed to say anything yet, but both the health inspector and the building inspector were there today and said they would approve the paperwork so we could open."

"That's great news, Chance," I exclaimed. "Let us know if we can help in any way."

Chance nodded. "Absolutely," he raised his wineglass. "I will need my favorite wine tasters to help me plan the opening," he smiled.

Syd scrunched up her face. "I thought Mindy was going to help you with your opening?"

Chance laughed out loud. "I wouldn't let Mindy Vanderbilt within ten feet of my opening. She would turn it into a pretentious party where my friends and family would neither be invited nor comfortable." He sighed. "I want a nice, relaxing opening where people will come and feel at home."

My heart melted a little more. Chance, I've come to realize, really cares about the people close to him. I've seen him help Marco out with some legal papers even though he's no longer practicing law. Syd told me that he came into the gallery and bought some of her watercolors for Two Cups. And Ricky said that they had been working out together at The Mercury on days that I didn't want to or couldn't go. I briefly wondered why he only worked out with Ricky when I wasn't there, but I was choosing to believe he was merely being a good friend to Ricky.

Maybe that's why he's my friend and no more, I thought. He was just being kind. I was more than a little disappointed at the thought that he might never be interested in me romantically, but at least I'd have another friend. An extremely attractive friend who made me weak in the knees, but a good friend nevertheless.

"Earth to Kat," I jolted back to the present and realized Ricky was calling my name.

"What?" I snapped, trying to cover my lapse.

"I was telling Syd about our workouts at The Mercury. What would you say is the hardest thing?"

I sighed. "For me, it's dealing with Cal Jr. He is a cross between a Marine sergeant and a creepy stalker."

They all laughed and then Ricky leaned in earnestly, "If he gets too creepy, Kat, let me know and I'll take care of him. My guns are really getting developed now." He flexed his biceps, or what would be biceps if there was any muscle there. I examined Ricky's skinny arms. Perhaps they did have a bit more definition, but I still don't think anybody would call them guns.

We spent the rest of the night catching up and talking about our plans for the coming week. I was not looking forward to the sorrow and anger I was sure to face at the vineyard tomorrow.

Chapter Nine

The tasting room was closed on Mondays through Wednesdays, but I had been taking advantage of those days to go in and learn more about both the vineyard and the import business. Today, I had a more important job – deciding whether it was time to harvest the grapes or not. I knew Marco would be back later today and would want a full report on the business and the police investigation.

I drove up the long driveway toward the vineyard and slowed down as I approached Pierre's house. I noticed there were still some police officers combing through the yard and what seemed like miles of police tape cordoning off the house. I waved at the officers as I drove by – yes, I knew most of them due to the murders at my high school reunion, but also from barbecues at Ty's house.

That was the thing about living in a small town. It often seems stifling and too small when you are growing up. Everyone knows your business and talks about you – but then again, we talked about them, too. As an adult, however, I kind of like the feeling of camaraderie and community – and the fact that I knew the names of every single checkout person at the grocery store. I like knowing the owner of the tearoom and bakery, Sunny Side Up. I also like knowing the top – or should I say only – realtor in town. Amelia and I had definitely not been friends in high school but we had bonded over the weekend of our reunion. I guess that's what happens when you survive a traumatic standoff with a killer.

I parked in the employee lot and climbed out of my car. Ty wandered over from where he had been supervising some of the officers. "Hey," he drawled, as if him being at the vineyard was everyday normal.

I sighed. "I suppose you want to interview the vineyard staff?"

He nodded. "Yeah, there wasn't much in the way of clues at Pierre's house, well, not that we've processed so far. Actually, there were so many conflicting clues that I can't make sense of anything yet. Maybe one of his co-workers knows something."

"Maybe," I shrugged. "I think Pierre kept to himself a lot, but I've only been here a few months."

"I don't want to drag them all down to the police station. Is there somewhere private here where we can conduct the interviews?"

I nodded. "There are some empty offices in the administrative area. How many do you need?"

Ty looked over at the police officers and removed his cap. He absently scratched his head while he considered who was there. "Just two. One for me and one for Officer Thermon."

"Okay, let me just double-check, but I'm pretty certain that we have at least two offices available."

Ty replaced his cap and nodded at me. He started walking away but stopped after a few feet and turned abruptly. "How are you doing, Kat? Sorry, I forgot to ask and Syd will kill me if I don't report back to her. She's already mad that my job made us cancel the barbecue last night. I've got a fridge full of meat that needs to be cooked." He smiled and I could see why Syd was still so in love with him. "I'm glad she got to spend time with you, though, even if it wasn't for a good reason."

I chuckled. Ty is a big guy and Syd is a petite woman, however, she is definitely the one in charge at that house. I knew she would give him all kinds of grief if she knew he had seen me and did not think to inquire as to my well-being. "I'll be fine. The initial shock was a bit much, but a night of drinking wine with friends made me feel slightly better."

Ty threw his right arm around my shoulders and gave me a half hug. Then he looked embarrassed and walked away, saying, "Let me know about the office space."

I walked into the import offices to try and avoid the vineyard staff. No such luck, however, as Giovanni and four of the interns were sitting in the recessed seating area for guests around an indoor fire pit that always reminded me of bad seventies sitcoms. All conversation stopped as I entered the room. That doesn't make me self-conscious, I thought.

I raised my hand and gave a small wave. Most of them just nodded back at me but Giovanni got up, crossed the room, and gave me a big hug. He stepped back and held me at arm's length. "How are you, *mia cara*?" He loves to throw in some Italian when he speaks to me. I was grateful it wasn't more as I didn't think my brain could keep up today.

I blinked back some tears – what was wrong with me? Again with the tears? I used to be a homicide detective. I should be able to deal with a dead body. Max grabbed a tissue box and brought it over to me. I hadn't spoken very much with him this summer but he seemed like a nice enough boy. I smiled gratefully at him and took the tissue.

"I'm OK," I sniffed. "Any news?"

"No," replied Giovanni, "Nobody has told us anything. We only know that Pierre," Giovanni made the sign of the cross and looked skyward, "was killed in his house sometime yesterday morning."

I looked around the room, trying to decide if any of them looked guilty. "Do any of you know if Pierre had any enemies?"

Almost everyone shook their head but I realized that Max had turned around quickly so I could not see his face. He also refrained from answering.

Giovanni sighed loudly and then said in a rush. "I don't know what to do, Kat. We are so close to the harvest. Max has volunteered to check the Brix for us today. Do you know when Marco is returning?

"Yes, I spoke with Marco last night. He was going to take a morning flight today and said he should be back by this evening."

"Good," Giovanni looked relieved. "I know a lot about wine and winemaking, but I don't want to make the decision about the harvest."

"I understand, Giovanni," I said. "Me either, but Marco asked me to review the data today to see if we are ready. I will definitely consult with you and everyone involved in the process before I make such a momentous decision for him."

Giovanni smiled wanly. "I'm glad it's your decision and not mine, Kat. Picking the grapes too early or too late could be disastrous for a vineyard."

I gulped at the enormity of the potential decision I might have to make. I had only been here three months. How could Marco trust me that much? I knew that I sure didn't trust myself that much.

"We'll do the best we can, for Marco and," I cast my eyes downward, "for Pierre." Giovanni and the interns nodded sadly. I turned slowly and then walked into my office. I suddenly remembered Ty's request and rushed back out to look around the suite. We actually had three empty offices, so Ty would have plenty of room.

"The police are here and want to interview everyone today, so please don't leave the vineyard until after you've been interviewed," I announced. Everyone looked at me with a look of fear in their eyes. The prospect of speaking to the police has that effect on a lot of people, even if they are innocent. I held up a walkie-talkie. "You can go work in the fields, I'm sure there's a lot to do after yesterday's deluge. Just make sure everyone has a walkie-talkie. The police will radio and request whoever they want to speak with. There will be two officers conducting the interviews, so it should go quickly."

Everyone nodded, grabbed a walkie-talkie from the charging stations, and started to leave. I grabbed an extra one and called out, "Can someone drop this at the barracks?" which is what they called the dorm housing. "Anyone with the day off will need to be interviewed, too."

Max took the device from me and ushered the other interns out the door. "Let's go! We've already lost a bit of field time this morning and these interviews will set us back even more." I looked at him and thought he definitely was a Type A, and then turned back to my office.

As offices go, it was pretty nice. Certainly nicer than the cubicle I had at the Boston Police Department. There was an old – probably antique – mahogany desk that faced the wall of windows and provided stunning views of the vineyard. Marco had bought me an ergonomic chair because he knew I had problems with my back – thanks to the meth addict who nearly killed me and ended my career. There were also two comfortable chairs for visitors across from my desk and a couch in the corner with a coffee table in case I wanted to have a more casual meeting. As if I ever had visitors.

As I did every day that I came into the office, I turned on my computer and then gazed out at the vineyard. I could also see the sparkle of water in the harbor in the distance. It was usually very calming. If only death hadn't followed me to the vineyard. I sent Ty a quick text to tell him that we had three offices available and he replied with a thumb's up emoji. I was surprised he even knew what an emoji was, but then again, he did have three kids.

My laptop roared to life and I started going through the emails that had accumulated since yesterday. I knew I would soon be distracted by the comings and goings of staff and police so I wanted to finish up quickly. Mercifully, there was nothing very important, just people inquiring about when the venue space would be open and wondering what types of unique wine tastings we would be offering. We had posted some teaser copy on our website and, happily, it had generated a lot of interest.

While I replied to emails, Ty came in and commandeered two of the empty offices. I pointed at the walkie-talkies and he understood that he should use them to call for the staff members he wanted to interview. By the time I finished replying to emails, he and Officer Thermon were interviewing the last two staff members.

Unlike Chance's good news, the email I received from the building inspector said we still needed to fix some compliance issues. I wasn't sure what he was talking about; the health inspector had approved all of the plans, so everything should be in compliance. I replied politely, asking him to please explain further and provide more details so that we could satisfy his requirements. He just pissed me off, though. Mac MacGill was the town's building inspector. He was also an entitled, power-hungry public servant who used whatever authority he had to make other people miserable. He had been at his job for nearly thirty years. Now, I know generally what public servants make, and his wife had never worked, so I was a little suspicious how he could afford the MacMansion – actually what he called it – on the posh side of State Street. I heard he had an

Olympic-sized pool and six-person Jacuzzi, as well as an indoor sauna, five bedrooms, six baths, a gourmet kitchen, and a landscaper who came every week. As I said, people talk in small towns.

I think that Marco and Chance had been experiencing so many problems with this inspector because they refused his not-so-subtle hints at wanting a bribe. I knew that Chance had actually threatened to go to the Town Council about the whole process last week, so I wasn't surprised that he had received his approval. When Marco returned, I would suggest that we do the same. At this rate, our construction wouldn't be finished until next season.

I finished with my emails and retrieved my lunch from the staff refrigerator. I looked forlornly at my ham sandwich and apple left over from yesterday and wished I had brought some of that leftover food from Ricky's the other night. It was still sitting in my refrigerator at home, rotting slowly.

My stomach rumbled and I made a snap decision. I threw my lunch back in the refrigerator and called Max out in the fields. He answered a little breathlessly. "Kat, I was just going to call you. I don't think we're quite ready to harvest yet, but I'll bring the Brix readings and you can decide for yourself."

"That's great, Max. I was actually calling to ask you to bring all of the interns to the office. I'd like to provide pizza and salad for the staff. It's a hot day out and I thought you guys could use a little break, especially after..." I trailed off, not wanting to reference Pierre's murder.

Max sounded a little hesitant. "OK, you're the boss. Just so you know, we're really close to the harvest so we do have a lot of work to do, *and* we missed some more work time being interviewed by the police."

"I know, but you still need to eat lunch and take a break. Why not do it in some air-conditioning?"

"Sounds great," said Max, and he sounded a little more enthusiastic now. "When would you like us to be there?"

"How about 30 minutes? I'm ordering online now."

"You're ordering from Roma's, right?" he asked. There was an ongoing debate in town about which pizza place was better, Roma's Pizzeria or Sammy's Special Pies. I was firmly in the Roma camp because I like traditional, Italian pizza. Sammy's usually had some new-fangled, new-age pizza that I just couldn't get behind. Forget the argument over pineapple and ham – they added toppings like pork rinds and okra.

I decided to treat everyone working today, not just the interns, with funds from petty cash, so I ordered five large pizzas with a variety of toppings. I was certain that Marco wouldn't mind.

After hanging up, I had another bright idea and ordered three more pizzas for the police working the scene. I knew they would appreciate it. I remembered working a crime scene and not having time to take a meal break. Mario Roma, the owner and cook of Roma's, had immigrated from Sicily and the pizza was divine. Nobody would turn down free Roma's pizza.

Chapter Ten

Thirty minutes later, I paid the Roma delivery person as the vineyard staff filed into the office suite. The administrative wing of Milano Importers has six offices, a conference room, and that delightful, recessed 1970s seating area. We were currently only using three of the offices, so the extra three were set up generically with desks and comfy chairs for visitors, the interns, or anyone who needed a quiet space to work. Today, the police had been encamped in two of the empty offices, but it was better than having the whole staff go down to the police station to make a statement and be interviewed.

The conference room has a wall of windows that overlook the vineyard. I had the pizzas brought into the conference room along with a variety of sodas and some bottled waters. May, one of the interns, went and got plates and utensils from the staff lunchroom while everyone settled in. There were ten of us spaced out in the conference room and we still had plenty of room. In addition to the interns and me, Giovanni, Justina, and Bud, our custodian, joined us for lunch. Bud brought the pizzas and beverages I had ordered for the police into the tasting room and then went outside to invite them in.

The interns fell on the pizza like they hadn't eaten in days. Of course, it was Roma's pizza and you didn't want to miss out on your favorite slice. Bud shuffled in rather quickly and grabbed two pieces of pepperoni and sausage. His face was blissful as he devoured the slices and reached for a third.

The conversation was casual over lunch and I looked around the table and thought what a great bunch of kids Marco had selected as interns this year. In addition to Max, there was Jayson from Korea, May from China, Alessa from Peru, Ava from Australia, and Louis from France. They all seemed to get along well, which was important as they had to spend a lot of time together over the summer.

After we ate, we cleaned up our mess and consolidated the few remaining slices into one box. Jayson put it in the refrigerator in the staff room so anyone could grab a slice later if they were hungry. We sat down to eat dessert – yeah, I broke down and bought some of Roma's cannolis, too – the best around, if I do say so myself. Everyone says you need to go to North Boston or North Providence to get good Italian food, but I know it's not as good as Roma's.

I hesitated for a moment about how to broach the topic of Pierre. I knew that a few of the interns had the morning off on Mondays and usually went into town for breakfast. As I fretted about the topic, May spoke up from the other end of the table. "Kat, have you heard anything about the investigation into Pierre's death?"

I shook my head somberly. "No, I was hoping one of you might have heard something in town today."

Jayson spoke up, "Nobody said anything to us and we all ate breakfast together at Starbucks." His eyes glistened. "He was a great guy to work with and always super helpful to us. He tutored us in English in addition to teaching us everything about the grapes and

64

vineyard. I learned more from Pierre this summer than I did in my four-year viticulture program at school."

May swiped at her eyes. "Me, too," she sobbed quietly. "He was a little secretive at times and liked to know where *we* were all the time, but I can't think of anyone who didn't like Pierre."

Ava was staring down at the table and wouldn't meet my eyes. "Ava," I inquired, "did you have any problems with Pierre?"

Ava looked at me with some concern. "No, Kat, he seemed to get along with everybody. There were occasional arguments," she looked furtively at Max, "but they were just general and usually blew over quickly."

Max blurted out, "He and I had some difficulty." He sighed. "I thought he was a little too friendly with the girls…"

Ava interrupted him, "We are women, Max, not girls."

Max held his hands up in self-defense. "I'm sorry, Ava, I didn't mean to be offensive. I was merely illustrating the difference in your ages. Pierre was about 55 and you *ladies* are between 20 and 25. Plus, he was your supervisor and I didn't feel it was appropriate for him to flirt so outrageously."

Ava snorted. "We may be young, but we are perfectly capable of defending ourselves, Max. We," she made an enveloping gesture around the table, "appreciate your concern but we had already handled the situation."

I blinked. Now it was a *situation*? How had I not seen nor heard anything about this over the summer? I certainly would have stepped in if I had noticed anything untoward. I cleared my throat. "How did you handle it?"

Ava stared at me intently for a moment. "Alessa and I met privately with Pierre in his office," she pointed in the direction of Pierre's office, "and told him that if he didn't stop the lecherous suggestions, we would go to Marco and the police if necessary."

Alessa jumped in. "Marco made it very clear when we started interning here that sexual misconduct, harassment, or unwanted attention was forbidden and he would fire anybody who acted in such a manner."

I nodded and thought that I didn't know Pierre as well as I had thought. I began to wonder if this could be why he was murdered. I looked at Justina who had been conducting inventory today. "Justina, did you ever have a problem with Pierre being inappropriate?"

She looked at me and shrugged. "You've met my boyfriend, and so did Pierre. Would you mess with me knowing that you might have to deal with Claude?"

We all chuckled. Claude was a trainer at The Mercury, my gym. I cringed as I inventoried my aches and pains, leftover from my workout this morning. Claude was six foot five and 200 pounds of lean, ripped muscle. He also sported a spiky mohawk and his arms were covered in tribal tattoos. Nobody would want to mess with Claude.

"Well," I hesitated, "can anyone think of any other reason someone might have killed Pierre?"

May shook her head slightly and looked over at Giovanni. Perhaps their long-standing argument about the best wine region had popped into her head.

I had noticed Giovanni becoming more and more agitated as Ava and Alessa revealed Pierre's predatory behavior. Finally, he blurted out, "You should have come to me. I had warned Pierre in the past and he knew that with one more complaint, he would be fired. That is unacceptable behavior for anyone, but especially for someone in a position of trust."

Giovanni angrily pushed his chair back and stomped out of the room without saying another word. We all looked at each other in shock. Finally, I stammered, "I guess that was a touchier subject than we thought."

Max nodded as he stood up and indicated to the other interns that it was time to leave. "I guess so," he said. "Thanks for lunch, Kat. Guys – I mean ladies and gentlemen – we've got to get back out to the fields." Ava chuckled and winked at Max. Everyone finished their last few bites of cannoli and started moving toward the door until it was just Justina and I left in the room.

I stood up and busied myself around the conference room, making sure it was clean. That was one of Marco's pet peeves – people who didn't clean up after themselves in the communal areas. Actually, Marco had a lot of pet peeves.

I smiled and my thoughts wandered just a little. I wouldn't mind being one of his pet peeves…and then I got a little angry with myself, remembering that soft, murmured voice in his room in Peru.

Chapter Eleven

I finished replying to business emails and then Max came in with a late afternoon Brix report. Let me give you a crash course in winemaking, as I know I've been talking about Brix a lot.

Brix is a measurement of the sugar content in grapes, must (unfermented grape juice), and wine that indicates the grapes' ripeness, or sugar level, at harvest time. Most table-wine grapes get harvested between 21 and 26 Brix. If you then want to determine the alcohol conversion level, you multiply the Brix by a number between .55 and .65, depending on other fermentation factors. Therefore, a Brix of 22, and using the lowest number in the conversion range, provides an alcohol level of approximately 12.1 percent ABV (alcohol by volume). I had learned that one degree Brix is the number of grams of sucrose present in 100 grams of liquid. It is measured on a scale of one to 100, using either a refractometer or a hydrometer.

A refractometer measures the refraction of light passing through a liquid sample that contains as little as the juice of one crushed grape. The refractometer compares the solution to the refraction of light through water and provides the Brix value. This is the preferred tool as measurements can be taken anywhere, even in a field of grapes.

Hydrometers are used to calculate a liquid's sugar level using the physics of relative density. A hydrometer uses a weighted floating glass tube placed inside a calibrated test tube that contains the liquid sample. The test tube calibration measures the amount of displaced liquid and this displacement determines how much sugar is present.

Brix is, however, only one of the factors that winemakers use to determine when the grapes are ready to harvest. A skilled winemaker, such as Pierre, looks at a wide variety of factors, such as the color of the grapes, stems, and seeds; how plump the grapes are; and their flavor. There were a lot of factors to consider, but Milano Vineyards had used their tried and true methods of wine production for over eighty years, producing very tasty, often award-winning, wines.

Without even going into the vineyard and looking at the grapes, the Brix numbers that Max showed me were not yet within range for harvest. I decided to walk the vineyards anyway just to keep an eye on things. I knew Pierre did that three or four times a day, especially when it was this close to harvest, and I also knew that Marco would ask me about it when he got home.

Justina was leaving for the day as I walked out the back door and I waved to her in the parking lot. I had to run back in for my little tool belt that everyone receives when they start working for Milano Vineyards. The tool kit contains some necessary tools for the vineyard, such as a refractometer, a small spade, and harvesting shears, as well as band-aids and organic bug spray. I climbed into the little golf cart that we used for VIP tours – and for when we were just feeling lazy. I drove up the hill to the top of the vineyard and looked down at all the grapevines happily growing in the sunny warmth of this late fall day.

I could see the interns spread throughout the fields and I watched them for a moment to see if anyone was behaving suspiciously. I realized what I was doing was insane – as if I could tell if someone looked suspicious from 100 yards away.

I saw Max in the pinot noir area of the vineyard and walked over to him. He pulled out the refractometer and the sample he had used for the Brix calculations and I agreed we were still probably at least two days away from the harvest. I looked at Max curiously. "Have there been any issues this afternoon?"

Max shook his head. "Not really. Giovanni has been helping out in the fields today because we're a little shorthanded. Besides for Pierre," Max grimaced, "Louis wasn't feeling well and went back to the dorms to lie down."

I felt a rush of concern. "Is it a stomach bug or dehydration? You know how Marco likes everyone who is working in the fields to carry a water bottle. It gets really hot out here." I looked down at my empty hands and grimaced. "I can't even follow my own advice."

Max grinned. "I'm sure he'll be fine. I think he was a little dehydrated to start with from drinking last night." He looked at me cautiously then took a deep breath and spoke quickly. "I don't know if you know this, but Louis' father was good friends with Pierre. That's how Louis got the internship without studying viticulture at university. Pierre put in a good word for him to Marco."

"I didn't know that." I thought for a moment. "I never heard Pierre mention any friends from France, or even from here. Did he

71

have any friends? Or a girlfriend?" Max looked at me sharply, "Or a boyfriend?" I hastily added.

Max chuckled mirthlessly. "It definitely would have been a girlfriend. You heard the stories at lunch. To answer your question, no, he didn't have anyone special in his life and not very many friends. Pierre lived for the vineyard. I think the bottles were his friends." He snorted a little. "Many times, I would see him walking down into the wine caves in the evening with a flashlight."

"Really?" I asked, surprised.

"*Ja*," Max nodded. "When we first arrived, he gave us a brief tour of the caves, as part of the general vineyard tour. I asked him for a more in-depth tour later, as those caves and tunnels are very extensive and I find their history fascinating." He looked pensive. "He told me I had no need to go down there without him and he had better never find me down there alone or with anyone else. He was quite adamant and stressed how dangerous they could be."

"Huh," I couldn't think of anything else to ask Max about Pierre, but then I looked more closely at him. "How about you, Max? Anyone special in your life?"

Max kept working on one of the vines that he was standing in front of and did not make eye contact with me. "*Nein*," he said slowly. "Nobody special in my life right now. This was my summer away from home and I just wanted to have fun and enjoy myself with no complications."

I lightly touched Max's shoulder and smiled kindly at him. "Sounds like you made a good decision." Max looked at my hand, stiffened up, and then took a step away from me. I think he thought I was coming on to him. I was mortified that I might unknowingly be committing sexual harassment. I withdrew my hand like it was on fire and stammered, "I hope you did have a good summer. Harmony is a great place to relax and unwind, even though it doesn't have as many bars and the culture of Boston."

Max visibly relaxed and grinned, a bit mischievously. "I certainly did. Boston is only an hour away and Louis and I went whenever we had enough time off to make the trip worthwhile."

I was learning a lot on my walk through the vineyard. "Really? What types of things did you do?"

Max shrugged. "Some things were really fun, like interesting restaurants and themed bars near Faneuil Hall, and the Theater District." He scrunched up his face. "Often though, Louis only wanted to go and visit museums. He dragged me to at least five different museums in Boston and to the Gardner Museum twice before I said, 'No more!'"

I was stunned into silence – but only for a moment. "Louis likes museums?" He was kind of quiet and I hadn't spoken much with him, but he seemed like more of an outdoorsy kind of guy.

Max nodded emphatically. "*Ja*, it is something he and Pierre had in common. Pierre gave him a list of museums to visit while he was here."

"Huh, I didn't think Pierre really liked art very much," was all I managed to add to the conversation. I didn't think I was coming off as very bright. "I'll let you get back to work. Thanks for your time."

I took a step away and then turned back. "Max, I'm sure that Chief Randall asked you already, but I know Marco will want details when he gets back, so…" I hesitated. I had no authority, but I thought I should have the information. "Where were you two nights ago?"

Max shook his head and sighed in exasperation. "I suppose you need to know." He took a deep breath. "Most of us were in the barracks. We all ate dinner together around six-thirty and then went our separate ways back to our rooms. Jayson and I played your friend's online game, *Call of the Wild*, until about nine o'clock and then I went to bed. Alone. I don't know what Jayson did after we stopped playing the game. I think I heard Ava and May chatting in the common area, but I don't know what happened to everyone else after dinner."

I nodded at him. "Thanks."

I wandered through the fields and stopped to speak with each of the interns. Everyone seemed fine, except for Louis who had already left, and Alessa who had the day off.

Jayson told me he continued playing *Call of the Wild* until midnight. I would have to remember to tell Ricky as he liked to hear about how long people played his game. Ava and May said they were in the common area until eight o'clock then they both went back to their rooms and FaceTimed with their families. I made a mental note to stop by the barracks and speak with Louis and Alessa.

I could tell that none of the interns were being completely forthright with me, but I had to remember that I wasn't a cop anymore and people, especially young people, don't always want to confide in an older person.

I stopped dead in my tracks. Did I just call myself an old person? I am not old, I thought. I'm only 38. I looked down at myself as I walked back up the hill. I was a little winded at the top, but that wasn't entirely my – or pizza's – fault. I believe I've previously mentioned that I had to leave the BPD after a meth head stabbed me ten times and I had part of a lung removed. I was working hard to get back in shape but knew I could never go back to the BPD. This job at Marco's winery had come at the perfect time for me.

Wait! Maybe that's why neither Marco nor Chance had tried to be romantic with me. Maybe they thought I was too old? Maybe they liked younger, more fit women, who weren't retired on disability. I shook my head. None of this was productive. If they didn't want me, I'd find someone else – not that I needed anyone else, but if I wanted someone else, I'd find him. I shook my head hard. Where were all these errant thoughts coming from?

I reached the top of the hill – and the golf cart, thankfully – and saw Giovanni waiting for me. He looked at me breathing a bit heavily from the exertion – and my diminished lung capacity – and asked with concern, "You are not sick, *mia cara*, like Louis?"

I smiled and thought that maybe I really was old.

"*Sto bene*, Giovanni." My Italian pronunciation usually made him smile. Not so today.

75

"*Cara,* I am concerned about what the interns reported today. I do not think he did, but I…" he wrung his hands and looked out over the vineyard, "but I am worried he got himself into trouble with the ladies. I would have stepped in if I had known."

I put my hand on his arm. I knew he wouldn't view it as harassment. "I think the ladies handled the matter well on their own." He looked at me hopefully. "I know you are old school and like to believe that women need to be rescued, but most times, we can handle sticky situations on our own."

Giovani nodded slowly. "*Capisco.* I understand, Kat. I just wish they had told me. I had given Pierre a final warning and would have followed through with terminating him."

I grimaced but Giovanni didn't comprehend his double entendre.

Giovanni continued, "Marco does not need a sexual harassment suit against the vineyard."

"I think everything is fine now, Giovanni. No worries." I stood on my toes and gave Giovani a big hug which he grudgingly reciprocated. "Giovanni, you're one of the good ones. Don't ever change."

Giovani straightened up and looked in Max's direction. "What did the Brix say today?"

"The Brix was only 20 this afternoon. Between the Brix and the condition of the grapes, I think we still have about three more days before we need to start the harvest."

Giovanni nodded. "If that's what the Brix number is, then I agree."

I looked sharply at Giovanni. "What do you mean?"

Giovani looked around nervously. "I shouldn't tell tales out of school."

"Now, you must," I insisted.

Giovanni sighed. "The Germans don't use the Brix system, even though it was invented there. They use the Oechsle scale which is a metric measurement and classifies German wine into nine quality groups from 44 to 150."

"Pierre didn't cover this in my introduction to winemaking," I frowned.

"He wouldn't. The French use the Baumé scale which measures the sugar content of grape juice by density. It is not as elegant though, so Pierre adjusted to the Brix scale when he moved to the United States."

"What does this have to do with Max?"

"Max wants us to convert to the Oechsle scale and he wants Milano wines to be a little sweeter, but Pierre was adamant that Milano Vineyards stay consistent with its roots. Marco agrees." He looked at Max apprehensively. "I just hope that he is not using Pierre's tragedy for his own plans."

I looked down the hill at Max who must have felt me looking at him because he looked up and gave a little wave. I then picked up the Brix report he had given me and looked at the small bag of grapes I had absently picked when I was chatting with each of the interns. I decided to go back to the office – after a quick run by the barracks to speak with Louis and Alessa – and run my own tests. Although I had a refractometer in my kit, I didn't want Max to see me check his work and I wanted to consult my notes to do it properly. I had seen Pierre run the test many times over the past few months. How difficult could it be?

Chapter Twelve

Around eight o'clock, Marco came breezing into the office. He had no right to look – and smell – that good after a ten and a half-hour flight and at least an hour drive from Logan Airport. He had his luggage with him so I knew he didn't stop home to shower.

I, however, looked like I had been dropped in a wine vat, then rolled in dust and dirt. I hadn't realized how dirty I had gotten when I was out in the vineyards. Then, I had a *little* mishap when I tried to test the grapes so I had to go out and pick some more. Then, I fell and rolled quite a ways down the hill, squishing pinot noir grapes all over my new white, now mottled red, T-shirt. I was not a happy camper. Nor a clean one.

Marco stopped, took one look at me, and burst out laughing. "I'm sure there's a funny story attached to your appearance, Kat, but probably not as funny as what I'm imagining."

I glared at him for a moment but found myself relaxing while picturing how I must look. On the plus side, Marco's laughter was infectious and brightened my spirits.

Marco tumbled into one of my visitor chairs – not that I ever had any visitors besides Marco – and his laughter subsided. He leaned forward, resting his muscular forearms on the edge of my desk, eying me intently. "Are you okay?"

Damn it, I felt myself tearing up again. What was my problem? Marco noted the tears in my eyes and was immediately by my side. He pulled me up from my chair and enveloped me in a soul-soothing hug. I felt myself melt against his hard chest and I slipped my arms around his trim waist. Damn, he smelled even better up close. I surreptitiously inhaled his masculine scent as his hands gently caressed my back. I could just stay here all night if the option presented itself.

I remembered my sweaty, dirty, wine-stained self and started pushing gently away. Marco looked down tenderly into my eyes and gently pushed my now stringy blonde hair away from my face. "Kat, really, are you okay?" he whispered huskily.

I stared up at him, unable to speak for a moment. He had the most amazing hazel eyes – then I remembered the *other* voice in his room last night, that female voice, and I pushed myself more firmly away from him. I took a few deep breaths and quickly composed myself. Marco was looking at me in confusion.

"I'm fine." I remembered the doctor's business card in the pocket of the jeans I was wearing last night. "I will be fine. I just need people to stop asking me how I'm doing."

Marco hesitated near me for another moment. It almost looked like he wanted to hug me again, but he took a deep breath and returned to his seat on the other side of my desk. He assumed a mock, business-like posture, "Why are you here so late, Ms. Snow? You know I don't pay overtime."

A small giggle slipped out – did I mention how charming he is? "I just thought I'd practice testing the Brix," I tried to sound dismissive, as if I had mastered the skill.

He looked perplexed. "Why? Didn't Max give you those numbers?"

I fidgeted. "He did..." I faltered and sighed. "It was suggested, however, that he disagreed with the scale we use and the Brix numbers we use as benchmarks. I thought it wouldn't hurt to double-check, plus," I gestured at the crushed grapes, puddles of liquid, and refractometer littering my desk, "apparently I need to practice using the refractometer."

He scanned the disarray on my desk and once again burst into uncontrolled laughter. When he finally caught his breath, he grinned impishly at me. "I guess if this was just a practice session, that's fine. I wouldn't place too much confidence in your numbers though."

I sat up indignantly and then regarded the untidiness on my desk. I sank back, defeated. "I'll never get the hang of this. I think I got a reading of two for the pinot noir and I know that's highly unlikely."

Still chuckling, Marco leaned forward again. "Why don't you clean up and I'll go over this again with you tomorrow. It just takes practice and," he stifled a chuckle, "it really isn't very difficult."

I nodded glumly and started cleaning up the mess.

"Why so sad? There are a lot of women who would love to spend some quality time with me."

Once again, I remembered that voice over the phone in Peru and looked at him sharply. Obliviously, Marco continued. "Don't worry about Max. He has a differing opinion, but he wants a permanent job here and he knows that means following the rules.

My rules. He wouldn't dare mislead you on the Brix numbers. He knows you're second in command."

My head swiveled so quickly toward him that I thought I'd give myself whiplash. "What?"

Marco shrugged. "Technically, Giovanni, then Pierre," Marco made the sign of the cross, "would be next in command if I'm not here, but Giovanni is basically my Human Resources department and doesn't want the responsibility. Pierre," he paused and sighed, "Pierre had a problem with boundaries, especially with the female staff. He was on his last warning and dangerously close to being let go. I don't care how long he had worked here. There is just some behavior that I will not tolerate."

I was stunned. Even though Giovanni had said the same thing, I had thought perhaps it was a bit of machismo on his part. To hear Marco confirm it, was dumbfounding. I frowned in consternation. "He was never inappropriate with me."

"You sound upset about that," Marco joked.

"No, of course not," I faltered.

Marco's eyes opened wide. "What, you feel left out?"

"No, of course not," I repeated more firmly.

Marco stared at me incredulously.

"I don't know how to explain it." I thought again about that voice in Peru. "I feel – just a little bit – like I'm not attractive enough to be noticed as a woman…not even as the object of sexual harassment."

Marco's mouth hung open.

"I know, it's weird. I can't believe I'm even saying it – but there you go."

Marco sat there with his mouth hanging open for at least five seconds. He finally shook himself from his stupor. "Kat, I don't know why you would *ever* think that you are not attractive enough to be noticed." He paused and thought about his words. "Please, don't take offense, I do not mean what I'm about to say in any way, shape, or form as harassment. I am saying this to you as your," he sighed, "your good friend, not as your boss."

I nodded slowly while looking at him suspiciously. Was this a setup for a joke? I mean, it's Marco.

He took a deep breath. "Kat, you are funny, bright, trustworthy, kind…" I rolled my eyes so loud I think they heard me down at the harbor. He held his hands up. "Okay, I get it." He took another deep breath. "You're also breathtakingly beautiful and sexy as hell." Marco sat back in his chair, flushing crimson. I had never seen him blush before. It was very charming.

Now it was my turn for my mouth to hang open. "Wh-what?"

Marco shrugged. "Come on, Kat. Don't make me say it again." He grinned. "Some past boyfriend *must* have told you how beautiful you are?"

I shook my head slowly and whispered, "Never."

"Then you've been dating the wrong kind of guy. Any real man would have told you every day how much they appreciated you, all of you, mind, body, and soul."

I looked away, embarrassed. "I haven't really dated very much."

Marco stared in disbelief. "What? Why not?"

"Well, I joined the army and between training and deployment and being soul-suckingly tired while stationed overseas, I didn't have time to think about it." I picked up a pen and began absently twisting the cap while I considered what to say. "Then, I moved to Boston and joined the BPD. Again, there was training, and learning, and long hours. My schedule was erratic and the only guys I met were other cops. Most of them had joined right after high school or college and I was older than them after my time in the army. Plus, a lot of them were already married and I don't mess around with married men. I did make some really good friends, and I dated a few interesting guys, just nobody I meshed with enough for a long-term relationship."

I could feel Marco watching me as I looked out the window. The space between us was filled with anticipation. Suddenly, the moment was broken when he clapped his hands together, startling me out of my maudlin thoughts. "That is enough heavy conversation and deep thoughts for tonight. I just got off a nearly eleven-hour flight plus the commute from Logan and you've worked a long day." He tried to suppress a grin. "Apparently, you've also been rolling in wine and dirt. I think I'm going to need to institute a dress code here," he quipped.

I chuckled quietly and finished clearing off my desk. I gathered my belongings and Marco joined me for the walk out of the building. Marco lived in a very modern, compact home he had built when he took over running the family vineyard. His mother still lived in the family homestead along with his sister, her husband, and their four children. Even though the house was big enough – it was massive – for Marco to have his own wing, there seemed to be constant chaos happening around the house and I couldn't blame him for wanting his own space. He was close enough to help if needed, yet separate enough to lead his own life.

Marco's house was very cool and it was perfect for him. He had attached two former shipping containers and used the space judiciously. There were two bedrooms, each with an *en suite* bathroom, a gourmet kitchen, a cozy dining room, and a very comfortable living room. The whole house was bright and airy with large windows, French doors, skylights, and a beautiful terrace that overlooked the vineyard.

Ever the gentleman, even after the recent awkwardness, Marco walked me to my car. I opened my door and paused for a moment while Marco looked unsure what to do. He made a slight movement as if to hug me and I put my hand up. "Wait, I'm gross, remember?"

Marco snorted. "You are not gross, Kat. Your *clothes* might currently be gross, though." He looked me up and down in the light of the moon. "You'll have to tell me tomorrow what happened to cause this state of affairs."

I smiled slightly. "I'll put it on the agenda."

He grinned then grabbed me in a quick-release bear hug. "Get some sleep. Tomorrow we work."

I thought he was joking, but the next day was one of the longest days in my life. Of course, that night, when I got home, I immediately called Syd and we dissected my whole conversation with Marco. Sometimes you need your best friend to help you sort out complicated feelings and situations.

Chapter Thirteen

I woke up the next morning with the sun streaming through the window. Apparently, I had been so tired last night, I forgot to close my shutters. I stretched carefully and cataloged my aches and pains. At this point, I wasn't sure which pains were caused by my exercise regimen and which were caused by my tumble down the vineyard hill yesterday. At least I didn't have a training appointment with Cal Jr. today.

I turned on the shower and waited for the water to heat up. The shower massage beat down on my battered muscles and the heat helped to loosen them. I looked at the clock and realized I had somehow managed to get ready early, so I decided to make a quick stop at Sunny's bakery to say hi to my friend and pick up freshly brewed coffee. Sunny imported a rare Costa Rican blend that I couldn't get anywhere else and I was addicted to it. I thought about what I had eaten yesterday and decided to throw caution to the wind. I hoped that there would still be some *pain au chocolat.* Most people used the Callebaut *pain au chocolat* sticks, but Sunny used a delightful liquid chocolate inside the croissant that just melted in your mouth. Even just thinking about it, I began to salivate.

Sunny Side Up was mostly full and there was a long line. Sunny spied me at the back of the line and gave me a nod and lopsided smile. Knowing the owner does *not* help you move to the front of the line at Sunny's shop. I think the other customers would physically attack me if I even tried.

Fortunately, Sunny had three wait staff and they were very efficient so the line moved swiftly. I got lucky and Sunny was able to serve me and have a quick chat. I ordered a double shot of espresso and was very disappointed that the *pain au chocolat* bin was empty. I scanned the other pastries to see what else looked good – seriously, what doesn't look good at Sunny's? – and then noticed she already had a bag for me with my coffee. I looked at her in confusion and she leaned in and whispered, "I put two aside when I saw you walk in." I peeked inside the bag and was deliriously happy when I saw two *pains au chocolat.* I won't lie. I felt better than anyone else in the bakery right then.

Sunny laughed when she saw my expression. "I know the way to make you happy, Kat." Her expression clouded over. "I won't ask you how you're doing because I'm sure everyone is asking you that and I know how annoying that can be."

I nodded. Sunny had barely escaped death earlier in the summer and still had some lingering health issues because of the attack. I was sure she had heard more than her fair share of "how are you doing" inquiries. I shrugged. "It's sad and maddening and a little tense at the vineyard. Ty said he hasn't found any clues yet and they already interviewed the whole vineyard staff. The kids were scared and not sure what to expect." I inhaled the aroma from the pastry and sighed contentedly. "Ty has trained his staff so well, though, that they put the staff at ease. I don't think he got anything useful out of them because Pierre was so secretive, but at least they're not all asking to leave, right before the harvest."

Sunny nodded with a distant look in her eyes. "Pierre used to come here sometimes for my authentic French pastry. I don't think he ever said more than ten words to me in total. He seemed nice though." She frowned for a moment. "Actually, he was in here last week with what must have been one of the interns."

"Really?" I asked, immediately suspicious. "Which one?" None of the interns had admitted to me that they had spent any time alone with Pierre.

"One of the young men. The French one," she said decisively. "He was very charming and complimentary." She grimaced. "Made me wish I was fifteen years younger."

I shook my head in sympathy. I knew that feeling. "Did you hear what they were talking about?" Louis had been so non-communicative with me all summer that I couldn't see him as charming.

"No, they mostly spoke in French and it's been a while since I had any practice speaking French. Plus, it was crowded in here and kind of noisy." She thought for a moment. "I kind of think they were talking about gardens and how amusing they are." She shrugged. "At least, that's what I deciphered."

I made a face. I really didn't know Pierre at all. Gardening? Fortunately, Louis was still around and I could ask him about his conversation with Pierre.

I pulled my debit card out of my wallet and Sunny waved me away. "Don't worry about it. I can spot you a coffee and pastry every once in a while." I gave her a quick hug and we promised we would get together for drinks later that week.

My cell phone rang when I was on my way to the vineyard, the scent of hot coffee and warm pastry wafting through my car.

"Hey, Kat," Syd boomed out over my Apple Play car connection.

"Hi, Syd. What's up?" It wasn't like her to call just to chat. Between her graphic design business, art gallery, and painting beautiful watercolors – in addition to taking care of her family – Syd never seemed to have much time.

"My design software wasn't working this morning and I have a rush job for a logo that's due tomorrow. I'm waiting for Ricky to get off a conference call so he can fix it." I smiled. Syd was not very technically gifted and Ricky hated to do computer maintenance and repairs. He made an exception for Syd and me, but I knew I'd hear about it later. Syd was famous for deleting her apps on her Mac and then claiming that they just disappeared. Ricky would lecture her about being more careful and Syd would solemnly promise to do her best – until the next time she deleted something vitally important. Sometimes, it's a good thing when one of your best friends is a computer genius.

"How are you feeling today?" she inquired.

"I'm okay, but I tumbled down the vineyard hill yesterday and that didn't help me much."

I could hear her trying to muffle her laughter over the phone. I'm not sure how I had been such a good soldier and cop in the past, but now, I could trip over my own two feet while standing in line. I'm going to blame it on the meth addict.

"Laugh all you want, Syd. Maybe I'll just skip your next art opening."

Syd snorted as she tried to rein in her laughter. "Okay. Have you heard anything about the case?"

I shook my head then remembered we were not FaceTiming. "No, but I should be asking you that question. You're the one married to the Harmony Chief of Police."

"You know Ty doesn't like to share information about cases with me. He did tear apart my sewing kit last night though. I'm not sure why and he wouldn't say."

"Your sewing kit?"

"Yes. I caught him with my pinking shears in his hand."

Now I started laughing at the mental image of Ty holding a pair of pinking shears. Something began needling at the back of my mind, but I couldn't quite put my finger on it. "That's strange…" I trailed off.

"I thought you would find that interesting."

Suddenly, I heard Ricky yelling in the background.

Syd laughed again. "I'm being summoned by his majesty. He's squeezing me in between meetings so I had better go and see what he wants."

I was still thinking about the pinking shears. "Okay, have a great day." I stopped at the red light on State Street and glanced over at the bus stop bench. Looking back at me, big as day, was Amelia Smythe-Jones-Beauregard's smiling face. I grinned as I noted that some hooligans had drawn on a mustache. "Hey, wait!" I shouted before she could hang up.

"What?" Syd began to sound impatient. Syd liked to have things proceed according to her personal schedule.

I knew she was on a work deadline though, so I decided to ignore the tone in her voice. "Let me know if you and Ricky are available to go to the soft opening of Two Cups. Chance sent me a text this morning to remind me about the opening for friends and family only, and he told me to bring you both."

"Okay. I'll ask Ricky while he's doing my repairs and text you later this afternoon. *Ciao!*" Syd had been using Duolingo to learn Italian for a trip next summer and tried to insert at least one Italian word into every conversation. Ty had been promising for years to take her to Italy, and he was finally following through. She clicked off before I could reply and I turned on Milano Drive and thought about my morning testing Brix session with Marco. This was either going to be fun ... or a disaster.

Chapter Fourteen

It wasn't quite a disaster, but I just could not seem to get the hang of a refractometer. Basically, a refractometer measures the water content of liquid. Liquids that contain sugar, such as crushed grapes, are denser than water and cause greater refraction as light passes through. This refraction index is measured on the Brix scale and vineyards use the scale to determine when to harvest their grapes.

Sounds simple, right? For some reason, I could not get an accurate reading while looking through the eyepiece. "I don't understand how it is that you cannot see the numbers! Do you need glasses?" Marco asked me this last question as much out of concern as frustration.

I sank into a chair in the conference room. Marco had decided to train me in refractometer usage along with some of the other vineyard staff and community harvest volunteers. Justina had gotten it right away. Claude had come in because he was scheduled to work the harvest when the grapes were ready and he also wanted to learn more about grape growing. I think he had dreams of becoming a winemaker someday – that is if he could ever get out of the gym. That man was seriously in peak physical condition.

To amplify my embarrassment at not being able to get an accurate Brix reading, Mindy and Julian were there. I had heard that Mindy was throwing her hat into the ring for mayor in the special election. Harmony had called a special election for mayor because our last mayor had resigned in disgrace after the events at our high school reunion. His solicitation of sexual favors in exchange for the promise of a job was really what did him in, though. People could have excused his wife's naked ambition.

Mindy was, and still is, my arch-nemesis. She was a lifelong bully and elitist who thought she was better than everyone else. Especially me. Her barbed comments and malicious taunting had not dulled at all with age. She may have felt superior to me, but I secretly pitied her. I had witnessed much marital discord at the reunion, as well as her drunken oblivion, and knew that she was a deeply miserable person. Not that I liked her any better, but I did pity her.

Now that she was running for mayor, she had engaged in a publicity campaign to make herself seem more likable. She ran a catering and prepared meal business and consistently received negative customer service reviews. The food was delicious, as I grudgingly admitted the other day at Ricky's condo, but she did not know how to act in a service business. Apparently, her publicity campaign involved attending anything where there might be local voters, so she had volunteered for the harvest and dragged her husband along.

Julian was a trader and, even though I had met him several times at, and since, the reunion, I could not describe his face or eye color. He was continuously watching the market on his phone, making trades, or, more probably, finding ways to avoid Mindy. She tried to project domestic bliss, but I had witnessed a bitter fight that seemed long-running. I briefly wondered how Julian was going to help with the harvest with his hands wrapped around his phone.

Mindy saw me watching them and her fake smile turned into a genuine sneer. "Well, Kat, looks like you landed on your feet." She cast a sidelong glance at Marco. "Marco did always like to care for strays." She made sure that nobody else heard her spiteful comment and smirked meanly.

You know when people talk about getting so angry, they see red? Well, I saw red. I felt my blood pressure shoot up to the stratosphere and my hands curled into fists. Slowly and deliberately, I stood up. Once again, I was covered in crushed grape juice. I eyed Mindy, casting a quick glance at Julian, and leaned over the table toward her. "I hear your husband did the same for you."

Mindy gasped and her mouth hung open. She wasn't used to people fighting back, which is generally the case with bullies. I turned around smugly and let out the breath I had been holding. The red drained from my vision. I wandered over near Marco and could tell he was holding back a grin. "Did that feel good?" he asked quietly.

I was shocked that he had heard me, and a little embarrassed. I wasn't usually mean, but Mindy just brought it out in me. I should have known that Marco would monitor my interactions with Mindy. He had dated her in high school and knew how malicious she could be. I nodded quickly.

"I hate to refuse volunteers," he whispered, "but I never thought such objectionable people would volunteer." He shuddered. "Unlike a fine wine, she does not get better with age."

I snorted, trying to keep my laughter in. I pulled out my harvesting shears from my personal tool belt. "I can't imagine her trying to harvest grapes with thi…" I regarded the shears contemplatively.

"Are you too tired to finish your words now, too?" Marco inquired.

I shook my head and started walking quickly out of the conference room. "I'm going to order a digital refractometer. They're more accurate anyway," I called over my shoulder as I moved out of the office suite. Marco opened his mouth to reply but I was already down the hallway and moving fast.

The tasting room was still closed today so there was nobody there when I burst out of the administrative hallway. I peered through the windows and saw that there were still some police officers searching the grounds and talking to the staff. Officer Freely was interviewing Louis in the tasting room and both were visibly startled when I arrived.

"Officer Freely," I wheezed – wow, I really needed to work on my lung capacity and cardio – "Is Ty, I mean, Chief Randall, around?" I was still holding onto the harvesting shears and hastily shoved them back into my tool belt pocket.

Officer Freely shook her head. "He went back to the station."

I waved and dashed out to my car. I started the car and began the drive down the hill, reminding myself to breathe and drive carefully. I didn't want to get into an accident before I could get to Ty and tell him my vital clue.

Chapter Fifteen

When I arrived at the station, I stopped at the entry desk and asked for Chief Randall. The rookie called Ty and then sheepishly asked for my name. "Kat Snow," I replied brightly. Geez, he was young. Was I ever that young? I tried to remember back to the new recruit stage of my life and it felt like a lifetime ago.

"Chief Randall said to ask you to have a seat, Mrs. Snow…"

"That's Ms. Snow. Never assume someone's marital status. Officer Stewart," I read off of his uniform.

"Uh, I apologize *Ms.* Snow. This is only my second week and I wasn't expecting to be assigned to receptionist duty." He was acting like they had asked him to clean port-o-potties.

"No problem," I replied. I leaned in conspiratorially. "Let me give you a tip." He leaned in but I could tell he didn't think I could tell him anything he didn't already know. "I used to sit where you are." He looked in confusion at his chair. "Not literally. I was a cop with the BPD."

That made Officer Stewart sit up a little straighter and lose the sneer that had crept across his face.

"You need to treat every job they assign to you as if it's the most important job in the world. The brass takes note of everything – your attitude, how you interact with the public, how you dress," I eyed a mustard stain on the lapel of his shirt. "You will not be successful as a police officer in any position if you believe that any job in the department is beneath you."

"I don't plan on being here in Harmony for too long," he stated snidely.

"Really?" I feigned interest. "Why are you here then?"

"Harmony was the only department hiring right now. I want to be in a big city where the real crime happens. Not some sleepy coastal town." He eyed me speculatively. "Why'd you leave the BPD? Couldn't hack the responsibility?"

Oh, this guy was a peach, I thought derisively. "Actually, I retired on disability after being the youngest officer to make detective in homicide – ever. Oh, and after I was ambushed, stabbed by a meth head, and lost part of a lung."

Officer Stewart had the decency to look chagrined and squeaked out "Oh." He then clamped his mouth shut and indicated the seating area where I should wait.

Ty came out a few minutes later and fist-bumped me. That's Ty – as sentimental as raw sewage. Except with Syd. He treated Syd like a precious commodity, but she treated him the same way so it only seemed fair. "Hey, Kat." He looked at my wine-stained outfit. "Did you fall into a wine vat again?"

I gave him my most outraged look. "That only happened once," I looked away, "or maybe twice! And I didn't fall in a wine vat. I tripped over the wine discard barrel from the tasting room and it spilled all over the place." Officer Stewart was staring at us open-mouthed. Ty motioned me to follow him into the back room. As soon as the door closed, we both started chuckling.

"What's with Officer Sunshine?" I asked.

Ty kept chuckling. "Officer Sunshine. I like that. That may be his new nickname except he probably wouldn't get the irony." We crossed the bullpen area and entered his office. It was fairly modern, for Harmony. Ty had a laptop and a personal printer on a sleek, glass desk. Well, I think it was a glass desk. It was completely covered in papers, file folders, and telephone message notes.

Ty shook his head. "I doubt that 'Officer Sunshine' is going to pass probation or his psych eval. He is definitely one of those people who want to become a police officer for the power it gives them over others, not to enforce order and aid the community. Most cops aren't like that, but we need to weed out the ones that are. The bad ones give us all a bad name."

I agreed. When I was with the BPD, Internal Affairs had swept through my precinct and identified some cops for retraining and some for termination. I had been a good cop, but even good cops occasionally receive civilian complaints. IA cleared me, but I still remembered that feeling of tension and dread.

"What can I help you with, Kat?"

I thought for a moment about how to proceed. Ty hated it when Syd shared information with me, but I couldn't see any other way to explain why I had rushed down to see him. I looked him square in the eye and said coolly, "Syd tells me that you're taking up sewing?"

The look of confusion that crossed his face was priceless. He looked down at his hands and we both pictured them trying to maneuver with a tiny needle and thread. "I have no idea what you're

100

talking about but obviously Syd said something to you that triggered a thought and you ran down here to share it with me instead of just calling me on the phone," he looked at me pointedly, "like a rational human being. Spill the beans!"

I grinned. "Okay, but first, can I ask what was used to kill Pierre?"

"You can ask," he shrugged.

I sighed loudly. "Fine. Syd said you were searching through her sewing basket and ended up with her pinking shears."

"That's what they're called?" he asked incredulously.

"Yes. So, I assumed that the murder weapon must have been some type of shear."

Ty opened his mouth to reply, but I held up my hand. "Let me finish." Ty sighed and I continued. "You obviously concluded that Pierre was not killed with pinking shears and I've had this nagging thought at the back of my mind. Today, while we were testing the Brix…"

"Oh, that's what you call rolling around in grape juice?" he pointed at my wine-stained shirt and snickered.

I growled at him, low in my throat, and he held up his hands in mock defeat. "Please continue, Kat."

"As I was saying, while we were testing the Brix, I pulled my harvesting shears out of my tool belt and it struck me that they are similar, but not identical, to pinking shears. You might want to look for one of these as the murder weapon." I looked at him expectantly. "What do you think?"

Ty sighed. "I think it's a good idea, and it might even be true, but we haven't found a set of shears that match the victim's wounds," I winced at the word victim, "so I don't know yet if you're right or not."

I sighed and leaned back, deflated, in my seat. Ty was staring at the shears still in my hand and reached out for them. "Can I see those shears, please?"

I leaned in and handed over my shears. He examined them closely and tapped the handles. "Does everyone have their own set of shears?"

I remembered that the shears were engraved with my name. "Yes, and they are all engraved with our names and our Milano Vineyard logo, too. Marco thinks of it as helping fledgling winemakers build their wine toolkit. He wants us to always remember our time at Milano Vineyards."

Ty cocked an eyebrow. "*Our* Milano Vineyard?" he tried to ask innocently.

"*The* vineyard where we work. You know what I meant."

"I do, and I'm going to love telling Syd all about your Freudian slip of the tongue."

I rolled my eyes and he giggled in a very non-manly manner. "The engraving makes it easier to return someone's shears if they misplace them. Happens all the time."

"I will tell you this, Kat, and only because you used to be a homicide detective and you know the people involved." He let out a long breath. "This was a messy killing. I don't think this was a crime of passion or of opportunity, but a long-standing hatred that culminated in Pierre's murder."

"Why do you say that?"

"Pierre was stabbed twenty-two times, that we could distinctly count. Some of the stab wounds overlapped the others and enlarged the wounds so there could have been more."

I scowled. Nobody deserved that. "Poor Pierre. He seemed nice. A little cantankerous and set in his ways, but nice." I decided to take advantage of Ty's generous mood. "Any suspects?"

"Everybody and nobody. Somebody interrupted him while he was cooking, lured him to the bathroom, slaughtered him, and then placed him in a hot bath. Pinning down the exact time of death is proving to be difficult." He gave me an appraising look. "Okay, I hate to involve you in this, Kat, but I could really use your help. First, can I hold onto these shears so Dr. Nilsson can compare the shape to the wounds?" I nodded, a little sick at the thought. "Next, you know the vineyard and the staff and, well, you found the damn body."

I shuddered slightly, remembering my walk through Pierre's house. "What do you need?" Maybe I needed to exorcise some of my demons to help me get on with my life.

"We've interviewed the whole staff at the vineyard. Pierre and Giovanni had a long-standing feud about wine, but it seemed to be congenial by all reports." I nodded. "Justina, and/or Claude, may have been upset about Pierre's previous sexual harassment of

103

Justina, but they would have had no reason to tear his house apart. I mean, what could they have been looking for?"

My mind reeled with the information that Pierre had sexually harassed Justina. She had definitely denied it to me yesterday. I mean, Pierre had to have met Claude and nobody would want to have him angry at you. "I can't think of what they would search for in Pierre's house." I made a rolling motion with my right hand.

Ty nodded. "Right. Then there are the interns. Apparently, there was some harassment there, but they seem to have taken care of it earlier. And that was just the females. Pierre seemed to get along well with the guys and, again, there was no need to tear Pierre's house apart."

I thought for a moment. "I did hear that he and Max had a disagreement. It was work-related and seems minor though. Not enough to stab someone twenty-two times and again, no reason to search the house."

"What was the disagreement?" Ty asked. "This is the first I'm hearing of discord between Pierre and any of the male interns.

"It was more of a methods argument. Pierre – and Marco – wanted to keep everything the same at the vineyard and Max wanted to update the scale we use to measure when the grapes are ready and when we actually pick."

Ty exhaled in disgust and I shrugged. "You asked. I didn't think he was a *good* suspect, but I know you need all the information about everyone." I thought for a moment. "Sunny said that Louis and Pierre were at her bakery a few days ago arguing about gardening."

"Gardening?" Ty asked in exasperation.

I shook my head. "Well, that's what she thought. They were speaking in French and the bakery was busy, so…" I shrugged.

"Yeah, thanks." Ty opened his water bottle and took a long swallow of water. "Well, now you know what I know. Let me know if you hear, or think of, anything else."

I nodded as I stood up. "I should probably get back to work, too. I ran out in the middle of some training."

Ty looked at me seriously. "Kat, don't act like you own the place yet. Wait until he puts a ring on your finger." Then he burst out laughing.

I stuttered all the way out past the bullpen and past Officer Sunshine, I mean Stewart. Damn! Ty knows how to shut me up – and that doesn't happen very often.

Chapter Sixteen

I tried to slip quietly into my office without being observed. No such luck.

"Kat! Where did you run off to?" Marco's voice boomed across the office suite.

I popped my head out of my office and looked around. Marco and Giovanni were in the conference room, leaning far back in their chairs, with a few empty bottles of wine on the table. I sighed and made my way across the suite to join them. Marco kicked a chair out with his foot and graciously indicated I should sit. I could tell he was drunk and in a bit of a snit and replied meekly, "I had an idea about the case and needed to go see Ty."

"Interesting, very interesting." He leaned toward me and asked, "Does your job description include investigating a murder?"

Giovanni snorted loudly and I realized he was sleeping. I began quietly counting the number of bottles on the table. I decided that the best way to de-escalate the situation was to apologize and ask for forgiveness. After all, I shouldn't have just taken off in the middle of training.

"I'm sorry, Marco. Please forgive my momentary lapse in judgment. I just want the killer to be found so Pierre can have justice."

Marco took a deep breath like he was ready to launch into a full dress-down when my words registered. He deflated immediately and just looked sad. "I was worried you were unwell, Kat. After what happened with Pierre, I couldn't stand to lose you, too."

My heart melted. I had been gearing up for him to make me feel badly about leaving when he had just been concerned. And a little drunk. I counted six bottles. Make that quite drunk.

"I *am* sorry that I worried you, Marco. It won't happen again."

Marco snorted then giggled in a very drunken fashion, "I doubt that." He leaned back and seemed to be settling in. He murmured, "I think I'll just sleep right here tonight."

It was my turn to chuckle. "That's not a great idea. Hold on." I ran to my office and looked up toward the interns' dorms. The twilight was creeping up and I noticed that they seemed to be getting ready to go on a hike. I dashed down the hall and out of the tasting room. I was already feeling a little winded, so I grabbed a golf cart and drove as fast as I could over to the dorms, skidding on the dirt driveway, and startling the interns.

"What's up, Kat?" Max called out.

I looked at the six of them. Some were wearing headlamps and others had large flashlights. "I need some help getting Marco and Giovanni back to their houses."

"Are they sick?" Alessa asked with concern.

I shook my head. "No, but I think they overindulged at their own private memorial for Pierre."

They nodded sadly. Alessa, who I had secretly called the quiet intern all summer, stepped forward. "I will help."

"Great. Two more would be fantastic so Alessa and I don't have to manhandle both of them…?" I trailed off.

107

Max sighed. "Okay. Jayson and I will help too." He looked at Ava, Louis, and May. "Bring the supplies down there and we'll meet you in about fifteen minutes." They nodded and continued packing food, water, and wine into backpacks.

Jayson, Alessa, and I climbed into my golf cart and I drove back to the main building. Max jogged over and got another cart and met me by the tasting room door. I paused with my hand on the door. "What do you all have planned for this evening?" I asked innocently.

Max hemmed and hawed a little and Jayson and Alessa wouldn't look at me. Finally, Max sighed and replied, "We are planning our own memorial for Pierre. In the wine caves. He spent so much time down there, we thought we would do some exploring in teams and then have a few toasts to his memory. We heard that the main tunnel runs directly down to the beach in Harmony." He looked around guiltily. "Please don't tell Marco. I'm not sure how he'll feel about our little expedition."

I nodded. "No problem. There is no way that he will remember anything I tell him now anyway. He's quite inebriated."

A look of intense relief washed over Max's face. "Thanks, Kat." He looked at the other two then looked at me slyly. "You know, you're welcome to join us if you'd like. We planned to go in teams of two but we could have a team of three…?"

I thought about it for a moment and then looked through the glass door into the tasting room. I could see Marco trying to open one of the wine refrigerators, but he was grabbing at the side that didn't have a handle. I shook my head in disbelief. "Let me see how everything goes with getting these two back to their houses first. This could be more difficult than I expected."

Everyone chuckled and we walked in the door. Max and I approached Marco while Jayson and Alessa went down the hall toward the office suite.

"Hey, Marco," Max called softly.

Marco spun around with a bottle of red in his left hand and a bottle of white in his right. "Max," he slurred loudly. "I need a new drinking buddy. Giovanni passed out and I hate to drink alone." Marco took a step forward and tripped over his own feet. He crashed to the floor but managed to keep the wine bottles from shattering. He giggled again, eying the bottles, "Phew, that was close."

Max looked at me and rolled his eyes. We both leaned over and grabbed one of his arms. Marco looked at me in surprise. "Kat, when did you get here?"

"Just now," I replied without missing a beat. I took the bottles and put them on a nearby table. He'd feel crappy enough tomorrow without me making him feel bad now for forgetting our conversation of only ten minutes ago.

"Will you drink with me, Kat?" He tried to sound alluring and sexy. He failed on both counts because what he actually said sounded more like, "Wi you drnk wi me, Ka?" and it was considerably more comical than flirtatious.

"Sure, Marco, but let's go drink at your house. It's much more comfortable there." I heard a loud noise and turned to see Jayson and Alessa literally dragging Giovanni out through the tasting room. He had an arm around each of their shoulders but was not moving his feet or supporting himself in any way. Jayson stage-whispered, "We'll meet you at the entrance in about ten minutes."

Max held up an okay sign with his hands. Marco looked around confused. "Max? You here, too?" he slurred.

"Max is just going to drive us to your house, Marco."

"Ok," he tried to wink but ended up blinking both eyes. "I might feel a little frisky tonight, Kat."

His drunken charm was wearing a little thin. This was really no time for him to be flirting with me. I once again recalled that female voice in his room in Peru. Did he want me to be one of his string of conquests? Not going to happen. Plus, there was Chance to consider. I shook my head. What was I doing even contemplating any of this? Chance was not mine to consider and Marco seemed to have at least one woman in Peru – who knew how many others there were? I guess that I would just have to go meet some new men if I wanted to start dating.

Max was looking at me with some worry. "Everything okay, Kat?

"Sorry, momentarily distracted. I think I've been working too many days without a day off."

"That can happen." He looked at Marco then back at me. "Let's get moving. I don't want to miss anything."

Marco looked at us both expectantly. "Well, leth go!" he slurred and headed toward the door.

Max and I looked at each other and ran to catch up with him. We each grabbed one of Marco's arms and steered him to the golf cart. Jayson and Alessa were still having problems loading Giovanni into the back of their cart, but he suddenly woke up and pushed them away. "I can hold on. *Andiamo!*" he yelled, as if he had not just been carried out to the cart. Jayson threw his hands up in the air and stalked around the cart to get behind the wheel. Alessa slid into the back next to Giovanni to make sure he didn't fall out. Jayson took off in a cloud of dust that left us all coughing.

Marco angrily raised his fist in the air and shook it at the retreating golf cart. Then he quietly got into the cart behind the wheel. Max looked at him and simply said, "*Nein.*"

Marco rolled his eyes – though it looked more like his eyes were rolling back into his head – and slid over into the passenger seat. By the time we reached his house, he was struggling to stay awake. Max and I walked him to his front door and got him inside. He fell onto his sofa and a bottle dropped softly to the ground. Damn! How had I missed that bottle? "Raincheck, Kat," he mumbled.

I smiled. He could be just like a little kid sometimes. Or, a rather annoyingly overgrown man-child, most of the time. I found a blanket in a linen closet and covered the already snoring Marco. Max turned to go. "I'm heading to the caves. Last chance – do you want to come with us?"

I paused for a moment. I really could use the sleep – but, I had also always wanted to explore those caves further. Who knew when I would have another opportunity? It would be safer in a group, too. I made up my mind. "I will go, but I need a sweater. It gets cool down there and I only have this dirty T-shirt."

"I'm sure Marco has something you can borrow."

I felt a little weird, rifling through Marco's closet but told myself I would grab the first sweatshirt I found. The closet smelled lightly of Marco's scent – kind of woodsy and musky with a hint of vanilla – it smelled almost like a warm hug.

I shook myself back to reality. What was with me today? I finally saw some sweatshirts folded neatly at the back of the walk-in closet. I swear, he has more clothes than me. I grabbed the top sweatshirt and hastened out while pulling it over my head.

Max stopped and stared at my chest when he saw me. "You are going to wear that?"

"I didn't read it," I said. "Why, what does it say?" I looked upside down at the wording on the sweatshirt and read "World's #1 Bikini Inspector" splashed across the front of the sweatshirt with a lewd picture of a woman and I quickly pulled it off. I shuddered and was about to go back to Marco's closet when I spied a black hoodie on a hook by the door. I had seen Marco wear this recently and knew there were no lewd messages on it anywhere that would embarrass me.

Wrapped in Marco's voluminous hoodie, I followed Max down the path to the tunnel entrance. Jayson and Alessa had just arrived and looked upset.

"What's wrong?" I asked with concern.

Alessa glanced at Jayson but he had wandered off to go talk to the others. She shuddered. "That was not fun." May walked over to see why Alessa was upset.

"What happened?" May inquired.

Alessa rolled her eyes. "Giovanni fell asleep on the short drive to his cottage. He then fell out of the golf cart and I didn't catch him in time so he began rolling down the hill." She put her hands on her hips. "Even that did not wake him up so Jayson and I had to drag him back up the hill and put him back into the golf cart. We were afraid he would fall out again, so Jayson rode in the back and held onto him."

"Oh, no!" I whispered.

"*Si,*" she replied. She looked around guiltily. "I am afraid he is going to be quite bruised and battered tomorrow morning. I hope he doesn't take it out on us."

May put an arm around her. "Don't worry, Alessa. Kat will make sure everything is okay."

I put my hand on her arm. "Absolutely, "I agreed. "He probably won't even remember what happened." I thought for a moment. "If he does though, and if he is upset with you and Jayson, I will step in. *You* were only trying to help him. It's not your fault he was too drunk to accept assistance."

Alessa seemed partially consoled and we joined the others. We stood in a small circle. Louis had opened two of the Milano pinot noir bottles and Ava passed out plastic cups. I sipped the wine as I listened to them discuss the evening's plans.

Max pulled out three handwritten maps and scowled. "I couldn't find any official maps of the caves except for these that I bought from those tour guides in town."

I looked at him quizzically. "Tour guides?" I thought for a moment and snorted. "You mean Danny and Robbie? The surfer dudes?"

Max nodded. "Are they not tour guides, too?"

I shrugged. "I guess they do occasionally take tourists on tours of Harmony." I leaned in to look at the maps. "This should be interesting."

Max looked at one of the maps. "They are not very detailed, but we should be able to follow them for a little while." He gestured at Louis. "Shine your flashlight over here."

Louis stepped forward and shone his light on one of the maps. Max continued. "About fifty yards in, the entrance tunnel opens into a cavern. That's where we store and age most of the vineyard's wine." He traced the route and then pointed at three additional lines leading away from the cavern. "We will split up into our teams here and each of us will follow a tunnel." He looked more closely at the map. "There are no tunnels shown that shoot off of these tunnels, but I have been a little ways down each of them and know that there are also some side tunnels."

He looked at the group. "I think we should add more details to the maps if we discover any new tunnels. Marco mentioned earlier this summer that he might like to add a 'Wine Tasting and Tunnel

Tour" for next season and it would help to have detailed maps to give the tourists."

Everybody nodded in agreement.

Max continued. "The maps don't show any of the tunnels leading down to the beach, but the two tour guides assured me they all lead down there eventually."

I was a little worried at the word "eventually."

Max looked at me. "We drew straws before to decide the teams. May is with me. Jayson and Ava. And Louis and Alessa. You can join whichever team you want."

Alessa took my arm. "I want Kat to come with us." She looked at Louis. "Is that okay?"

Louis nodded. *"Bien sûr."*

Max nodded again. "That's settled then." He looked around. "Any questions? Remember, our goal is to find the tunnel down to the beach." Nobody said a word. *"Allons-y!"* he said with an exaggerated French accent that sounded extra funny with his slight German accent.

Chapter Seventeen

It felt a little bit like a party. Everyone had their plastic cup full of wine, a flashlight, and a great attitude. There were three headlamps – which of course, the guys decided to commandeer – and they led the way.

I hadn't been in the caves recently and noticed a lot of the racks were empty in the main cavern. "Max," I called out. "Why are there so many empty racks?"

He waved his arms around. "We have been making room for the new wine, after the harvest and the crush. We will need to store the newly pressed wine to age before bottling and this is the best place we have." He held his hand up and then pointed at some sophisticated meter on the wall. "As you can feel, the temperature is stable and cool and there is a consistent humidity level." He smiled fondly. "*Parfait*," as Pierre always liked to say.

Everyone held their glass up in a silent toast to Pierre and then we separated into our groups. Louis indicated the far right tunnel. "This is the one we're supposed to investigate." He held up a clipboard and handed it to Alessa. The clipboard had a copy of the map and a pen attached. "We can use our phones to track the distance so we can be as accurate as possible on the map."

Alessa nodded and we started down the tunnel with Louis in the lead, followed by Alessa, and I brought up the rear. The tunnel was about ten feet wide and one side had additional racks of casks that were aging wine. Louis pointed at some of the casks. "These are the pinot noir casks. Milano Vineyards ages their pinot noir wines for approximately eleven months."

Louis had been here as long as Alessa and only slightly longer than me, so his tour guide routine was more than a little condescending. I wondered if Alessa thought the same as me – until she turned around and rolled her eyes. I chuckled softly as we padded down the tunnel.

After about fifty yards, the tunnel started to descend slightly and there were no more casks. Not a shar descent, but enough that you had to be more careful about where you stepped. Fifty yards after that, we came to another tunnel, branching off to the right. Louis shined his light down the tunnel. "Is this on the map?"

Alessa nodded and then must have realized it was difficult to see her in the dark. "Yes. This one is here." She pointed at the map and peered down at it. "It looks very short, maybe only ten yards or so, then it opens into a small cave."

Louis nodded. "I think that is where they store the pinot grigio bottles." He pointed down the dark tunnel. "Let's go further down this main tunnel."

I noticed that Alessa was wearing a pair of flip-flops and thought that this terrain must be hard on her feet. "It's not a race, Louis. Why are you rushing'""

He turned to face me, the headlamp temporarily blinding me. "It is a race. Max bet Jayson and me that his team would reach the beach first. A hundred dollars to the team that makes it to the beach

117

first *with* the most complete map." Without waiting for a response from us, Louis turned and started walking quickly down the tunnel.

Alessa rolled her eyes at his behavior once again and sighed. "He likes things to be his way, but he's basically a nice guy."

I smiled. "I'll let you in on a secret…they're all like that."

Alessa grinned and then we shuffled off after Louis.

Chapter Eighteen

Three hours later, Alessa and I were exhausted and our feet ached when we finally emerged onto the beach. We had lost Louis about two hours ago and mainly navigated by our wits. After a certain point, the map was useless and the batteries in the flashlight began to die. We had split up to check out a couple of side tunnels, Alessa and I going down one and Louis another with the agreement that we would meet back in the main tunnel in fifteen minutes.

Alessa and I had gone down several additional side tunnels, some of them dead ends, and eventually got a bit lost, so it had taken us at least a half hour to find our way back to the main tunnel. Louis wasn't there, and after waiting a while and even going as far as we dared down the side tunnel he had taken and calling his name, we decided to keep going.

We agreed to stick to the main tunnel and just keep walking what felt like downwards. The tunnel was bound to lead us out somewhere near Harmony – we hoped. I also hoped the exit wasn't underwater. Either way, we faced a *long* hike back to the vineyard if there was no exit. We had tried to use Google Maps to navigate, but could not get a signal. I wasn't sure if it was due to the fact that we were underground or that the signal could not penetrate through the stones in the tunnels. We were able to use our phone flashlights, but they weren't very bright and our batteries drained quickly.

We saw what we hoped was moonlight about twenty yards ahead of us and were startled when someone came stumbling out of another tunnel. It was Jayson.

"Wow! You guys are a sight for sore eyes!" Jayson was out of breath and shaking.

Alessa peered up the tunnel he had just exited. "Why are you alone?"

Jayson crossed his arms and started to pout. "Ava didn't want to work on the map. She was focused on being first to the beach so she could win the hundred dollars." He huffed noisily. "I told her the bet needed both a completed map and to be first to the beach, but she didn't care. She took off and left me there with just the headlamp. She even took the map." He looked at us again, somewhat gratefully. "I've been wandering around this tunnel for hours, I think."

Alessa smiled and linked her arm through his. "Yes, we've been in these caves for about three hours now. There is light ahead and Kat and I hope it is moonlight coming through the cave exit."

"Let's go then," Jayson prompted and began tugging at Alessa, anxious to get out of the caves.

We needed no additional encouragement either and we all walked as quickly as we were able for the last thirty yards. Nothing ever looked so good to me as the sight of Max and Louis sitting on the beach next to a crackling bonfire.

Despite our lengthy journey, we were not the last ones to arrive – I didn't see Ava or May either. The three of us hurried over to the fire and began warming ourselves over the flame.

Louis was lounging on a piece of driftwood and casually ventured, "What took you so long?"

Alessa turned and glared at Louis. "We spent a good half-hour looking for you after waiting at the *rendezvous* for nearly twenty minutes. Where were you?"

Louis shrugged dismissively. "I got turned around and couldn't figure out how to get back to the main tunnel. I finally found my way down here and I've been here for about a half hour."

Max looked at him doubtfully and shook his head forcefully. "*Nein!* You've been here maybe for fifteen minutes."

Louis shrugged again. "Maybe it felt longer because I was stuck here with just you."

A look of disgust flitted over Max's face.

I turned to Max. "Where's your partner? Where's May?"

"She said she had a migraine about a half-hour into the expedition and wanted to head back to the dorm. I offered to walk her back but she told me that she would be fine. I gave her my headlamp so it would be easier to navigate." He picked up his phone and looked at it. "She was supposed to text me, though, when she got back to let me know that she was okay." He grinned sheepishly. "I was going to ask her to come to get us in the Cherokee so we don't have to walk back."

Oh, crap, I thought. We hadn't planned this expedition well at all. Suddenly, Ava stumbled out of the tunnel exit. She was filthy and had a few bloody cuts on her face.

Jayson and Louis stayed by the bonfire while Alessa, Max, and I went rushing to help her over to the fire. She smiled gratefully at us and sank down onto another piece of driftwood.

Alessa pulled some wet wipes and a bottle of water out of her backpack. She gave Ava the water and used the wipes to dab at her face and staunch the blood flow.

I found a spare hair tie in my pocket and gave it to Ava so she could pull her tangled tresses into a ponytail. She downed the water, sighed softly, and seemed to relax by the fire.

I asked her gently, "What happened, Ava?"

She shook her head in disgust. "It's my own fault. I left Jayson because I was feeling competitive." She looked over at Jayson and smiled ruefully. "I'm sorry. I should never have deserted you."

Jayson looked ready to argue with her but I could tell he felt bad at her bruised and bloodied condition.

Ava rolled her head around to loosen the kinks. "I was traveling at a pretty good rate and thought for sure I would get here first. I saw some bobbing lights down a cross tunnel and called out, but nobody replied and I got nervous." She looked around. "Whoever it was, they must have heard me. It's basically an echo chamber in there." She shuddered. "So, I wanted to put as much distance between me and the lights as possible, in case it wasn't one of you. I began to jog and…" She sighed and rolled her eyes. "And I tripped and rolled down a steep part of the tunnel for what felt like a mile but was probably only twenty feet or so, maybe less. I must have hit my head and blacked out because when I opened my eyes, I was in total darkness and couldn't find my flashlight."

"Oh, no," Alessa cried. "How did you find your way out?"

Ava took a deep breath and closed her eyes. "Very carefully. I walked slowly and kept my hand on the cave wall to help guide me. I must have tripped over a million rocks and then my hand touched something sticky that I think was probably bat guano…" She grabbed the package of wipes from Alessa and frantically began cleaning her hands. She stuffed the used wipes into her own backpack.

"That's horrible," I murmured. It was good I hadn't considered bats before going into the tunnel or I might not have gone. I was traumatized by bats in my mother's house as a child and now I stay as far away from them as possible.

Ava looked around and did a quick calculation. "Where's May?"

Max shrugged and explained again. "Migraine. She went back pretty early."

"Really?" asked Ava. "At one point on my descent in the darkness, I thought I heard her voice from a long way off."

Max looked worried. "Maybe she got turned around. She hasn't texted me to say she made it back to the dorm okay."

Louis sat up and threw a few more pieces of wood onto the fire. "I'm sure she's fine," he said dismissively.

Max gave him a dirty look and pulled two bottles of wine from his backpack. "Well, let's have a drink and warm up while we think about how to get back to the vineyard. I don't think any of us want to walk back through the tunnels."

We all shook our heads emphatically and Alessa whispered, "No."

Max walked around and filled up our cups. "Does anyone know where we are – in relation to the vineyard?"

I looked out at the water. "I think we're north of town, maybe about a mile or so."

Jayson looked at me then looked up at the steep hill behind us. "How do you know?"

I pointed out at the water. "I can see the Newburyport Harbor Light and I know how it looks from Harmony." I shrugged. "We're further north than that, probably about a mile."

Max still looked worried. "That doesn't help us get home though."

I pulled out my phone. "I'll call my friend to come pick us up."

Jayson pointed at the steep hill. "Do we have to climb up that?"

I smiled. Sometimes I forget that the interns weren't local and didn't know their way around. "No, we just have to walk up the beach around that giant rock and there's a public beach about a half-mile away."

Everyone sighed with relief and began cleaning up the beach. Jayson and Louis kicked sand onto the fire to put it out and Max collected the garbage.

We began a slow hike up the beach and I could tell that everyone was exhausted. I pulled my phone out and said, "Call Syd."

I grimaced as I noted that it was almost eleven o'clock. Fortunately, she sounded wide awake when she answered the phone.

"Want to take a ride?" I asked cheerfully.

Chapter Nineteen

Never underestimate the value of your best friends. The fact that Syd didn't even question why I wanted her to bring her van to pick up me and five friends at a closed public beach twenty minutes from her house after eleven o'clock at night meant the world to me. I would, of course, fill her in on the details later – but everyone needs to have that one friend they can always count on. I could have called Ricky too, but his Tesla would not have fit all six of us.

Syd pulled into the parking lot just as we trudged across the beach and stomped the sand off our feet. Being a mother, she had thought ahead and brought bottles of water and snacks. We fell on the food like we hadn't eaten in days. I had missed dinner, but really, I should be able to skip a meal without acting like an animal.

We all took turns telling Syd our tales of the evening. She thought it was very adventurous and brave of us, but she was also a little disappointed to have missed the journey. When Ava mentioned the bat guano, Syd looked at me sharply – she knew about my aversion to bats.

Max continued calling May but she didn't answer her phone. We pulled up to the vineyard about a half-hour later and basically fell out of the van. Syd informed me that she would be driving me home and that she would bring me to work in the morning. I pretended to be annoyed but I was secretly pleased. Everyone wants to be mothered sometimes.

We waited while Max ran up to the intern dorms to look for May. He was back in less than five minutes, in a frantic state of mind. "She's not there. It doesn't look like she's been back either."

As the enormity of his words weighed down on us, I began to panic, too. Fortunately, Syd was well rested – and married to the Chief of Police – so she calmly pulled out her phone and called Ty.

"Honey? I believe we have a missing person to report."

I could hear Ty mumble in the background. I hoped he wasn't sleeping. I know how exhausting murder investigations can be and he probably hadn't slept much in the past two days.

Syd began speaking again. "I'm at the vineyard. Kat and the interns went on an adventure this evening and one of the interns didn't make it back."

There was some low rumbling coming over the phone speaker.

"We can discuss that when you get here, but please alert the Search and Rescue Team and tell them to be ready to explore the cave network to the north of town. We'll all wait at the vineyard..."

I gestured toward the tasting room.

"Yes, we'll be in the tasting room." She got out of the car and we started walking toward the building. We all looked at each other wearily and followed after her. We stood there dumbly for a moment until I remembered that I had the keys. I fumbled them out of my backpack and we spread out at the five tables in the tasting room.

Alessa jumped up. "I need something warm to drink. Coffee?" she asked, looking at the group.

"I'll help you," Syd offered. "We'll make some coffee, hot chocolate, and tea. Knowing Marco," she gave me a knowing look, "and Kat, there's sure to be snacks back there too."

I smiled weakly at her; happy she was there to take charge for the moment.

Ten minutes later, Syd brought out a tray with hot coffee, creamers, and sugar. I noticed she had found my supply of Snickers bars but decided that I could share in this situation. Alessa came out with the pizza box from the other day.

"There's enough for everyone," she announced. We all grabbed a slice. Even cold pizza was good from Roma's, I thought as I sank my teeth into the buttery crust.

The police arrived as I took my second bite of pizza. Ty came striding in, looking even more tired than me, if that was possible. He came straight over to me, followed by the Captain of the Massachusetts State Police Missing Persons Division, Clark Kent. I don't know if his parents were huge Superman fans or if they were clueless, but I know Captain Kent had endured much good-natured ribbing over the years. I had met him when I was with Homicide at the BPD. We took over a missing person case after the body was found murdered in a drainage ditch. He gave me a small nod of recognition. I noticed that he had been promoted. He had only been a sergeant when I met him.

"Ms. Snow, could you please tell us what you know about the missing person?" It always made me smile a little to hear Ty in his professional role. I had seen him rolling around the floor and pretending to be a horse for his kids when they were young. It was difficult to meld the two images of the man.

"Her name is May…" I looked over at Max with uncertainty.

"Lee," Max whispered. I knew he was feeling guilty for letting May go back through the caves on her own.

"Right. May Lee," Ty murmured to himself as he wrote the information into his notebook.

Captain Kent took over the questioning. He asked some identifying questions such as May's age, address, and physical description.

I looked to Max again and he waved at me dismissively. "I got this, Kat." He pulled out his mobile phone. "I have all the interns' information as well as pictures on my phone." Ty and I walked a few steps away while Captain Kent and Max huddled over his phone.

"What were you thinking, Kat?" Ty demanded angrily.

His sudden change in demeanor threw me off and I stammered, "Wh- What?"

He was incredulous. "There was a murder just a few nights ago. One of those interns could be the murderer and you thought it was a good idea to go wandering mindlessly through the unexplored tunnels and caves of Harmony at night without a detailed map or

129

cave exploration equipment? Without telling anybody what you were doing?"

I stared at Ty with my mouth open for a few moments. "I guess I never thought they were suspects," I finally muttered. "They barely knew Pierre."

Ty continued, angrily whispering to me, "You don't know how well they knew him, Kat, or if they had a long history with him. You've only worked here a few months and Pierre had a whole long life before you arrived on the scene." He scowled and glared out the window, watching the local and state police arrive and break into groups. "I shouldn't have to tell you this, Kat, but everyone is a suspect – even you."

I sputtered. "What? How can you think I'm a suspect?"

Ty shook his head. "Come on, Kat, think clearly. You were a cop. You know that everyone is a suspect until they're completely cleared and alibied out." He shook his head sadly and put his arm around my shoulders. I angrily shook him off. "Kat, come on. I *know* you didn't kill Pierre, but I have to keep you on my suspect list until I can completely clear you. Otherwise, I'll be accused of bias and possibly removed from my job."

I calmed down enough to see the logic in his words. "Alright. As long as you *know* I didn't do it."

Ty turned me to face him and put a hand on each shoulder. "Seriously though, Kat, you need to be smarter. We have no idea right now if May is just lost, playing a joke, hurt, or…" he looked around carefully, "if something bad happened to her." He looked at me earnestly and I think I saw a tear in the corner of his eye, "Syd would be devastated if anything happened to you. She was a wreck when you were attacked in Boston."

I nodded. "Right. Syd would be devastated."

He grinned at me crookedly and then turned when Captain Kent called his name to beckon him over to the police groupings. I noticed that Danny Winters and Robbie Branson were handing out what looked to be maps. They led boat tours around Harmony harbor and the surrounding area in the summers. A few brave souls went scuba diving with them as well, but I think the scuba trade dropped off a lot when all the great white sharks started coming closer to shore a few years ago. I don't know if they were actually coming closer or if we just knew they were coming closer now that so many had been radio-tagged. Regardless, I wasn't going in any deep water – nor shallow water – any time soon. I learned my lesson from *Jaws*.

Danny and Robbie were well known around town. They would be called surfer dudes if we lived someplace with actual big waves to surf. They were about five years younger than me, their skin dark and hard, like leather. They had been regulars at my mother's bar – and probably every other bar in town, if you know what I mean. They were also well known to both the local and state police and their names were often printed in the police blotter of the *Harmony News* for disturbing the peace or for being drunk and disorderly. As far as I knew, they were both single. I don't think anyone would put up with their shenanigans, female or male.

131

I grabbed Ty's arm. "What are they doing here?" I pointed at Danny and Robbie.

Ty snorted and shook his head. "Believe it or not, those two have quite extensive knowledge of the caves and tunnels." He whispered conspiratorially, "Probably because they used to smuggle in some marijuana before it was legal in Massachusetts. You know there are stories about secret rooms and caverns in the tunnels."

"That's an old wives' tale," I scoffed.

Ty shrugged. "I'm really not sure, but they do know their way around in there. Marco's father used to call the police on them for trespassing whenever he caught them in there. He was afraid they were stealing his wine."

I laughed. Wine was the last thing those two would drink. Ty continued. "So, we asked them for maps to guide us so we can hopefully find May Lee as quickly as possible. They agreed – probably to gain favor with us before their next brush with the law."

Ty gave me a half hug and then pointed outside. "Do you want to come with us or are you waiting here?" He looked around quickly. "By the way, where is Marco?"

I rolled my eyes. "Drunk as a skunk and probably snoring on his living room couch where I left him about four hours ago." I looked at all the police outside. "I'd wake him up, but I don't think he'd be any help in his current state." I considered whether I wanted to go back into the caves and then thought about my aching feet. "I'll wait here in the tasting room." I looked at the interns who were yawning but seemed to be firmly encamped there, too. "I'm sure we'll all be here until you find May."

Ty nodded grimly and went outside to join one of the search parties.

I went and sat with Alessa and Max as the teams headed out in the direction of the cave entrance.

Chapter Twenty

Waiting for May to be found felt like an eternity but really was only two hours. We sat quietly most of the time – it didn't feel right to have casual, lighthearted conversations when May was missing. We all had assumed that she would be found, lost and disoriented, wandering through some distant tunnels, but that hope faded as time wore on.

As soon as Ty walked into the tasting room, I knew that May was dead. The interns realized it as well barely a moment after I did. Alessa began quietly crying and Ava sobbed loudly. Max moved to sit closer to Ava and put an arm gingerly around her shoulders. She collapsed against him.

Max was trying to put on a brave face, but I could tell that he was upset, too. His eyes were glassy and his movements were robotic. Jayson and Louis looked shell-shocked and sat in their seats stoically.

Ty cleared his throat. I had grabbed Alessa's hand and she was squeezing it like it was a life preserver and she was stranded in the middle of the ocean. Even though I knew what was coming, I still felt sucker-punched. "We found May," he reported quietly.

Jayson tried to stay hopeful. "How is she?"

Ty looked carefully at each of us before he shook his head sadly. "I'm sorry. May is dead."

A collective gasp went through the room and it felt as if all the oxygen was being sucked away from me. I squeezed Alessa's hand as desperately as she squeezed mine. Syd leaned in and hugged both of us.

Max was still holding Ava against him but sounded hoarse even after he cleared his throat. "What happened? Did she fall or trip over something?"

Ty looked at everyone individually for a moment before answering. "I'm afraid not. May was murdered."

Ava gasped loudly and stood up shakily. Suddenly, her body went rigid and she fell to the floor before Max could reach her. The shock of the impact woke her up, but there was a small pool of blood on the floor under her head. Ty and Max knelt next to her as we all gathered around. I finally came to my senses and my training kicked in.

"Everyone, step away and give her some air." Apparently, I could still command a modicum of authority, and Jayson, Louis, and Alessa backed up. I pointed them to tables across the room and they podded over and sat down.

There had been an ambulance sitting in the parking lot in case May had been found with injuries, so the paramedics were fortunately on hand. They rushed in and pushed Max and Ty away. They loaded Ava on a stretcher and immobilized her head to ensure no further damage, then wheeled her quickly out to the ambulance.

I noticed that Ty motioned to Officer Freely and she peeled away to climb into the ambulance with Ava. I was sure she would wait at the hospital and take Ava's statement after the doctors cleared her.

I went in the back and brought out a case of water, then sat at my own table to wait. I knew that the police questions and witness statements would eat up the rest of the night.

Ty assigned officers to interview myself and the interns. He went to sit with Max. Officer Thermon, whom I had met at my reunion, sat across from me. No, she didn't go to school with us, but there were some murders at my reunion, and, well, that story can wait for another time, but trust me when I say that *Reunions Can Be Murder.*

Before Officer Thermon began asking questions, I realized that Marco really should be here, even if he wasn't entirely clear-headed. I called out to Ty, "I need to call Marco. He needs to be here now."

Ty considered for a moment and then nodded. I picked up my mobile phone and hit the speed dial for Marco. It rang for a long time and voice mail finally picked up. I sighed in exasperation. Why did Marco have to pick tonight to get so hammered? He should be here, dealing with all this. I left him a quick message to call me back, no matter what time he got my message. After hanging up, I shook my head at Ty's inquiring look.

Ty sighed and motioned Officer Sunshine over. He had been standing by the door, trying to joke around with the other cops. By his hand motions, I decided that he was sending the officer to Marco's. I grimaced. Hungover, tired, and frustrated was not a good combination for Marco. Being woken up by the police was going to

136

make matters even worse. I couldn't think of a better cop to endure Marco's wrath.

Ty also had one of his officers drive Syd home. Her van would have to be searched for evidence in case one of the interns had tracked anything in after she picked us up. She turned toward me and made the signal for me to call her later. I smiled weakly and nodded at her.

I sighed and turned to Officer Thermon. She began asking me questions and I took her through the events of the evening from the time I had left the police station, to getting Marco home, and all through the time we spent in the tunnels until Syd drove us back to the vineyard. Officer Thermon shook her head occasionally – I think she was amazed at our stupidity.

Just as I finished my statement and answered a few follow-up questions, Officer Sunshine returned with Marco. I could see his bloodshot eyes from across the room. He stormed across the room toward Ty. His voice sounded ragged as he rasped, "What's the meaning of this, Randall? Why are there cops all over my vineyard and why was I dragged out of my house under threat of arrest if I didn't accompany this idiot immediately?"

Ty looked questioningly at the officer who merely shrugged dismissively. Ty sighed loudly. "I apologize, Marco. Officer Stewart had no authority to threaten you with arrest and he will be reprimanded later." He shot a withering glare at the young officer. "I asked him to request that you join us as I knew that you would want to be here."

Marco was slightly placated, but his complexion was still not right and he was having a bit of a problem standing upright. He exhaled loudly. "What was so important that you had to wake me up in the middle of the night?" He looked at his watch pointedly. "Did you find Pierre's killer?" He looked around the room. "Why is everyone here?"

Ty shook his head slowly. "I'm sorry, no." He looked around, unsure how to continue. "I'm afraid that I have some more bad news for you, though."

Marco grasped onto a chair for balance and regarded Ty warily. He whispered, "What's happened now?"

Ty laid his hand on Marco's arm. They had played football together in high school and had remained friendly over the years. "I'm sorry to tell you that one of your interns," Marco looked quickly around the room, "May Lee, was found dead in the caves a short while ago."

Marco sat down hard in the chair. His head sank between his knees and he held his hands up as if to ward off the information. "Whoa! What? Why was she in the caves?" He took a ragged breath then continued his barrage of questions. "Who found her? How did she die?"

Ty pulled a chair up next to Marco and began speaking to him quietly. Hard as I tried, I could not overhear the conversation. Marco raised his hands and scrubbed at his face. He pulled his hands down and looked around the room, finally resting on me. I could see the hurt and confusion in his eyes, as well as the anger. I grabbed a bottle of water and brought it over to him as Ty walked away to join the cops outside.

"What were you thinking, Kat?" he asked quietly.

I handed him the water and sat down. He opened the bottle and drank thirstily. I caught Alessa's eye and mouthed "black coffee" at her. She understood and went to get a large mug for Marco.

I sighed in frustration. "That seems to be the question of the day."

He looked at me sharply and I explained, "Ty asked me the same thing."

"Why would you take those, those…" he looked desperately at the interns, "kids down into the caves when Pierre was just murdered and his murderer is still on the loose?"

His question flipped my anger switch and I began whispering furiously at him and ticking off the reasons on my fingers. "First of all, those *kids* are actually adults. Second, it was their idea to go into the tunnels, not mine. Third, they would not listen to me when I suggested they shouldn't go. Fourth, I was thinking of protecting you, them, and this vineyard when I agreed to go with them. Fifth, we were in teams so nobody was ever supposed to be all alone. Sixth…" I ran out of steam and sat back in my chair angrily, crossing my arms over my chest. Alessa crept over with a giant mug of coffee and Marco accepted it gratefully.

Marco regarded me for a moment. "Feel better now that you got that off your chest?" He blew on the coffee and took a loud, slurpy gulp.

I looked at him hotly and suddenly deflated. I had officially used the last of my energy reserves.

"Good," he nodded. "I need you on your 'A' game."

Now, I was confused. "What?"

Marco sighed. "Look, Ty and the cops are great at their jobs, but they don't know the people involved." He looked at the growing number of police in the parking lot and exhaled loudly. "Plus, people talk to you, Kat. You have a way about you. You find random facts and string them together somehow to create a valid solution – like at the reunion." He blew on his coffee some more. "That's why you were such a great cop and that's certainly one of the reasons I hired you."

I stared at Marco with my mouth hanging open.

He looked at me and flashed a quick grin. "That and your ability to catch flies."

I snapped my mouth closed. I was about to respond snarkily when I noticed a commotion across the room. Ty was handcuffing Max and reading him his rights. What the heck was going on?

Marco and I both jumped up – though I had to stifle an inappropriate giggle as I watched Marco wobble – and walked over to Ty and Max. Marco held up his hand. "Hold on there, Randall. What do you think you're doing?"

Ty turned to Marco with gritted teeth and growled, "That's Chief Randall, Mr. Milano, and I'd advise you not to interfere. Maximillian Keller is under arrest for the murder of Pierre Berger." Ty started leading Max through the tasting room toward the doors.

"But Ty…" I attempted to ask.

Ty just held up his hand in a stop motion while Max looked back at us, his eyes filled with terror.

Marco sighed and pulled out his phone. I checked my watch and looked at him suspiciously. "Who are you calling at this time of night?"

"Chance. I know he doesn't practice law anymore, but he may be able to help us out. At the very least, he can refer me to a reliable lawyer."

"Oh," I mumbled weakly. Why didn't I think of that? My thoughts drifted to Chance and I pictured him waking up and wiping the sleep out of his eyes. He probably slept without a shirt on and maybe boxer briefs… Whoa! I had to shake myself. This is hardly the time to think about Chance – I looked sidelong at Marco having a whispered conversation – or Marco in anything but a professional manner.

Marco hung up and swore quietly.

"What did he say?"

"He said that they will just charge, book, and process him tonight. Harmony is not Boston so he probably won't be questioned until morning when they've collected more evidence, though I can't imagine what evidence they could have on Max. He's a good kid, or

141

adult, or whatever." Marco scrubbed at his face and I could see the exhaustion settling in on him. "Chance said he'd head down to the police station anyway and register as his lawyer. He wants to make sure he meets with Max and is present when they question him."

I smiled fondly. Chance really was a great guy. He had just retired from law to pursue his dream of opening a wine and coffee bar which was supposed to open in – I looked quickly at my phone – tomorrow, and here we were dragging him back into a profession he hates. Plus, he wasn't ever a criminal attorney. Even though it probably wouldn't be me, he would definitely make someone a great husband someday.

Marco looked around at the remaining interns – Louis, Jayson, and Alessa – and then back at me. "Can you take Alessa to your house for the night? I can't imagine they'll be allowed into the dorms with the cops crawling all over the place. I'll take Jayson and Louis."

"Of course," I agreed. "It'll be, well, not fun, but nice to have someone around."

"Thanks, Kat." He looked around to see who was now in charge of the scene. The Missing Persons team had left after finding May and now there were just Harmony officers and a few state police officers. He spied an older officer who seemed to be directing the younger officers. "Let me just go clear it with Sergeant Crandall." He walked off while I stared in disbelief. Sergeant Crandall had been around forever. I remembered him coming into school and giving safety demonstrations and tips on saying no to drugs. He had seemed old then. How could he still be working?

Marco came back and held out a small, reddish booklet. "The sergeant said it was okay for you to leave but he asked if we could drop off Max's passport. For safety reasons, I keep all the interns' passports in my office safe. Do you mind? It will just be a slight detour for you…?" He asked hopefully.

"No problem." I certainly was in better shape than Marco to drive down to the police station and deliver the passport, even if I was almost falling asleep on my feet. Marco looked like he was about to drop. Alessa came over as Marco walked toward Jayson and Louis.

"You don't mind being stuck with me?" she asked shyly.

"Of course not," I replied. "Let's go, before we get stuck here any longer." I looked at her. "And don't worry. I have clothes for you to sleep in and extra toiletries at my house."

Alessa looked relieved. We walked out the door and I remember thinking that I didn't know when we'd be able to come back. I had a distressing thought about missing the harvest, but really, bringing a murderer to justice was far more important.

Chapter Twenty-One

I could not stop yawning as I drove down the vineyard's long driveway onto Route 1A. Both Alessa and I averted our eyes from Pierre's house as we drove by it. I drove the short distance into town and pulled in front of the police station. I checked my dashboard and saw that it was nearly four in the morning.

"I'm just going to run in and drop off Max's passport to the desk sergeant. I'll be right back out."

Alessa looked like she wanted to come with me, but nodded her head meekly. I'd like to say I bounded out of the car, but that would be a lie. I hauled myself out and felt every ache, pain, and bruise resounding loudly. I'm sure the creaks and cracks were audible for quite some distance – not that there was anyone on the streets of Harmony at four in the morning.

I didn't know the desk sergeant, so I didn't feel the need to hang out and chat. I made sure to get a receipt for the passport and turned to go back to my car when the outside door opened and Chance walked in.

Nobody has a right to look that good at four in the morning. He took one look at me in Marco's baggy hoodie with my dirt-smudged pants and stringy hair that also seemed to be knotted beyond belief and smiled. Suddenly, the night didn't seem quite so bleak. I felt myself smiling back at him and then a few tears ran down my cheek. Fatigue, I told myself. Or maybe dry eye.

Regardless of the reason, Chance dropped his briefcase, stepped close to me, and enveloped me in his arms. I inhaled his masculine scent that was woodsy and fresh and thought that he also did not have the right to smell that good at four in the morning. His large hands caressed my back and my aches and pains seemed to melt away.

We finally stepped away from each other a few moments later. He tucked an errant strand of hair behind my ear and let his hand rest on my shoulder.

"In the thick of things again, I see?" he teased as he idly played with a strand of my hair.

His voice was soft, smooth, and very soothing but his actions were heating me up. "It's not my intention, that's for sure."

He smiled. "I know. Some people just have a knack for being in the wrong place at the wrong time." He pulled me in for another hug. "I guess you're one of them and I'm going to have to keep a closer eye on you."

I grinned against his warm, hard chest and mumbled into his shirt, "That's fine by me."

He kissed the top of my head and grudgingly – or so I hoped – pulled away. He had his hands on my shoulders and looked intently into my eyes. "I need to see if they'll let me speak with my client and get his story." He stole a quick look at the desk sergeant who was trying very hard to ignore us. "Also, I want to ensure they don't question him without me."

"Okay," I said meekly. By now I was functioning on fumes and I remembered that Alessa was out in the car. I gave him a small wave and began to turn toward the door.

"I do want to talk to you though, Kat." My heart lifted a little and I felt a surge of excitement surge through my veins. It was soon dashed as if cold water had been injected. "I need to get your version of tonight's events and background on everyone. You've been working with them now for a few months so you probably know them fairly well."

I felt my shoulders sag a little and turned toward him, a bit dejectedly. "I can make time whenever you're free. I'm sure we won't be able to do much around the vineyard tomorr…Wait! Your opening is tomorrow night! How are you going to represent Max and make sure all the last-minute details are ironed out?"

Chance sighed slightly. "My sister is just going to have to shoulder some additional responsibility for the next few days. Plus, almost everything is ready. We've had a lot of time with all the building delays to plan what we needed."

"If you or your sister need me for anything tomorrow, let me know." I looked at my watch and gasped. "Today, I guess. As I said, I doubt we'll be able to do anything at the vineyard until they wrap up their investigation. Investigations." My shoulders sank lower.

He took a step toward me and gave me another quick hug. "Thanks, Kat. That really means a lot to me. I'll let my sister know and my bet is that she will definitely have something for you to do. She likes to delegate." He looked at the sky beginning to lighten outside. "Go home and get some rest. We'll talk some time tomorrow and I'll also see you at the opening. I have a table reserved

146

for you, Syd, and Ricky." He looked around. "Ty, too, but I doubt he'll have time.

I walked out of the police station with more of a bounce in my step than I've had in a while, even if I was basically sleepwalking,

Chapter Twenty-Two

I opened the car door and Alessa jolted awake. Whoops! I guess I had been gone longer than anticipated. She blinked her eyes at me several times. "I was going to be angry with you for taking so long until I saw you hugging that very fine man inside. Is he your boyfriend?"

My mouth dropped and I stammered, "N-n-no, we're just friends."

"Hmm," she pondered. "I do not hug my friends like this." She looked at me again. "Maybe you are friends with benefits, as you say here in the USA...?"

I shook my head, a little bit sad. "No, just friends."

Alessa was staring at me hard as I started the car. I tried to stop myself from squirming as I had never enjoyed close scrutiny. "Is it because of Marco? You are together?"

I noticed that her Spanish accent was a little stronger when she was tired. Or maybe it was the stress. I shook my head again. "Nope. Just friends, too."

"*Oh, Dios mío,*" she exclaimed and threw her hands up in the air – at least as far as my car ceiling would let her. "You do not like hot men? Perhaps you like women...?" She narrowed her eyes at me. "It is okay if you do. I like both men and women."

I think I drove the next mile with my mouth opening and closing, trying to find words. I don't care that she's bisexual, it's just the events of the day had finally overwhelmed me and my ability to speak coherently. Finally, I managed, "Nope. Definitely men – not that liking women is wrong – I'm just not into women."

She snorted. "So, what is the problem? You have two very attractive men who both seem to like you. Yet you do nothing with them?"

I sighed. "It's complicated."

She waved a hand at me dismissively. "I do not understand you Americans. You are so *reprimida* – what is that word in English?" She thought hard for a moment.

I knew that word. One of the guys I had dated when I tried a dating app had said the same thing to me when I didn't want to have sex in the restaurant's rest room on the first date. Apparently, he was into some kinky stuff that certainly did *not* interest me. I looked it up when I got home. "Repressed," I translated for her. "I am *not* repressed." I shrugged. "I've just been busy." I could see her taking a deep breath to reply so I hastened, "We're all busy. Chance, that's the guy from the police station, has been renovating a wine bar that is opening tomorrow night. And Marco…" I groaned. "I don't know what's up with Marco." I thought for the thousandth time about the female voice that I had heard in his room in Peru. "I don't even know if he's dating anyone else."

She made a rude noise. "No, seriously," I argued. "I can't figure out if either of them *is* interested or if they just want to be friends. Chance is hard to read and Marco is always so flippant." I could actually hear her roll her eyes. "It's not like I've turned either of them down. Neither of them has tried *anything* with me."

149

"Why are you waiting for them?" she asked incredulously. "This is the 21st century. Women can initiate intimacy as well as men. I ask both men and women for dates."

I stared dumbly out the window. Huh, I thought. I was scared to admit that that idea had never even entered my head. Maybe I am repressed. I stole a glance at Alessa who seemed to have lost her will to argue with me. She was almost falling asleep again as we pulled into my driveway.

"We're here," I said brightly, as much to wake her up as to change the subject.

Alessa climbed out of the car and stretched. "I cannot wait to close my eyes and sleep."

"Me, too," I said enthusiastically, although I had a strong suspicion that I might be awake for a while contemplating whether I was *reprimida* or not.

We entered the house and I set her up in the guest room and showed her where I kept the towels and toiletries in the guest bathroom. I grabbed her a nightgown to sleep in and some clothes for the next day and placed it all on the guest room bed. "Good night," I yawned as I padded back down the hall to my room. I think I heard a muffled "good night" from the guest bath, but I was past the point of caring.

I did a rush job on my bedtime preparations and made a silent wish that one night without flossing wouldn't upset my dentist. I glanced at the clock as I fell into bed and saw that it was nearly five a.m. I set the alarm for ten o'clock and thought I'd be awake the whole time with various thoughts and deductions racing through my head. But even my brain was too beat to fight the allure of sleep and I think I may have been out before my head even hit the pillow.

Chapter Twenty-Three

I awoke a few hours later feeling … not refreshed. It was before the alarm went off, but I couldn't get back to sleep. I knew that only roughly four hours of sleep after the day I had yesterday was not nearly enough. Plus, Alessa's comments were running through my head and today was probably not going to be an easy day either.

I took a long, hot shower and then stumbled downstairs to the kitchen. Alessa had made coffee and looked a whole lot better than I did, even in the baggy sweats and t-shirt I had loaned her. She had also made scrambled eggs with crispy potatoes and assembled a small fruit salad. I know they were all ingredients I had on hand, but I couldn't have turned them into such a delicious feast.

I climbed onto a stool at the kitchen counter and began serving myself some food – after I poured myself a large, black coffee. Alessa gestured at the food. "I hope you don't mind. I cook when I'm upset."

I paused with the fork midway to my mouth and looked at her sideways. "Not at all," I said hurriedly and continued devouring my breakfast.

Thankfully, she waited until I had shoveled in at least half of my breakfast and, more importantly, moved on to my second cup of coffee before attempting more conversation.

"Do you think I will be able to go back to my room today?" she inquired.

I shrugged. "I really don't know. It depends if they have wrapped up their investigation and are ready to release the scene. I doubt it though."

"But May and Pierre were not killed in the dorms..." she persisted.

"No, but that is where their chief suspect at the moment lives and I'm sure they think that they will find some evidence in there." I was quiet for a moment while I tried to make the pieces fit in my mind. "I just don't see Max as the killer, though. I can't imagine why he would have wanted both Pierre and May dead." I was mostly talking to myself, but Alessa listened intently. "He's not stupid. He would know that he would be the obvious suspect in May's death because they were partnered, so that makes it even less likely that he actually did it."

It was Alessa's turn to shrug. "Max is German," she said dismissively. "Maybe he has a fiery German temper and it just happened."

I regarded her curiously. It was odd that she had so easily accepted that Max was the killer. Of course, I didn't know any history between them over the summer, so who knows where her attitude was coming from.

I picked up my phone. "I'll ask Chief Randall if the dorms have been released yet." I used Ty's speed dial number but his mobile went straight to voicemail. I called the station and was told he was not available. I gave up and asked the desk sergeant if he had

153

any information. He told me that the scene was not released yet, but they hoped to release it by morning.

I relayed the information to Alessa then excused myself and went out to the back patio to call Marco. I did not need Alessa to further analyze my relationship with him, I thought, a little grumpily.

Marco answered his phone without even saying hello. He started speaking like we were in the middle of a conversation.

"What are you doing up already?" he demanded.

"I was just calling to ask if you need us today."

"Always," he said, "but I know that you both need to take a break today more than I need you. Take the day off and come in tomorrow."

"I definitely need you early tomorrow though. Both of you. There is a lot to do to prep the vineyard for the harvest and we are severely short-staffed. I know that sounds a bit callous, but the grapes will need to be harvested soon no matter what else has happened around here. It will be all hands on deck!" He boomed.

I groaned inwardly. "Okay, see you in the morning."

"Great, and Kat," he hesitated.

"Yes?"

"I also need you to put together a wine tasting station for the Two Cups opening tomorrow night. Chance asked me to do a tasting for those invited to the event and I haven't had a second to plan it, what with Pierre, and now," he paused, "May."

I gulped. "Uh…"

"Great! Thanks!" Marco enthused to my non-answer and hung up.

I closed my eyes and counted to ten. How was I supposed to plan a wine tasting when I didn't even know for certain what wines Chance had stocked at Two Cups? Did I have to bring the wines from Milano Importers? Tomorrow just became way more stressful and now it seemed like I'd have to work at the opening tomorrow night. So much for that cute black dress I had bought for the occasion. I would have to represent Milano Vineyards & Wine Distributors and that meant logo-wear. I certainly couldn't work in that dress and the kitten heels I had planned to wear.

I trudged back into the house and told Alessa that we had the day off. She asked if she could use my washer to wash her clothes so she would have her own clothes to wear. I nodded absently then decided to go back upstairs and sleep some more.

I woke up a lot later and had that groggy feeling I often got after a nap, especially a long nap. I stumbled back downstairs and found Alessa sprawled on the couch, watching television, and eating my ice cream. I didn't mind. Well, not very much.

We ate the leftovers from breakfast, watched some mindless rom-com movie, and then we both went to bed early. I had a feeling we would need our rest to get through the next couple of days.

Chapter Twenty-Four

We both got up early the next morning, although Alessa had gotten up earlier than me and made breakfast again. I fleetingly wondered if she wanted to be my roommate. The kitchen hadn't been used this much in months.

We talked about everything that would probably have to be done in the vineyard today. I was not looking forward to it, but Alessa seemed excited. I looked at her suspiciously.

"I do not like to be bored. Staying busy at work will be very helpful for me, especially with everything that has happened."

"I'm glad you feel that way," I muttered as I turned to walk away. "I need to go get dressed." I turned back and looked at her. "You found everything you needed to wash your clothes yesterday?"

She smiled and nodded so I trudged upstairs to prepare to meet the day.

I realized that I had not done my own laundry in some time so I had to dig in the back of my closet to find a pair of skinny jeans that had shrunk in the dryer. I laughed mirthlessly as I looked down at my stomach and noted that perhaps the dryer was not the problem. It had been difficult to really exercise hard since I was stabbed, and I had been drinking a fair amount of wine – and let's not forget Sunny's delicious chocolate croissants. I don't think even Cal Jr.'s brutal training program could counteract all of that.

I thought wistfully about a croissant but decided that Marco had already been very generous in giving us yesterday off. I didn't want to push the limits of his patience. I wiggled into my clothes and we were ready to go ten minutes later. Good thing I was not a high maintenance, wear a lot of makeup, kind of person. I caught a glance of myself in the mirror by the front door and thought that maybe I should become that type of person.

Alessa and I were quiet in the car. We drove by Pierre's house and both looked the other way again. I did note that the crime scene tape had been removed, so that was a step in the right direction.

Damn! Ty had arrested Max. He must really believe that Max was the murderer. I didn't understand why, though. There's no way Max would be so stupid as to murder his own cave exploration partner and besides, he was the first one who made it to the beach. He had no spare clothes and his clothes were still relatively neat and clean, albeit a bit dusty from the caves. It couldn't have been him.

I glanced quickly at Alessa. I knew it wasn't her, either. She had been with me the entire time in the caves. Two potential suspects eliminated – at least in my mind.

I started feeling a little better. I had eliminated two suspects, well, three if you counted me. I seriously doubted that anyone considered me a suspect, even though I had discovered Pierre's body. I shivered, picturing that awful tableau.

"I wonder how Ava is doing," Alessa interrupted my thoughts. "Did Marco say if he heard anything from the hospital?"

"No, he didn't. I'm sure she'll be fine." I thought for a moment. "She was able to walk out of the caves and to the parking lot where we met Syd, so it was probably just shock that caused her to pass out." I was pretty sure I could eliminate Ava as a suspect, too. I don't think she would have cracked herself over the head quite so hard in the caves as a distraction.

I pulled my car into the winery parking lot and had to navigate past a half dozen news vans and a swarm of local and state police cars. I guess the word had spread about the two murders associated with Milano Vineyard. Alessa and I ducked our heads and did our best to ignore the reporters as they shoved microphones in our faces and shouted questions at us. We squeezed in through the doors and I locked them behind us.

I heard raised voices coming from down the hall. Alessa and I looked at each other and I nodded toward the hall. Alessa vehemently shook her head. "No, Kat! We do not want to get involved, or arrested," she hissed.

"Nobody is going to arrest us," I asserted, sounding braver than I felt. "We were together the whole time in the caves. Neither of us could have, or would have, killed May."

"Unless they think we killed her together," she argued.

That brought me up short. I knew we didn't kill her but what evidence did we have to clear us? Unfortunately, it wasn't always innocent until proven guilty. Still, I wanted to see why Marco and Ty were shouting at each other. I shrugged as if her comment hadn't made me a little bit concerned and walked down the hall toward the offices.

"You are disrupting my business and causing me to lose customers and money!" Marco shouted as I entered the office suite.

Ty had his hands up in a placating manner. "That is unavoidable. We are trying to gather evidence and get out of here as quickly as possible so you can revert to business as usual."

"Business as usual," Marco sputtered. "Two of my staff have been murdered and one was arrested. How many people do you think want to buy wine from someone who hires murderers? We could lose our family business!" he cried.

Lose the business? Crap! I really liked this job and all the people I worked with. Still, Ty had to do his job and follow the evidence. Speaking of evidence…

"Ty?" I asked hesitantly.

He turned sharply to look at me and frowned. "Stay. Out. Of. This. Kat." He growled at me.

I could see that he had not gotten any sleep last night. His eyes were bloodshot and the exhaustion had etched deep ridges on his face. I felt bad for him, but I couldn't lose this job. I really liked it, notwithstanding being covered in wine most days.

"Ty," I tried to sound reasonable, "I'm not trying to get in the way. I know how difficult your job can be when there are constant interruptions and people who think they know better than you." He seemed slightly mollified but still looked at me suspiciously. "I just wanted to make sure you knew that there was no way Max could have killed May."

Ty took a deep breath and looked ready to launch a verbal assault on me. I held my hand up in a conciliatory gesture. "Please just listen for one minute, then you can yell all you want." Ty slowly released the breath and nodded at me once.

"Max was already on the beach when Alessa and I came out of the tunnel. He was perfectly clean except for some dust – not a drop of blood – and he had no change of clothes with him. He couldn't have carried a change of clothes because his small backpack held only water, a flashlight, and a map."

"Did you ever think that perhaps he had a second backpack, hidden in the caves?"

I nodded my head impatiently. "Yes, of course I considered that – but he was wearing the exact same shirt as when we entered the caves. It was quite distinctive."

Ty sighed. "Come on, Kat. T-shirts are a dime a dozen. He could have two of the same t-shirt."

I shook my head emphatically. "Not two of this t-shirt. He was wearing a 1994 vintage Green Day tour t-shirt. They go for about $140. I wouldn't normally remember what anyone was wearing, but, well, you know they're my favorite group and we had quite a long discussion about it the first time I saw him in it." I exhaled the rest of my breath. That was a lot of talking for me.

Ty nodded slowly. "You make a good point. It doesn't completely exonerate him, but it's definitely a point in his favor."

160

I nodded quickly, making a mental note to tell Chance about my evidence as soon as possible. Ty looked at Marco who was struggling to keep a straight look on his face. He shook his head as he turned to leave the office. Marco's grin spread across his face. "Kat!" he shouted joyfully, earning a scowl from Ty as he walked away.

I looked at Marco expectantly but he seemed to be speechless – a definite first for Marco. He grabbed my shoulders and pulled me close to him in a bear hug. I could hear him muttering "thank you" repeatedly into my hair.

"It's okay, Marco, we'll solve this," I said as he finally pulled away.

"I didn't think Max did it, but I was a little worried. Probably lack of sleep."

"And about eight bottles of wine," I sniped, a little maliciously.

He at least had the good grace to look repentant. "Yeah, that was not one of my better ideas." He took a ragged breath in. "Unfortunately, grapes do not stop ripening when tragedy occurs." He glanced up at the acres of vineyards. If you concentrated, you could smell the grapes, almost ready to be harvested and release their juice. "I think we still have another day or two before harvest, but let's go take some quick samples, test the Brix, and pray that I'm right. I don't think anyone could function well if we had to harvest today." He looked around. "I'll give everyone the rest of the day off after we complete the absolutely essential tasks."

161

I nodded. I knew that I needed some downtime. A thought popped into my head and I slapped my forehead with the palm of my hand. "Crap!" Marco looked at me quizzically. "Chance's opening is tonight and you asked me to prepare the wine tasting we're running."

Marco scrubbed at his face. "That's an easy fix. First, go into the office and look in the filing cabinet under 'red varietal tasting.' There's a wine tasting in there that we did two years ago for a local charity – *Save the Bay* or *Save Dolphins* or something like that. Then, call Chance. Tell him about the evidence you just shared with Ty. I'm sure that will be enough, with your sworn affidavit, to get Max out of jail. Next, ask him if he has those wines. If he doesn't, I'll have them sent over from the warehouse. Just read through the notes and Justina will do fine tonight."

It was my time to look confused. "Justina?"

"She's going to run the tasting, I just want you to set it up and get it ready for her. I know you want to be a guest tonight at Chance's grand opening. You deserve a night of fun and Justina is always looking for extra hours."

It was my turn to throw my arms around Marco and give him a huge hug. "Thanks, Marco," I murmured.

Marco's strong arms held me tightly. The hug lasted a few seconds longer than a conventional thank-you hug, but I think we both needed the comfort. It had been a long, soul-sucking week. We pulled apart and I wanted about to say something gracious. Marco, however, couldn't resist his impish nature, and patted me on the

162

back with a quick grin. "Go get the wine tasting ready. You're going to need as much time as possible to get ready tonight." With that parting remark and a snarky smirk, he turned on his heel and stalked off toward the vineyard, calling Alessa, Louis, and Jayson to join him in the fields. He pointed Justina in my direction and she joined me by the door.

Alessa caught my eye and shook her head sadly at me while pointing at her watch and looking toward Marco. I think she was trying to convey that my time was running out to make a move before I got old and shriveled up, but I could have just been projecting my own feelings of inadequacy.

Chapter Twenty-Five

Justina and I went into the office and I went straight to the file cabinets. Justina fell into my office chair and looked at me pointedly while I tried to ignore her and search for the red varietal wine tasting plan.

I freed the file and went to my desk. As I opened the file, I cleared my throat, still avoiding Justina's eyes. I scanned the file and felt better immediately. I was certain that Chance had these wines on his wine list and that would make setting up the tasting much easier.

Justina couldn't hold her tongue any longer. "What was that?"

I looked up innocently. "What?"

She scoffed. "What? That was some hug from Marco, or should I say hugs?" She grinned.

I shrugged and still avoided her eyes. "They meant nothing. Just a friend providing support to another friend."

Justina rolled her eyes. "Please. I know this vineyard has been going through some tragic times, but those were *not* just comfort hugs." She got up and started dancing around, singing, "*Marco likes Kat! Marco likes Kat!*"

I had to get this under control before someone else came in and overheard her being silly. Plus, it wasn't appropriate to think about my social life when Ava was in the hospital and May and Pierre had been murdered. "Enough, Justina." I used my cop voice and that seemed to work as she abruptly stopped dancing around and sat down. "I don't really know what those hugs were and now is not the time to think about it. We've got work to do and precious little time to get it done." Justina tried to look chagrined, but I could see her grinning. I showed her the wine tasting list. "I know Chance has these in stock, but Marco asked me to call him to make sure he has enough in stock for the tasting."

Justina perked up and rubbed her hands together. "The plot thickens. One minute you're hugging Marco. The next, you're off for a chat with Chance." She looked at me coyly. "Who will Kat choose?"

"Stop!" I demanded, more than a little frustrated at the constant needling. "It's not my choice to make. Neither of them is actually interested in me as anything more than a friend." Having to constantly explain that I was not a choice for either of them was starting to give me a complex. I felt a wave of sadness wash over me and my shoulders sagged. In a more subdued tone, I added, "Can we please just focus on the wine tasting for now. I don't have the energy to debate my love life, or lack thereof."

Justina opened her mouth to respond, but I quickly interjected, "I asked if we could *please* stop?" Justina nodded.

"Okay, but I'm rainchecking this conversation." I nodded in defeat as she mimed putting something into a pocket on her shirt. She took the list of wines from my hand and scanned it quickly. "I can easily talk about each of these tonight. Call Chance," she couldn't help her smirk, "and then let me know if I need to grab anything from the warehouse. Then you can go." She grinned again.

"You don't need any more stress if you want to wow those two hotties on your tail tonight."

It was my turn to roll my eyes in exasperation as she wandered out to the kitchen to grab us coffee. Justina was definitely good for my ego, although she could also be highly irritating. I found Chance in my contacts, took a deep breath, and clicked to call him. The phone rang twice and then he picked up, sounding a little breathless. My heart beat a little quicker in return.

"Hey," I tried to sound casual.

"Hey back at you," he replied. I could feel his grin through the connection.

"Are you ready for your big opening tonight?"

He chuckled. "Nope. It doesn't matter how much time anyone has – I don't think anyone is ever truly ready." I heard him inhale deeply and slowly exhale. "Not that I don't love chatting with you, Kat, but is there something you need?"

"Sure, I'm sorry to bother you. Two things." I told him quickly about the information I had shared with Ty about Max. He sounded pleased.

"That is wonderful news. I'm going to try to get him released today. He shouldn't have to sit in jail when he is clearly innocent."

"Glad I can help. I'm not sure how you'll have time to get everything done though.

"I'll manage somehow. I'm used to multitasking," he bragged.

I laughed softly. "Okay, next, I'm just getting things ready for the wine tasting station tonight and wanted to be sure you have enough of these wines on hand. If not, we have them here in the warehouse and can deliver them or we can swap out one of them for another bottle if you prefer." I rattled off the list.

"I do have those red wines. That sounds like a fun tasting. I've got some food samples we could pair with them as well to really round out the wine tasting."

"That sounds gr…"

"Wait!" he interrupted me. "Is Marco making you work at my opening tonight?" He sounded incredulous – and a little bit peeved.

"No, no," I hastened. "Justina is working the event. I'm just making sure everything is set up so it will run smoothly for her."

"Okay," he sounded appeased. "I really want you to relax and have a good time tonight. You've had a rough couple of days."

His concern choked me up a little. "I wouldn't miss it for the world."

It was awkwardly silent for a moment and then he cleared his throat. "I should get back to the final staging for tonight. Please come early so I can spend a little time with you before I have to mingle with the rest of the guests."

My mouth went dry, but I managed to croak out, "Sure thing. See you later."

I leaned back in my chair and could feel a dreamy smile creep across my face. Justina walked in and smirked again. "Now if that isn't a cat that ate the canary smile, I don't know what is."

I sat up abruptly, not willing to talk about my personal feelings for Chance right now. "Chance has all five wines and he's going to prepare some food samples to pair with them." Justina clamped her mouth closed, but I knew the matter wasn't closed.

She sighed. "I need the banner and promotional materials for Milano Importers. We usually set up a table and give those promotional cards so people can order directly from us for their home wine racks."

I nodded. "They should be in the warehouse. Let's go get them and put them in your car. Chance will have a table and wine glasses, so we don't need to bring those."

"That's good," Justina looked relieved. "I hate when I have to cart in a table and crates of wine glasses. This should be an easy and fun night."

I stretched and my body made a few odd creaking noises. It had been a rough few days. Justina chuckled. "As soon as we load my car up, you are going home. You need a nap and a hot shower before you get all dressed up tonight."

"Dressed up? I was going to wear a pair of jeans and a sweater."

Justina made a face that let me know that was a bad idea. "You will not wear jeans and a sweater. You're going to a wine bar opening where there will be *at least* two hot guys checking you out.

I had better see you in that little black dress you told me you picked up two weeks ago. You had better be wearing make-up, too, or I *will* cause a scene." She grinned. "Well, more of a scene than usual."

I stammered. I did not like dressing up. The new dress was a little tight, very low cut, and extremely revealing. I had hoped to lose a few pounds before I wore it out in public. I opened my mouth to protest, but Justina waved me away.

"No arguments, Kat. Now help me load my car and then go home."

"I need to stay. Chance told Marco to invite the interns tonight and Alessa wanted to come back to my house after Marco is done with the interns in the fields."

"I'll bring her to your house when they're done. You're going to need all the extra time to cover up those big, dark circles under your eyes." She laughed and struck a pose. "You don't look this great without putting some time into self-care."

I gave up. I could use a nap. And another hot shower. I conducted a mental inventory of my make-up drawer at home and decided I needed to make a quick trip to the drugstore so I could replenish my supplies. I caught a look in the mirror as we walked out to the warehouse to get the promotional materials and shuddered internally. I *was* going to need a lot of work. I smiled. This sounded like a job for Ricky.

Chapter Twenty-Six

Syd picked me and Alessa up at six o'clock. The official opening wasn't until seven, but Chance had asked me to come early. Plus, I thought he might need some extra, last-minute help.

Alessa, in all of her twenty-two-year-old glory, needed only a half-hour to get ready, from shower to bombshell. Damn, thirty-eight didn't feel old until I compared myself to someone sixteen years younger.

Ricky had come and gone, promising to meet us at Two Cups later. He had worked as much magic as possible and I felt a lot better than if I had tried to transform myself on my own.

Syd let out a low whistle as I came down my stairs. I was nervous enough without her calling attention to me. I had been happy that my little black dress fit. Happier still that my training with Cal Jr. and work in the fields had given me some nicely-defined biceps and triceps – no flab there. I was a little wobbly in the heels…well, most people wouldn't call two inches on a shoe a heel, but I could trip over my own feet in flats, so they were as high as I was willing to go.

Syd looked down at herself in her leggings and beautiful, artsy tunic. "I feel under-dressed. I didn't know we were supposed to dress up," she said accusingly.

I began to feel insecure. "I didn't plan to dress up. Justina forced me." Syd looked around. "Okay, she didn't physically force me but she threatened to make a scene if I showed up and wasn't dressed up."

Syd and Alessa exchanged a knowing look. "Well, if that's the only reason…" Syd giggled and then approached me, looking critically at my face. "Your make-up is flawless. When did you learn to do that?"

I blushed with embarrassment. "Never. Alessa saw my first attempt at applying make-up. I looked like a clown."

Alessa chimed in. "It was not a good look."

"Ricky came over and saved the day." I glanced in a mirror over the fireplace. "I'll never be able to replicate this on my own, but I'll enjoy it tonight."

Syd glanced into the mirror. "You are way more glamourous than me tonight, but," she shrugged, "I'm already married so who cares." She smiled at me to take the sting out of her words. "I told Chance we'd be there early though, so let's go."

"You spoke with Chance?"

"Do you think that you're the only one he speaks to in town?" Syd teased.

I stammered, "N-no, of course not."

Syd wound her arm through mine. "Relax. We were talking about some of my artwork that he's hanging at Two Cups. He wanted to be sure that it was lit correctly."

"You don't have to explain yourself to me," I tried to pull off a nonchalant tone.

Syd and Alessa looked at each other again and Syd winked at her. "Hmm, really?"

I was really embarrassed now and tried to deflect as we all walked out of my house and climbed into Syd's car. "Nice night, isn't it?"

Syd and Alessa burst into waves of laughter that lasted all the way down the hill to Harbor Street. Fortunately, Syd was able to score a parking spot close to Two Cups. I did not want to walk very far in these heels.

Syd and I walked in and came to an abrupt stop. It was absolutely unrecognizable from The Harbor Bar, my mother's old dive bar. I had been inside at the beginning of the renovations, but not for a while now. There was a clear demarcation between the two sides of the place – the coffee bar and the wine bar – but they flowed nicely together. I'm sure my mouth was hanging open as I gaped around the place. In the wine bar, there were several old photographs of Harmony and many of The Harbor Bar under different owners through the years. You could almost see it decaying as the years progressed. There were also old photos showing the shipping industry, the marina, and Market Street, which was mainly an empty street with just a few businesses in the early 1900s.

I turned toward the coffee bar and noticed all of Syd's bright watercolors hanging on the walls. She was an incredible artist and where the old photos in the wine bar seemed darker and grittier, the watercolors were bright and optimistic. I cannot stress enough that even though the two sides were so different, the entire place was stunning and both sides played off of each other nicely.

172

I saw Chance across the floor and my heart skipped a beat. He was dressed in a tailored black suit with a black silk shirt open at the neck. With his dark wavy hair, well-built physique, and stunning smile, he could easily have graced the pages of *GQ*. At that moment, he looked across the bar at me and his smile spread even wider, eyes crinkling. He walked across the bar toward me and it was as if we were the only people in the bar. Our eyes were locked on each other and I was completely mesmerized. My body was tingling and I was finding it difficult to catch my breath.

When he reached me, I discovered that Syd and Alessa had melted away and were speaking with Justina at the Milano Importers table. My mouth was dry as Chance stood in front of me. He reached down and took both my hands in his. I felt a jolt of electricity flash through my body. "Kat," he said huskily, "You look spectacular." I noticed a stray thought flit through his mind. "I mean, you always look great, but tonight..." He exhaled a ragged breath.

I think I forgot how to breathe for a moment, gazing into his deep, emerald green eyes. He leaned in slowly and I thought he might actually kiss me. I took a shallow breath in anticipation but he veered to the side at the last moment and enveloped me instead in a more-than-friendly embrace. My arms snaked around his neck and I clung to him like a life preserver.

The magical moment was broken when one of his staff, I think his name was Karl, cleared his throat loudly. We wrenched apart and Karl smiled wryly at the two of us as he quirked an eyebrow. "Sorry, but there's an issue with the cash register in the coffee shop. Hope can't get it to print receipts for the customers."

Chance still held my hand. "Okay, I'll be right there." I was a little embarrassed as I could see Karl chuckling as he walked away. Chance turned to me once again and squeezed my hand. "Can you stay after the opening? I probably won't have much time over the next two hours to spend any time with you."

"Of course," I murmured, still not trusting myself to speak coherently. Chance grinned and leaned in to kiss me softly on the cheek. I felt his warm breath graze behind my ear as he inhaled my scent. Damn! My body would not stop tingling!

"I'm really glad you could make it, Kat." He turned to go and realized he was still holding my – sweaty – hand. "You'll probably want this back," he grinned at me as he released my hand and walked off toward the coffee bar cash register. As I stood there stupidly, enchanted by the past few moments, Ricky came up behind me and put a glass of prosecco in my hands.

"Damn, girl! I think I'm a little hot and bothered after that public display of affection. I'm glad to see my makeup magic worked."

I laughed nervously, afraid that I'd made a fool of myself. I took a long swallow of my wine and physically shook myself. As calmly as possible, I retorted, "I don't know what you're talking about, Ricky."

He was wise enough to merely chuckle and then dragged me over to Syd, Alessa, and Justina. I downed the rest of the prosecco and looked at Justina. "Are you all set? Can I help you with anything before the crowds show up?"

Justina smirked and Alessa cleared her throat, preparing to speak. Syd beat them to it though. "*What* was that?" she demanded eagerly.

I fidgeted nervously and tried to downplay the moment that would be running on an endless loop through my brain for at least the next few days. "Just two friends saying hi."

Ricky slung his arm around me. "I'm friends with that man too, and he has *never* said hello to *me* like that."

I sighed in defeat. "I don't know. It's like a cat and mouse game. He seems interested…then he backs off and I don't hear from him for weeks." I looked around as the front door opened and people started trickling in. I noticed Giovanni and the interns were part of the first wave of guests. Giovanni waved at me and then their group broke up. Giovanni and Ava went to the coffee bar and Louis and Jayson wandered toward the small stage where the band was setting up. I was happy to see that Ava was out of the hospital and looked okay. "Can we talk about this another time though?" When it looked like Syd was going to argue, I pleaded, "*Please?*"

There was a collective sigh and Justina jumped in. "Okay, we'll raincheck that conversation – but only because I want to practice my talking points about these specific wines before we get really busy."

I smiled at her gratefully. "Okay, shoot." I looked at the five bottles displayed on the table in front of her and tried out my best, inquisitive customer voice. "Ooh, these look interesting. Is this a tasting? Is it *free*?"

Justina tried not to smirk, though a small one slipped through her professional demeanor. "Yes, ma'am. Let me tell you about these five, delicious red wines. We will be pairing each of the wines with food that will complement the wine. Shall I start?" She looked at my little group expectantly.

Syd stepped forward and smiled encouragingly. "Of course. I never pass up good wine and food pairings."

Justina smiled back at Syd. "All five bottles are available here at Two Cups so you'll be able to enjoy a glass when you're out with friends, or want to sneak away for some alone time." She pointed at a Milano Wines & Importers brochure. "If you prefer to enjoy wine in the comfort of your own house, you can order from Milano Wines and we'll deliver locally right to your door."

Ricky got into the spirit. "What can you tell me about Milano Wines? Do they make all of these wines?"

Justina was warming up. She liked to talk about the history of Milano Wines. I had learned a lot, working with her in the wine tasting room. "The current owner is Marco Milano; he should be here shortly if you would like to meet him."

I made a grunting sound that earned a sharp look from Justina. As friendly as Marco is, he doesn't like meeting new people. Justina continued. "We are going to taste a variety of red wines today from across the world. The wine bar does stock some Milano Vineyards wines if you are interested in trying any of our locally produced wine." She grinned and continued. "Marco's great-grandfather came over from the Umbria region of Italy in the 1880s. His relatives still have a vineyard there and we import their wines as well as wines from other vineyards for distribution in the United States."

She took a breath. "Great-grandfather Leonardo was a fisherman, but he planted some of the grapevines that he had brought over from Italy on his small farm in Harmony. Leonardo made enough money fishing – though many believe he also smuggled tobacco and other contraband – and bought all the land that the Milano family now owns, most of which is planted with grapevines." She leaned in conspiratorially, "There are rumors that some of Leonardo's treasures are still hidden in the tunnels and caves that run beneath the vineyard all the way down to the beach, just north of Harmony."

I shuddered as I remembered my time spent in the caves. That was an experience I did not want to repeat any time soon. I glanced at Alessa and saw that she had the same reaction as me. Jayson and Louis had wandered over and joined our group for the wine tasting.

Justina continued, "If you would like to know more about the Milano family history, take one of these brochures. We will also be running historic cave tours to explore the caves starting next spring." She winked at the group. "Maybe you'll be the one to find Leonardo's lost treasure."

I was distracted by the sudden shift in Louis' demeanor. His brow furrowed and he crossed his arms while a frown crept across his face. Jayson leaned over to make a comment – presumably about the inappropriately-dressed woman who had just sashayed past our group – and Louis pushed him away, then stalked off toward the restrooms. I caught Jayson's eye and raised my eyebrows. He shrugged and whispered to me, "He's been really moody lately. I think it's the stress of everything that's happened with Pierre, May, and Max."

I whispered back, "How are you doing, Jayson? We haven't had much time to talk, but please let me know if there's anything I can help you with."

Jayson nodded gratefully. "I will. I'm fine. Stressed, but excited for the harvest."

Justina looked at both of us pointedly and cleared her throat. I mouthed, "I'm sorry," to her and she resumed her spiel.

"We are going to highlight the cabernet sauvignon grape tonight. We'll be tasting cabernet sauvignon wines from five different countries so that you can try to discern the influences that different terroirs – mainly soil and climate – have on each bottle. I think you will be surprised at the differences in wines from different regions that are all made with the same grape."

Ricky raised his hand and Justina chuckled. "Yes?"

"Which countries do the wines come from?" he asked innocently.

"Good question. Tonight, we will be tasting cabernet sauvignon from Argentina, Chile, South Africa, Spain, and New Zealand. As a special bonus, you will also taste Milano Vineyards own version of the delicious cabernet sauvignon wine.

Justina handed out a condensed version of our tasting notes paper so we could take notes on each of the wines. She also suggested we download and use the Milano app on our smartphones to digitally store our notes.

Even though I had been working in the tasting room, I decided to enjoy being a guest tonight and took some notes, too.

Two Cups' Cabernet Sauvignon Tasting

presented by:

Two Cups & Milano Vineyards

	Argentina	Chile	South Africa	Spain	New Zealand
Name	Bodega Norton Reserve	Baron Philippe de Rothschild Escudo Rojo	Rust en Vrede Stellenbosch	Marques de Grinon Dominio de Valdepusa	Vina Robles Estate
Color	Ruby red	Garnet red	Crimson red	Purple	Dark garnet
Bouquet	Red fruit mint dark chocolate	Strawberry cherry black currant	Strawberry cherry currants	Black cherry berry nutmeg tobacco chocolate	Cassis Cherry Mocha Licorice
Taste	Fruity & spicy	Cherry mocha hazelnut	Earthy & fruity	Intensely fruity & hints of chocolate	Dark fruit & mocha
Price	$20	$28	$33	$30	$20
Rating	91	94	90	90	91

Chapter Twenty-Seven

After we finished the tasting, I excused myself to use the ladies' room. It was peaceful and calm in there with an essential oil diffuser that made it smell both spicy and relaxing. Chance and his sister had completely gutted the old bathroom, which was great because it had been very nasty and probably a health hazard.

I touched up my lipstick, spritzed a little perfume, and fluffed my hair. I didn't look half-bad, I thought wryly, despite all my bumps and scrapes. I headed back out and nearly screamed when a hand reached out and pulled me into a semi-darkened office. I barely had time to notice that the office had also been completely renovated as well before I looked up into Chance's smoldering eyes.

"Kat," he murmured softly, yet intensely.

I smiled shyly, "Hi," I replied somewhat awkwardly.

Chance wrapped his arms around my waist and pulled me close to him. I wound my arms around his neck and ran my fingers through his thick hair. About a millisecond later, he was kissing me with a burning passion that left me weak in the knees. It was a good thing he had such a tight grip on me, I thought briefly as I pushed myself closer to him. This kiss was exactly what I had always imagined it would be – passionate, sensitive, demanding, and tender.

When we finally came up for air, he buried his head against my neck and nuzzled me gently. I thought I could just stay locked in his embrace forever. As if from a distance, however, I heard Chance's annoying staff member, Karl, calling his name. We hastily pulled apart as Karl opened the door and flicked on the light switch.

I was pleased to note that Chance was a little out of breath. He cleared his throat and looked pointedly at Karl, who at least had the good grace to look embarrassed at interrupting us. "Karl, you should always knock before entering a room with a closed door. This could have been an important business meeting."

Karl smirked, and I decided I really didn't like him at all. "No problem, boss. We need more Spanish cabernet sauvignon for the tasting. This crowd is really thirsty."

"Okay, I'll bring it right out," Chance looked at him pointedly until Karl got the hint, turned around, and walked out – but not without first giving me a thumbs-up signal.

I was mortified, but Chance merely chuckled. "He may end up being the first casualty of Two Cups if he keeps up that insolent attitude. Nobody should be that rude to you. Ever." His hand entwined with mine and he brought my hand to his mouth for a soft kiss. He looked at me ruefully. "I probably should go, though. It *is* opening night of my new wine bar."

I grinned at him then stood on tiptoe to kiss him chastely on the cheek. "Yes, you should go." I purred and then smoothed my dress back into place. "And I should go enjoy your new wine bar."

He leaned down and kissed me gently, and way too briefly, before pulling away. He whispered in my ear, "I think you need to fix your lipstick. It seems to have gotten a little smeared." He grinned rakishly and reluctantly moved toward the door. "We'll pick this up later." His slow wink as he walked out the door promised many more intimate embraces in the future.

I followed him out and went back to the ladies' room where I walked into Sunny. She looked at my disheveled clothes and smeared makeup. "Girl, what have *you* been up to?" She leaned in conspiratorially. "Or should I ask *who* have you been up to?"

I flounced my hair like I had once seen in a movie and looked into the mirror. I really was a sight. "I don't know *what* you're talking about, Sunny," I said lightly. "Must have been the wind."

Sunny let out a boisterous hoot. "Wind inside the bar?" She shook her head, still smiling. "If you don't want to tell me right now, that's fine, but you will tell me over wine some night soon."

I grinned at her and just nodded. I really couldn't put into words how deliriously happy I was at the moment.

We walked out of the ladies' room together and rejoined our friends. Justina looked at me strangely. "Was there a line? That took you quite a while."

I shook my head and refused to make eye contact. I knew she could read me like a book. "I saw some people I know and stopped to talk to them on the way," I said lamely.

Ricky looked around at our little group. "Who else do you know that you would talk to here? Certainly not Mindy and Julian."

Our whole group turned to look at Mindy and Julian. They must have felt the weight of our stares because they turned to look at us. Mindy sneered and Julian, who had just looked up from his phone, gave us a friendly wave. I don't care if it was rude, it was just so comical that we all burst out in uncontrolled laughter.

A few moments later, I felt an arm drape lazily across my back. I turned, fully expecting Chance to be standing next to me – though that would have been uncharacteristic of him – and startled to see it was Marco. His familiar grin and spicy scent comforted me for a moment, but maybe it was the wine. Justina had been very generous with her tasting pours.

Marco looked rested and ready for a night on the town, dressed in a red silk shirt and an expensive-looking black suit. He once told me that he only had two suits, each of which had been hand-tailored in Milan. This suit certainly fit him like a glove. I felt a familiar tingle throughout my body as I leaned into him slightly.

"Hi, Kat," he whispered softly into my ear. "You look fantastic." I could feel his warm breath like a gentle caress and my body shivered. "This might have to be our new work uniform."

All I wanted was for Marco to pull me close and... Wait! I shouted inside my head. You were just passionately kissing Chance! And remember, Marco was just with someone else in Peru. You'd just be one of a long line of conquests. My body tensed up immediately and I stepped away from Marco. "Thank you, Marco. You look fantastic, too," I muttered, a little stiffly.

He looked confused. "What's the matter, Kat?"

I noticed that everyone else was paying close attention to my exchange with Marco. I sighed and pulled him off to the side of the room. I guess I was going to have to put on my big girl pants and have the conversation that had been brewing for months.

When we were at the side of the room, under the historic photos of Harmony, I noticed Syd and Ricky watching me intently. I turned my back to them so that I was facing Marco directly.

Marco had a look of confusion on his face. "I repeat, what's the matter, Kat?"

I looked at Marco, took a deep breath, and exhaled slowly. "Marco," I sighed, "What's the deal?"

"The deal?" he asked, perplexed. "What do you mean?"

Okay, more direct. "Since we became reacquainted at the reunion, you've been sending me mixed signals. One day you treat me like a sister, the next day, you treat me like your employee, and the next day, you're all flirty and..." I struggled for the word, "suggestive."

"Suggestive? What the hell does that mean?" he demanded indignantly.

"Quite simply, I don't know if you want to be my friend, boss, or boyfriend," I cringed as I uttered those words. I really hated confrontations. "Based on your companion in Peru, I assume you already have at least one woman in your life..."

"My companion in Peru..." he trailed off, looking increasingly more confused.

I huffed, "The night I called you in Peru to tell you about Pierre, there was definitely a lady in your hotel room and she was whispering to you in the background."

Marco wrinkled his forehead, "I didn't stay at a hotel in Peru. I stayed with family friends." Suddenly he burst into laughter. "The

185

voice in my room!" He laughed harder and doubled over, barely able to catch his breath. He slowly stood, still struggling to stop laughing. "Kat, that was Madeleina – the 90-year-old matriarch of the Fernandez family. She heard my phone ring and popped her head in to bring in my laundry."

"What?"

He shrugged. "They put me up every time I go to Peru. They would be insulted if I stayed at a hotel. They treat me like family and Madeleina insists on cooking for me and doing my laundry every day." He chuckled a few more times. "She also comes and goes as she pleases. I can't tell you how many times I've woken up to discover her in the room's attached bathroom, searching for dirty towels to wash."

"Oh," I said meekly, wishing I could crawl under the nearest table and hide.

"I can't believe you thought I was hooking up with Madeleina. I can't wait to tell Carlos, her son, the next time I speak with him." I opened my mouth to beg him to keep it secret, but he grinned at me and continued, "Okay, what was the next issue? You're confused by how I treat you?" He thought about it for a moment. "Fair enough. However, it's difficult to know how I should treat you when you have so many suitors in line."

"Suitors? What are you talking about?"

He made a placating gesture with his hands. "Maybe not so many, but I'm not sure if you're interested in me or Chance or Cal Jr."

"Cal Jr.?" I sputtered, picturing the buff gym owner. He had the intellectual capacity of a twelve-year-old and lived in his own world where treating women like possessions was still acceptable. "Cal Jr.?" I demanded again.

Marco started laughing again. "Okay, obviously not Cal Jr. You have to admit though, that was funny." He sobered up. "So, what's going on with you and Chance? Are you dating, casual, or...?" He put his hands up in a questioning gesture.

Now, I felt flustered, but I was determined to be an adult. I looked Marco straight in the eye and shrugged. "I have absolutely no idea." I thought for a moment about the kiss. The steamy, knee-knocking kiss. "Not dating or casual." I eyed him thoughtfully. "The situation is kind of like with you. We flirt and then I go home confused." I flashed back to the kiss. Maybe I wasn't confused any longer.

Marco grinned, "I guess that's how life works now." He sighed. "Look, Kat, I'm probably a little flirtier with you than most women because I really do like you. You're funny, smart, tough, and not bad on the eyes."

I felt the blush blossoming all over my body and made a self-deprecating movement.

"Enough," he asserted. He took a deep breath. "I hadn't planned to go to the reunion last summer. I was dating someone kind of seriously – I was actually thinking about proposing. Then, out of the blue, she dumped me and ran off with one of her co-workers."

I leaned forward and rested my hand on his arm. "Marco, I'm so sorry. Why haven't you told me this before?"

He shrugged. "I didn't really want to tell you now, either, but you need the background so that what I'm about to say will make sense."

I nodded at him to go on and gave his arm an affectionate, supportive squeeze.

Marco grimaced and continued, "Syria broke my heart..."

"Wait, Syria? The wine parts representative at our supplier, Elite Vineyard Supply Systems?"

Marco scowled, "Do you know any other women named Syria?"

"Sorry, I'm interrupting, but we are *so* going to talk about this someday soon over a bottle of wine. Or two."

He rolled his eyes. "As I was saying, she broke my heart and I was moping around the vineyard and around Harmony. One day, I ran into Amelia and Bo at that little food court. They dragged me into Sunny's bakery for a coffee and we ended up chatting for a few hours. They talked me into going to the reunion." He smiled at me. "I didn't think I was going to have fun, but then I reconnected with Chance, Syd, Ricky," he shook his head and grinned at Ricky's name, "and you. I stopped moping around and I started enjoying life again."

I swallowed. "I understand. You're not ready to date anyone yet."

He grinned awkwardly. "Well, I am ready to date again casually, but you're not a one- or two-date kind of person. You're someone I would want to commit to – and *that* is what I'm not ready for."

It was my turn to grin. "I understand and thank you for not being a jerk. A lot of men in your situation, and women, wouldn't consider other people's feelings."

"*But*, when I am ready to do more than date, if you are still single, watch out. I'll sweep you off your feet."

I grinned at him. "I'll keep that in mind, Marco."

"Don't think I didn't notice that you haven't explained your relationship with Chance…"

I gulped, unsure of what to say. I didn't want to jinx what might be developing with Chance by talking about it – yet. Marco laughed and swung his arm around my shoulders as we started walking back to the group. He leaned in close and whispered, "So, friendly flirtation is not off the table for the present, then."

"Agreed." I sighed, relieved to be moving forward in finding my footing with two of the more important men in my life. Syd pressed a glass of cabernet franc into my hands and looked at me with a million questions in her eyes. I shook my head slightly and caught Chance glaring at me and Marco from across the bar. When he saw me looking at him, he resolutely looked away as I slipped out from under Marco's arm.

That was the last I saw of Chance that night, as he turned his back on me and started chatting with a group of twenty-something women who were all gazing at him adoringly.

Chapter Twenty-Eight

I tried to have a good time the rest of the night, but I felt badly that Chance seemed to have the wrong idea about Marco and me. I didn't want him to think I was encouraging a string of men, waiting for the best offer. I didn't get a chance to speak with him as he moved from one group to the next throughout the evening. I hoped to alleviate any concerns he might have about my relationship with Marco. As the opening wound down, Karl brought over a note to me that read:

Kat,

Can't meet you tonight – problems with the walk-in cooler. We'll chat soon.

Chance

I didn't believe that for a second, but there was nothing I could do. Man, being an adult is frustrating sometimes!

Marco gathered Giovanni, the interns, and me to tell us he had taken a Brix reading before coming to the party and he knew in his bones it would not be ready the next day. He told us to sleep in and come in by eleven o'clock, which sounded heavenly to me. He then announced that the vineyard would only need minimal maintenance and asked for volunteers to start packing up Pierre's house.

My hand shot right up and I dragged Alessa's hand up with mine – though she didn't look very happy about it. I knew there had to be some hidden clues as to what Pierre had been involved in somewhere in that house. I also knew that Alessa had nothing to do with either of the murders as she had been with me the whole time in the caves and could not have killed May. Louis said he would help us, too, so I thought it would go rather quickly.

Marco had plans for Jayson to sanitize the fermenting tanks, so he would not be available to help. Ava was taking another day to rest after her blackout and hospitalization. Marco had offered her and Alessa his wing of the family house so they would not be alone and could feel safe with his mother, sister, and her family.

Syd and I dropped Alessa and Ava off at the barracks so they could pick up some clothes and toiletries. They promised to stay together for safety. I had quickly pulled Alessa aside to explain that I had volunteered her to help me with the packing as I wanted to snoop but I also wanted someone I could trust there with me. She wasn't thrilled at the idea but said she would help anyway.

Syd drove me home and she forced her way into the house for a glass of wine so that she could get the full story about what happened with Chance and Marco. I was glad for the company and the opportunity to dissect my evening, the good and the bad. She ooh'ed and aah'ed, nodded at all the right places, and asked probing questions. Sometimes, you just need your best friend's help to analyze a confusing situation.

I kicked her out by one o'clock – after all, what good was having a late morning if you didn't get to bed early enough to enjoy a sufficient amount of sleep? I feel safe in my house, but that didn't stop me from making sure that all my doors and windows were locked before going up to bed. I also made sure my gun was loaded in my nightstand. As a retired police officer, I was entitled to carry a concealed weapon and I made a mental note to continue carrying it with me until the killer could be found.

Despite going to bed by one-thirty in the morning, ten a.m. came early. I think that my body was sleep-deficient. I stretched and turned in every direction to try to loosen up my muscles. I finally resorted to some yoga moves and that seemed to help – well, that and a hot shower.

I arrived at Pierre's house and found that Alessa and Louis were already there. They had started putting boxes together to make it easier for us to start packing. The mood seemed a little tense between them and I soon discovered the reason. Max had been released from jail and was now staying at a local hotel, courtesy of Marco. Marco knew there was still some mistrust by the other interns and thought it best that they all had some space. Max would be working in the vineyard today, though, helping to prepare for the harvest which we were all sure would be tomorrow or the next day.

I discovered that Louis thought that Max should have stayed in jail. He thought there was still a possibility that Max was guilty. Alessa, on the other hand, was convinced of Max's innocence. Apparently, they were in the middle of a heated debate when I arrived. I decided that we could all use some space and sent Louis to the kitchen with some boxes to begin sorting what could be donated and what should be thrown out. Marco had tried to contact Pierre's family, but they hadn't heard from him since he moved to the United States so they didn't want any of his belongings. We were planning to donate the items that could be used to a local shelter that helped families in need. The furniture that had not been damaged would be retained in case the next vineyard manager needed it.

Alessa went upstairs to the bedrooms to pack clothes and miscellaneous items. I decided to start in the dining room which Pierre had also used as a home office. His filing cabinet had been searched by the police and re-locked in their search for clues. I eventually found the key taped under a whimsical snow globe of the Eiffel Tower on his desk. Most of the files seemed to be old bills and ancient check stubs. I threw out anything old and kept the more recent items in case they were needed for his taxes or estate.

Marco had told me that the police did not find a will – not that Pierre seemed to have had anything important to leave anyone, but that made me sad, too. After emptying the file cabinet, I started sorting through the accumulated papers in his desk drawers. I found a bunch of old museum brochures that looked well worn. Most of the museums were located in France, but there were a few from the Isabella Stewart Gardner Museum in Boston. I remembered Max mentioning that Pierre had recommended the museum to him and Louis. The brochures seemed a little out of place with the rest of his paperwork, so I put them on top of the "keep" pile so I could look at them more closely later.

Alessa came down the stairs with garbage bags full of clothes as I finished up in the office and dining room. Louis emerged from the kitchen a few minutes later and we all went into the living room. This is where the most damage had occurred. Most of the furniture had been destroyed and would be carted away in the dumpster being delivered later. All of Pierre's prints had been torn off the walls and were lying among the shredded furniture and books that had been pulled off of the bookshelf.

Before we started packing, we had to tidy up a little. We picked up everything that was strewn about and threw the garbage into large trash bags. Louis held up what looked to be a Monet canvas and looked at the torn-up prints on the wall. "Obviously a fake. Why would Pierre hang a cheap painting by a forger on a wall with these beautiful prints?" He peered closer at the painting. "This artist even used Monet's name and signature style." He shook his head. "Forgers and fakes infuriate me, as do the people who buy and promote their work." He threw the painting in a garbage bag. "Pierre must have been going senile," he declared arrogantly.

We finished cleaning and sighed as we looked at the shelves of books. Pierre had *a lot* of books, most of which would be donated to local schools or libraries. Alessa and I gave the books a cursory glance, but I noticed that Louis was painstakingly fanning each book and examining the bindings. I nudged Alessa to look at what Louis was doing. She was apparently still steamed about their earlier argument and shouted, "Louis, we don't have all day. There's no time to read the books. Sort them by genre and move on."

Louis looked at her angrily and I could see him trying to get his temper under control. "Excuse my thoroughness, Alessa. If you must know, I have an obsession with books. Some of these art books are from museums that I visited while I have been here in the United States and there's one from a museum in France that I also visited. I was just going to ask Kat if she thought I could take a few books to keep in memory of Pierre."

I thought for a moment and shrugged. "I guess so. They are just going to be donated somewhere if we don't take them." I looked at a lower shelf. "There are a few cookbooks here that I would like to have as well, especially Artusi's *La scienza in cucina e l'arte di mangier bene* – the bible of Italian cooking. It's the Italian version but I think my language skills are good enough for me to follow a recipe." I looked at Alessa. "You can take a few books, too, if you'd like."

Alessa made a condescending noise and waved her hand dismissively. "I have no room in my baggage for books." She pulled out her phone. "All my books are on the Kindle app on my iPhone."

I smiled and shook my head. Youth. I still liked the feel of a book in my hands, though I did often use my Kindle app when I was stuck somewhere with nothing to read.

I put my four cookbooks on the coffee table and glanced at the five books Louis had chosen. The former cop in me mentally noted the titles:

- *Museum of Fine Arts, Boston: A Guide to the Collections*

- *The Treasures of Monet (Musée Marmottan Monet, Paris)*, by Michael Howard
- *Confessions d'un voleur d'arte* by Stéphane Breitwieser
- *Stolen* by Isabella Stewart Gardner Museum
- *The Isabella Stewart Gardner Museum: A Guide* by Christina Nielsen, Casey Riley, et al

I thought it was an interesting array of books that he had chosen, but then again, I had no idea that Pierre had been such an art connoisseur. I looked thoughtfully at the destruction of the prints that were still covered with a fine layer of fingerprint dust. Pierre had framed them nicely so that they actually resembled the authentic paintings. I noticed that Louis was staring at me and I turned back to the bookcase, a thought elusively tickling the edges of my consciousness.

We finished what we could by six o'clock and I dropped Alessa off at Marco's family house. Louis said he could use the walk up the hill which suited me just fine. I hadn't spent much time with him over the summer, but he was starting to give off a weird, creepy vibe.

When I got home, I turned on my laptop and started doing some research. That elusive thought was starting to solidify and take form and I wanted to investigate and compile some facts before I went to Ty with a half-formed theory. I spent the next three hours researching my idea and then thought about how I should proceed. My hypothesis was a little outlandish, but I was now fairly certain that I knew why Pierre had been killed. My theory on May was circumstantial, but I thought it fit with the facts. I just needed to return to Pierre's house for a key piece of evidence.

Chapter Twenty-Nine

I drove about one hundred yards past Pierre's house and parked behind a large rock. My car wasn't completely hidden, but it would be difficult to see. I'm not sure why I decided to hide my car, but I thought it could be a prudent measure.

I hiked down the hill and went around to the back door. Of course, it was past midnight on a Friday night, so there shouldn't be too much traffic on the vineyard's long driveway, but it seemed better to be safe than sorry.

I still had the key to the door so I let myself in quietly. I remembered seeing a book that seemed a little out of place and I thought it would surely hold the clue I needed to prove my theory. I used a penlight and picked my way past all the boxes to the living room. I didn't want to advertise my presence by turning on the lights.

We had stacked the packed book boxes in the living room and we had tried to sort them by genre, but some of them just didn't fit any genre so they were haphazardly packed. I realized we hadn't labeled the boxes very well, so this could take me a little while. I started with the box closest to me and started sorting through. I could ignore all the box of cookbooks as I knew the book I sought wasn't in there.

On the sixth box of books, my back started to ache and my eyes began to feel the strain of reading book titles with just a penlight. Damn! I hated getting older. Soon, I'd probably have to wear reading glasses – ugh! I ran my index finger down the spines of the books, swiftly reading each title and then moving on to the next. I spied the book I wanted, pulled it out of the box, and flexed my shoulder muscles as I stood up. Did my shoulders make that popping noise?

I started to flip through the book and located a loose paper that was taped to a page midway through the book. My eyes widened when I realized what I was looking at and I got so excited that I let down my guard. Suddenly, I heard a quiet shuffling sound behind me. Before I could turn around, I felt a heavy weight strike my head and I dropped to the floor, out for the count.

Faint sunlight was trickling in through the window as my eyes fluttered open. Where was my soft pillow? All I could focus on was my stiff neck and splitting headache. For some reason, I was lying on the floor, face down with my cheek resting on something sticky. Maybe I fell out of bed? Wait! This wasn't my floor...

I slowly pushed myself into a sitting position and realized that was a bad idea as my head felt like it was about to explode and I saw red. Literally, blood red. There was a small puddle of blood on the floor that had pooled under my head after I fell.

My hand went slowly to my head. I felt around gingerly and touched a sticky, congealed mess and a knot the size of a golf ball. I pulled my hand away quickly and looked at the blood. My head started to spin and I felt like throwing up. I rested my forehead in my hands with my elbows supported by my knees. I took some deep breaths and my head started to clear a little, but all I could smell was that metallic scent of blood. I still hurt like I had been hit over the head with something hard, but at least I didn't feel like vomiting anymore.

My eyes wandered over to a hammer on the floor. It looked like it had been painted red and then dipped in straw. Oh, crap! That was my blood and hair. I could no longer contain the bile and vomited repeatedly on the floor, each soul-sucking retch feeling like it was tearing my head apart.

There was finally nothing left inside of me. It felt like I must have puked up some internal organs as well. I glanced at the mess on the hardwood floors around me and slowly crawled to the other side of the room where I saw my purse. I turned the phone on and noted it was five-thirty a.m. There was only one person I knew who would drop everything without demanding a huge explanation, so I asked Siri to phone Syd.

It seemed like it took her forever to pick up, but my throbbing head had lost the ability to track time. Finally, I heard, "Kat? What's wrong?"

I smiled a little inside and then briefly explained to her where I was and asked her to bring Ty and possibly an ambulance. Then I passed out.

Chapter Thirty

I woke up as I was being wheeled out to an ambulance in Pierre's driveway. Syd was by my side, looking more worried than even the time her son had built a set of wings and tried to fly off of the roof in the middle of his sisters' tenth birthday party. He was young and surprisingly only sprained his ankle. She had been equal parts worried and angry with him. Right now, she just looked scared.

She exhaled a sigh of relief when she saw my eyes flutter open. She leaned around the paramedics and squeezed my hand. "Kat!" she whispered. "Thank God!" I could see the trails her tears had left on her cheeks. "They couldn't wake you up and we were so worried."

I looked up and saw Ty standing behind Syd, his hands on her shoulders, squeezing tightly. He must have been worried, too, based on his white knuckles. He attempted to speak and only a croaking noise came out. He cleared his throat and swiped at his eyes. I could see the conflicting emotions racing across his face – relief, anger, concern, fear, anger. I always brought out the best in people, I thought wryly. "Kat, I won't ask you any questions right now as they need to get you to the hospital, except, did you see who did this to you?"

I started to shake my head but realized that my head was immobilized. I tried to wet my dry lips, but I had no saliva. That's when my eyes tracked to the IV bag which was attached to my right arm. I hissed a quiet no and felt myself being loaded into the back of the ambulance. I saw the flashing lights of more police cars arriving as the doors closed on Syd's anxious face. The paramedics did what paramedics do and I safely arrived at the hospital about ten minutes later. This was not an experience I had ever wanted to repeat after the attack in Boston, but at least I knew what to expect.

They wheeled me back to a room in the Emergency Room and cut my clothes off. I didn't remember this part of the ER entry after I had been stabbed in Boston and think I liked being passed out better. It was quite undignified. The ER doctor was very professional, even if he had no bedside manner to speak of. My head wound was examined and the doctor explained that they were going to take a CT scan to make sure there were no brain bleeds. Yuck! Brain bleeds. I could have lived the rest of my life without that thought tunneling into my brain.

Fortunately, it was a slow night at the hospital. My bloodwork was analyzed and the CT scan thankfully showed no brain bleeds. They shaved the area and sewed my wound up with fourteen stitches. I wondered how I'd ever be able to cover that up and decided I'd have to start wearing a hat, at least for the short term.

After asking me a series of questions, such as "Who is the President?" and "What's the date?" the doctors insisted I remain hospitalized because I had lost consciousness and vomited. I think they called it a Grade 3 concussion. They left me in the ER but allowed visitors, so Syd and Ricky rushed in, relief flooding their faces.

Ricky was still in drag from the night before which was causing quite a stir among the hospital staff. His make-up, usually impeccable, was smudged and I noted that he was missing one false eyelash. I wanted to smile but the pain was so great, that it came across as a grimace instead. Syd grabbed my hand and Ricky stood next to her, resting his hand gently on my leg.

Silent tears streamed from Syd's eyes. Ricky took a deep breath and exhaled loudly. "Kat, I'm getting tired of seeing you in a hospital bed." He tried to sound cross, but only managed to sound panicky.

I smiled weakly at the two of them, thinking for about the millionth time how lucky I was to have two such great friends. "I never want to be in another damn hospital bed either." I tried to look at Ricky critically. "Where the hell were you when Syd called you?"

Ricky groaned and buried his face in his hands. "Having the time of my life with a Russian programmer named Vlad, thank you very much, Miss Snow."

I chuckled, but that hurt my head and I winced. I whispered, "Sorry," and shrugged my shoulders slightly.

"No worries," Ricky grinned mischievously. "Vlad isn't going back to Russia for a few more weeks. I'll make it up to him." He patted me on the leg gently.

Syd swiped at her eyes with a tissue. "Kat, what were you doing at Pierre's house in the middle of the night."

"I can't remember. I only know that it was important that I went there after I did some online research at home. I'm sure the information is on my laptop at my house." I felt my eyes fluttering. "I really appreciate you both being here, but I'm exhausted." They both still looked anxious. "The ER doctor said I have a concussion, but I'll be fine. The CT scan came back negative. They're only keeping me for observation tonight. We can talk more tomorrow."

Ricky swallowed hard. "Ok, Kat." He glanced at Syd. "Is it alright if I stop by your house and look through your laptop? I'm not tired, but now I'm dying to know why you felt it necessary to go there without one of us."

"Sure thing," I nodded. "You still have my key?"

He reached into a sleek evening bag and pulled out a set of keys. "Never leave home without them." He winked at me which was a little scary with the missing false eyelash. "With you, I never know when I may need access to your house."

They both leaned in and gently kissed my cheek. Before the door closed behind them, I was already fast asleep.

Chapter Thirty-One

I had terrible nightmares as I slept in the hospital. I didn't actually get much sleep between the nurses coming in to check my vitals and the food service workers delivering my food trays even thought I didn't feel much like eating. My stomach was achy after all that vomiting last night. I stared mindlessly out the window as I felt my strength slowly return. Maybe it was the drugs they gave me for my head wound, but I wasn't as sore anymore either.

Around 5:30, Ty came strolling in. "Feel like talking?"

I turned to look at him. "Not really, but I know I can't avoid it." I glanced at him. "Last night is still very fuzzy though, so I'm not sure how much help I will be."

Ty nodded. "I understand." He took a deep breath and looked at me sternly. "I need to start with this, Kat. What the hell were you thinking, going to Pierre's house in the middle of the night – by yourself – when there is a killer on the loose?"

I knew better than to interrupt him. He seemed to be on a roll.

"Do you know how much you worried Syd, Ricky, and," he looked away, but not before I saw a glisten in his eyes, "and me? Syd would be inconsolable if anything happens to you and..." he choked up, "that would make my life miserable," he muttered gruffly. He took a step closer to me and squeezed my hand. "We got through it once when you were attacked in Boston. Don't make us ever go through that again."

I nodded meekly. I knew it had been a stupid idea, but I also know I'm single-minded and stubborn. I would inevitably make another stupid decision in the future. I silently vowed that I would try to think things through better next time. Or, I'd stay more alert.

Ty seemed to sense where my thoughts were wandering – the benefits of knowing someone for most of their lives. "I mean it, Kat. You need to wise up." He cleared his throat. "Okay. Do you know why you went to Pierre's house last night?"

I felt that elusive idea, still tapping at the back of my mind. I started to shake my head and realized it still hurt when I moved my head too much, so I stopped mid-shake. "I don't, but Ricky went to get my laptop to check what I researched before I went. I know I usually take notes so I can review them later."

He nodded and started sending a text. "I'll text him to let me know what he found." He finished the text and looked at me. "Do you remember anything about the attack last night?"

I was about to shake my head but stopped at the memory of pain. "No. I've been trying and trying to remember something, but I can't. I know I was looking through Pierre's books, but I don't know what I was looking for or if I even found it."

"How about any smells? Sometimes our other senses can remember things that our minds cannot."

I closed my eyes and pictured myself standing near the stack of book boxes. I inhaled deeply a few times and suddenly, a memory popped into my head. "I smell mustiness," I blurted out.

Ty looked at me quizzically. "Mustiness? What does that smell like?"

I shrugged slightly. "The best comparison I have is the scent of an old cellar. There's a faint tinge of dust and a coolness." My eyes opened slowly. "I'm sorry, Ty. That's the best I can do right now. Maybe something will come back to me later."

He nodded slowly. "When something does come back, what is the first thing you are going to do, Kat?"

"I'm going to pick up my phone and call you," I answered obediently, holding up three fingers as a sign of my intent.

He grinned. "I know that's not true, but at least make sure I'm in the top three."

I smiled up at him. "Will do. I promise."

Ty leaned down and kissed my forehead. "I'm sure Syd and Ricky will be here later to take you home. The doctor said he would release you this evening. I know Syd is planning on staying the night with you." He paused on his way out. "By the way, I have your gun. I took it before they put you in the ambulance. Not that it helped you any. Syd can bring it to your house later." He waved as he walked out the door and was almost pushed aside as Syd and Ricky rushed in, followed more slowly by Chance.

"Do you feel any better, Kat?" Syd asked anxiously. She looked at Ricky. "She looks good, doesn't she?" She fretted about the hospital bed, straightening the covers and adjusting the bed so that I was sitting up straighter.

Ricky shook his head. He knew better than to try to stop Syd from fussing. "She certainly looks better, but she still looks tired."

Chance stepped up, but I noticed he was having a hard time looking me in the eyes. What was that about? I hoped I would remember that as well. His opening! I remembered going to the Two Cups opening. Did something happen at his opening?

"Kat," he finally looked at me and I could see the concern in his eyes. His voice broke and he cleared his throat. "Is this a part of being your *friend*? Do I have to get used to you being attacked?"

Was it my imagination or did he emphasize the word friend? What does that mean? Wait! "What do you mean getting used to me being attacked?" I demanded indignantly.

The corners of his mouth lifted slightly. "Well, I found you in the stairway at the reunion after you had been attacked…"

"I stopped the killer from killing Sunny…"

"And got attacked in the process."

I nodded.

"Then, I came upon you being held at knifepoint in the resort kitchen…"

"It wasn't just me…"

"I know," he said patiently, "but it does seem to be a habit."

I looked away. "Not one I care to keep repeating."

He leaned in and squeezed my hand. "I know that, too. It's your nature to help people and, unfortunately, I don't think this will be the last time I see you in a hospital bed."

"I hope not," chirped up Ricky. "I'm still hoping she'll have babies and we'll have to visit her in the hospital then."

My eyes opened wide and Chance and I stared at Ricky, open-mouthed. I shook my head, muttering "No way!" and couldn't tear my eyes away from Ricky.

Syd sensed the tension and chuckled. "Shut up, Ricky," which effectively diffused the tension and made Ricky bring forth his "who me?" expression.

I slowly raised my eyes to look at Chance and he was grinning at my discomfort. I closed my eyes and sighed. The problem with having such close friends is that they felt entitled to freely voice their opinion about your life, even if that opinion contradicted everything you had ever said.

Ricky looked momentarily deflated, but then perked back up. "I texted Marco, but he said to tell you to stop slacking and get back to work." Ricky snickered like a twelve-year-old boy. "I told him you'd do anything to get out of doing work."

As soon as Ricky mentioned Marco, I saw Chance close down. He leaned in and kissed the top of my head and rested his hand on my right cheek, careful to avoid the stitches and general bruising. "I need to get back to Two Cups," he murmured. We've been busy since the opening and, if I want time off to help with the harvest, I need to butter my sister up."

I nodded slightly. "Thank you for coming. It means a lot to me."

Chance just stared into my eyes for a moment and I could see the conflicting emotions running through his mind. Silently, he kissed the top of my head again, waved at Syd and Ricky, and walked out.

Ricky, oblivious to everything, kept prattling on. "Marco also said to tell you that the grapes aren't ripe yet, but they're really close. He wants you to rest up so that you'll be ready to work the harvest. He said he thinks now that it will be a few days still, based on the weather and something he called bricks."

I looked at him in exasperation. "Brix, and we've talked about it before. Probably when you were applying make-up."

Ricky just shrugged. "Whatever."

They stayed with me until the doctor came in and gave me one last cognitive test. He told me to take it easy for a few days, avoid screen time, and that I should have some help washing my hair, at least for the first day.

Syd held up her hands. "Nope. You know how I feel about hair, and stitches."

Ricky practically squealed. "I'll do it! I LOVE hair."

I nodded then closed my eyes, not sure what I had just gotten myself into.

Chapter Thirty-Two

Ricky and Syd took me home. I was never so happy to see that cottage in my whole life. I realized that I had actually started to think of Harmony as home again. When I first got back to town, after I recovered from the attack, all I could think about was getting out of here and getting back to Boston. Now, I didn't even go into Boston once a month and I had started appreciating the lack of rush hour traffic and relative quiet of Harmony.

After Ricky carefully washed my hair in the sink and Syd combed it out, I took a long, hot shower. Nothing had felt so good in a long time. Just washing the smell of the hospital off of me felt wonderful. And the stink of dried blood. Hygiene complete, I was now ravenous.

Amelia came over with some garlic bread, a salad, and a lasagna she had made. I offered everyone wine even though I couldn't drink any with the painkillers, but they decided to suffer in unity with me. We devoured the food while we talked about our lives and things happening around town. Syd told us about Sarah's plans to go to the Royal Academy of Music next year. Sarah was her youngest child. She was getting a full scholarship, so it made sense, but I knew that Syd and Ty were going to miss her.

"We'll just have to cross the pond and visit her then," I said reasonably.

Syd looked at me hopefully. "Really? You'll go with me?"

"Of course," I said. "I love London."

Ricky chimed in, "Don't leave me behind. I love a man with a British accent."

I had a brief memory of a former English boyfriend that I still thought about fondly from time to time. He was the biggest regret of my life and I wondered how differently things might have turned out if I hadn't joined the army.

Amelia laughed and broke me out of my momentary traipse down memory lane. "Me, too. Maybe I'll go as well. I need to start pushing myself to do more things and I've never been to London."

Amelia's husband had been one of the victims at our high school reunion. She has recovered remarkably well in three months and seemed almost back to normal. She was working a lot, but I think that she needed to focus on something and work was a great outlet. She had even talked about running for Mayor in the special election. That post was currently vacant in Harmony.

Amelia looked curiously at Syd. "Unless Ty wants to go with just you."

Syd, Ricky, and I looked at each other dumbly for a moment and burst out laughing. It hurt my head but the thought of Ty getting on a plane and flying over the Atlantic was absolutely hysterical. Ty may be a big, macho, man's man, but he was deathly afraid of flying. They had to cancel their honeymoon trip to Hawaii because he could not get himself on the plane. We decided to move into the living room so we would be more comfortable.

Syd quickly explained Ty's problem to Amelia, who nodded knowingly. "Bo used to be severely claustrophobic – he couldn't go into our walk-in closet. He saw Dr. Capshaw and worked with him for a few months. He got hypnotized a few times and learned some coping skills. Within three months, he was able to spend five whole minutes in the closet on his own." She looked at us to see if we understood how big of an accomplishment that was. "I know it doesn't sound like much, but it was a huge step. Bo was even talking about exploring the caves and tunnels under Harmony." She reached into her purse and pulled out a business card. "I know Ty will want to go visit Sarah. Maybe Dr. Capshaw can help him, too…?"

Suddenly, my brain started to hurt. Jumbled images started flitting around, trying to form a sensible thought.

Syd accepted the card. "Thanks, Amelia. I'll see if I can get him to do this. Normally, seeing a therapist would be a little out of his wheelhouse, but I know he's going to miss Sarah terribly if he has to wait for her to come home on holidays and vacations."

Ricky nodded. "He can sit with me on the plane. I'm sure I can distract him."

The images slowed down as what Ricky said registered. I giggled as I pictured Ty being trapped by Ricky for nearly seven hours in a flying tin can.

Ricky slapped his forehead. "Man, I can't believe I forgot to tell you about this!" He pulled my laptop out of his bag. "Talking about claustrophobia made me remember."

I stared at my laptop, trying to jolt my memory back in shape. That wasn't working, so I just looked at Ricky expectantly.

"Okay, first of all, based on your recent search history, you have an unholy obsession with the Gardner Museum in Boston. Especially the heist in 1990. You had about five pages of notes and timelines all laid out in an open Word document."

My thoughts again started tumbling over themselves, trying to make sense of what he was telling me. Ideas formulated and coalesced. It was all beginning to make sense to me again and now I remembered why I had gone to Pierre's house.

Ricky was still scrolling through my Word document. "You also had some information here on art thefts in France." He looked at me suspiciously. "What's up? Planning a new career as an art thief?"

I held up both hands. "Nope, but I think I knew an art thief. Pierre," I declared triumphantly.

I had three sets of eyes, laser-locked on my face, their mouths hanging open. "What?" Syd was the first to recover. I guess she was used to recovering quickly, being a police chief's wife.

I settled back into the couch cushions and looked longingly at my wine refrigerator, exhaling in frustration at not being able to tell the story with a luscious glass of pinot noir. I mentally shook myself and saw the other three leaning in so they didn't miss a word.

"I went to Pierre's house," I had to think what day it was after everything that had happened, "yesterday morning with Alessa and Louis to start packing up his stuff. We each took different rooms and met up at the end in the living room to pack all his books and sort through the mess that the murderer left behind. Louis and I both chose a few books as mementos of Pierre – you know that Pierre was a family friend of Louis' father?" I asked as an aside.

"Does it matter?" demanded Ricky, impatiently.

"Uh, yeah," I replied in exasperation. The final piece of the puzzle popped into my head and I jumped up but regretted it instantly when I started feeling woozy. "I'll tell you the rest on the way. Let's go."

The three of them looked at me in confusion.

"Go? The only place you're going is back to bed, Kat," Syd tried to sound authoritative.

"If we wait until tomorrow, it may be too late," I pleaded.

They all looked at each other and looked at me. Syd felt Ricky and Amelia siding with me and crossed her arms, looking pissed off.

"Look, once I explain why we need to do this, you'll understand why it needs to be done today. Trust me, the art world will thank us and appreciate our effort." I knew that by appealing to Syd's love of art, I could get her on board as well. I saw her shoulders soften and her arms slipped to her side and knew I had won.

I grabbed a heavy sweatshirt that read "BPD" and started lacing up my hiking boots.

Amelia began to look a bit concerned. "Hiking boots? I only have these flats…" She trailed off and looked at Ricky and Syd's feet which were clad in sneakers. "I don't know…"

I looked at Amelia's feet. "What size are you? A seven or eight?"

"Seven and a half," she offered.

"I reached into the back of the hall closet and pulled out my old gardening sneakers. "Here, try these. They're an eight but should work out well. I'll grab you a thick pair of socks." I bounded – okay, I climbed slowly – up the stairs to my room and returned with a pair of thick, wool socks. I noticed that she had worn a fashionable autumn jacket, so I handed her another sweatshirt that I had also grabbed from my upstairs closet. This one was a deep maroon color with the Milano Vineyards logo on the back. Ricky and Syd had their own sweatshirts so we all walked out and climbed into Syd's mini-van. I grabbed a notebook on the way so I could organize my thoughts.

Syd started the van and then sat there for a moment.

"What's the holdup?" Ricky inquired.

"Where are we going? I need to tell Ty." She pulled out her phone.

I groaned and then I thought about my promise to Ty in the hospital. I sighed in resignation. She was right. "You drive," I said as I pulled out my phone. "I'll call him."

"Again, where are we going?"

"Drive up to the vineyard. I'll tell you my plan after I call Ty."

I called Ty. He picked up but sounded very irritated. "Kat, what's up?" He must have pulled the phone away from his face because I heard him screaming, "Make way for the ambulance!" He started speaking to me again. "Whatever it is, can it wait? I'm at the scene of a four-car accident and it doesn't look too good for two of the drivers. I've got Officer Sunshine on traffic duty and he can't even do that well."

I shuddered. I always hated responding to motor vehicle accidents when I was a cop. "Yeah, I'm calling because I said I would, but it can wait."

"Who are you with?" he demanded, but I could tell I didn't have his full attention.

"I'm with Syd, Ricky, and Amelia." I paused. "Look, I know you have to get back to the accident, so I'll text you what you need to know. Get back to me when the accident is cleared up."

"Sounds good," he said and then started screaming at someone that must have been Officer Sunshine. I heard, "Get your ass off of that stone wall and start directing traffic. There are no coffee breaks…" The phone abruptly turned off.

I filled everyone in on what Ty had told me, though they had figured it out based on my side of the conversation. I sent a quick text saying that we were headed to the vineyards to explore the wine caves and would text him when we were done. "We have fulfilled our vow to keep him informed." I leaned into the middle of the car. "Now let me tell you what I have planned for us."

Chapter Thirty-Three

We parked behind the tasting room at Milano's Vineyards so that nobody would easily see our car from the driveway. As I climbed out of the car, my throbbing headache almost made me rethink my decision to come out tonight. Almost.

Syd searched through the back of the minivan and only came up with one flashlight. I thought for a moment and remembered that Jayson had taken the headlamps back to the intern barracks after our last foray into the caves. I pointed Amelia and Ricky toward the cave entrance and moved toward the barracks with Syd. My plan was to get in and out quickly without being noticed.

We arrived at the door and I pulled out my keys. Marco would probably kill me if he knew I was using the keys to break into the barracks, but, it's always easier to ask for forgiveness rather than permission. It was only nine o'clock but I had barely slept at all the night before – unless you counted the time I was passed out on the floor in a pool of my own blood. I thought I would be more fatigued, but the thrill of the hunt had pumped some adrenaline into my veins and I was raring to go.

I unlocked and opened the outer door and walked right in – right into Max, that is. I was shocked that he was there. Last I knew, he was staying at a hotel along with Alessa and Ava.

"H-hi," I stuttered.

"Hey, Kat. Great to see you! I've been wanting to thank you for helping clear my name. Nobody ever trusts the German dude."

I stared at him for a moment, wondering how I would explain my presence. He apparently believed that I thought his joke was inappropriate because he continued on in a rush of words. "Sorry, I make bad jokes when I'm nervous."

That stopped me. "Why are you nervous?"

He shrugged and glanced at Syd. "You're Sheriff Randall's wife, right?"

Syd smiled and stepped forward with her hand extended. "I am. Syd Randall. Nice to meet you, Max."

He continued. "It's really nothing. It's great that Jayson and Louis said I could come back as they were the only two staying here and they knew I hadn't done anything."

"I don't understand why that makes you nervous?" I asked, quizzically.

"Everything was fine until last night. Jayson had worked on sanitizing the tanks all day. Louis had helped you pack Pierre's house. We were all in good moods. We ordered pizza and had a few beers. Nice and relaxing. Normal."

I was growing aware of time passing and Max had still not gotten to the point. I know that patience is not one of my virtues, and I really, really try hard to get it under control, but I couldn't help myself. I made a rolling motion with my right hand to get him to speed the story's pace.

"Right. We all went back to our rooms around ten, but I woke up around one and felt a little hungry. I got up to see if there was any leftover pizza and bumped into Louis. He was dressed all in black and had on a wool hat." He looked around uncomfortably and I stared at him until he continued. "I asked him where he was going at the time of night and I could see how angry it made him that I had asked. He muttered something about 'No privacy here!' and then pushed past me as he left."

"At one in the morning, you said," I asked innocently.

"*Ja*," he nodded vigorously. "And he never came back. I checked his room this morning and the bed hadn't been slept in." He shrugged. "He didn't show up in the fields today either and Marco nearly blew a basket."

"Gasket," I corrected.

He smiled in agreement.

I blew out the breath I had been holding. Now I was certain that my theory was correct.

Max suddenly looked at me differently. "Weren't you in the hospital after getting attacked at Pierre's last night? What are you doing here?"

I nodded. "I was. I can't sleep and Syd volunteered to go on a hike to help clear my head. I came to look for the headlamps so we don't kill ourselves in the dark."

"Oh, okay," he said. "I think I saw the box of flashlights and headlamps in the common area." He turned around and went into the common room. "How many do you want? Two?" he yelled.

"Four," I yelled back.

"Why do you need four for the two of you?" he asked. A perfectly reasonable question.

Jayson wandered out of his room. "What's all the noise out here?" he demanded. He did a double-take when he saw Syd and me standing there. He recovered quickly but was still curious. "Hi, Kat. What are you doing here?"

I started to answer as Max came back into the foyer with the headlamps in his hand. "Sorry, Jayson. I didn't mean to disturb you. Kat just came for some headlamps for a nighttime nature hike." He looked down at the headlamps. "I don't know where the flashlights are, though. Do you know where we put them, Jayson?"

He nodded vigorously. "Louis took the box into his room. I'll grab them." He walked down the hallway but came back quickly. "I'm sorry. His room is locked."

I looked down at the keys in my hands. "I wonder if any of these work?" I tried to look earnest as I continued to lie. "I'd really appreciate having a flashlight as well as the headlamps, just in case."

Max shrugged, indifferent. "Let's go check."

We followed Max and Jayson down the hall. I tried a few keys and the fourth one unlocked the door. We all squeezed into the tiny room and I saw the clue that confirmed my theory. The flagpole finial – originally stolen from the Isabella Stewart Gardner Museum in 1990 and later used as a stairway finial at Pierre's house – was just sitting on Louis' desk. I remembered admiring the bronze eagle when I had been invited over for dinner. It was magnificent! It stood nearly a foot tall and had been used by Napoleon's First Regiment of Imperial Guard.

Max shouted, "Here they are!" and picked up the box of flashlights. As we all started moving toward the door, I maneuvered so that I was the last to leave. I quickly grabbed the heavy finial and put it awkwardly into my messenger bag. I was not about to leave a valuable piece of stolen art just lying around the barracks!

We traipsed back out to the common area and I grabbed a few flashlights from the box. I looked solemnly at Max and Jayson. "I think you should call the police and report that Louis is missing."

Max looked uncomfortable. "We don't know that he's missing. Maybe he's off on an adventure."

"Perhaps," I agreed, "but I would rather err on the side of being over-cautious than not cautious enough. Remember, two people have been murdered."

Jayson and Max looked at each other and I could see that I had scared them. Jayson nodded and reached for his phone. "You're right, Kat. I'll call them right now."

Max leaned over and touched my arm. "Maybe you should postpone your night walk, Kat. It might not be safe."

Syd grinned. "Anyone that tries to attack the two of us will be in for a rude surprise." She pulled her jacket back to show the concealed Glock she always carried around. "Kat's armed, too."

I looked at her in surprise. I didn't know she had seen me strap on my holster and Sig Sauer that she had brought back to my house. I did feel better knowing she was also armed.

Max took a step back and Jayson paused with his phone midway to his face. "O-okay," Max stuttered. "I think you two are all set to go."

Syd and I grinned at each other and let ourselves out of the barracks. My adrenaline was still spiking and I was trying not to think about the throbbing jackhammer pounding into my brain. I was only mildly successful.

Chapter Thirty-Four

After leaving the barracks, I steered Syd back towards her car.

"What's up? Aren't we meeting Ricky and Amelia at the caves?"

I pulled the eagle finial out from my bag and presented it to her. "From the Gardner Museum heist. My theory has been confirmed."

Syd's eyes widened and she looked closely at the finial, reaching a hand out to stroke its head. "It's gorgeous," she whispered.

We stepped up to the car and she opened the back. We hid the finial under some beach blankets and a collapsible shovel she always kept in there, no matter what time of year it was.

After we both felt that the finial was sufficiently hidden, we hurried over to the tunnel entrance. Amelia and Ricky were talking about my theory as we approached.

"…I don't think I ever met Louis," Amelia said thoughtfully. "It's hard to believe one of Marco's interns could be a killer, though." She sighed. "After the reunion, I guess I need to be less trusting of people."

Ricky agreed. "I only met him once and he seemed okay, for a Frenchman." He grinned quickly to let her know he was joking. "I guess that anyone could be a killer with the right motivation. A fortune in art is as good a reason as any."

"What good is it though?" Syd asked. "I know the paintings, or at least the pictures I've seen, are beautiful, but what good is owning – or rather, possessing – art if it can never be shared with anyone?"

She shook her head sadly. "Art thieves make me so angry. They steal rare and priceless artwork that is on display for everyone's benefit in a museum and then they sell it to the highest bidder or keep it locked away where only they can enjoy it." She looked at Kat. "What makes you think Pierre didn't sell the pieces from the Gardner?"

I thought for a moment. "I considered that he may have sold some of them but I think he kept the artwork from the Gardner. I saw some of the expensive wines he had in his wine refrigerator and pictures of himself all over the world." I looked away guiltily for a moment. "I also looked through his bank statements the other day when we were packing his house. The balances were more than you would expect for a vineyard manager, but there was no indication of priceless painting wealth. I think he was an art thief for hire in his earlier heists and decided to keep the paintings from the Gardner Museum."

A collective gasp went through the group. I secretly felt a thrill at having solved the mystery. "According to everyone, he spent a lot of time in these tunnels and was very protective of them. He told the interns not to go there without him, ostensibly for safety, but we store wine in there. It's safe." I shook my head. "No, if he sold any stolen art to finance his secretive, luxurious lifestyle, it was from his thefts in France, including the Monets from the *Musée Marmottan* in 1985. I am reasonably certain that there is a secret chamber somewhere in these tunnels that holds priceless artwork."

Syd shook her head. "The paintings from the *Musée Marmottan* were returned. I read about the heist and recovery in college."

I shook my head. "Yes, they were recovered in Japan five years after the heist, but I don't really think the *Yakuza* committed the theft. I think they hired Pierre to steal the paintings for them. I also think that at least one of the recovered paintings is a forgery."

Ricky looked confused. "Wouldn't the museum have reported that a recovered painting was a forgery?"

Syd made a face. "No, not always. The museum and the investigators received a lot of good press after the paintings were recovered and people started flocking to the museum again." She looked at me questioningly. "Why do you think that at least one of the paintings is a forgery?"

"Because Pierre had an actual watercolor painting hanging on his wall. I thought it was just in the style of Monet, but it didn't fit the theme of the rest of his prints. Pierre had first-rate, museum-quality prints hanging on his wall. When we were cleaning, I noticed that one of them wasn't a print, but actually a canvas. I had missed that when I went for the dinner party earlier in the summer" I sighed. "I didn't think about it as we were cleaning, but then I remembered it after I was done researching art thefts. When I went to Pierre's house alone, I found the painting that we had put into the trash and put it aside while I looked through the boxes of books. I think Louis must have come to the same conclusion as me and he's the one who attacked me at Pierre's house the other night."

I could tell Amelia was contemplating what I had just revealed. "Okay," she said slowly, "but why Louis? How does Louis fit into all this? Why would he kill Pierre and May?"

I nodded. "If you read the description of the Gardner Museum thieves, one of them definitely fits the description of Pierre, or rather, Pierre from thirty years ago. The other sounded a lot like Louis, who I bet bears a strong resemblance to his father. I think that Pierre and Louis' father were partners in the museum art heist business but that Pierre decided to keep the paintings from the Gardner and so Jean-Louis, Louis' father, never got paid."

Ricky's eyes lit up. "That's why you were researching the Fontaine Vineyard. Louis' family owns it. When I read through your research, I couldn't figure out why you were interested in an obscure vineyard that appears to be on the brink of going broke." He thought for a moment. "Based on your research, there were improvements made in the 1980s, but nothing since."

I nodded. "Right. My guess is that Jean-Louis, Louis' father, used his portion of their art heists' money to make those improvements. Pierre and Jean-Louis were either paid a fee or Pierre might have sold artwork pieces from previous thefts every few years and sent half of the proceeds to Jean-Louis. Then, for whatever reason, Pierre decided not to sell the Gardner paintings. Maybe he became too attached to them or liked the feeling of his big secret.

Maybe he just knew they were too hot to move. Jean-Louis, without the trickle of art heist money, eventually went broke and his vineyard is currently up for sale. I think Louis came to get his father's share of the Gardner's paintings and Pierre underestimated just how desperate the family's monetary situation had become." I shrugged. "Or he didn't care. I'm sure he thought he could keep gaslighting them for some future payday that he never intended to make."

Syd looked sad. "It's a shame that his greed led to his death. I can't really blame Louis for wanting his father's fair share, but murder is never the answer."

Amelia still looked confused. "Why do you think you know how to find this 'hidden room?'" she put her fingers up, pantomiming air quotes.

"I remembered that Pierre had a book of maps in his library. That's what I really went back for that night." I stopped for a moment. "Last night." I did a few easy stretches to get ready to explore the caves. "Pierre was a little peculiar. I thought that he would probably think it was funny to hide the map to his treasure in plain sight. I had just found a handwritten map in a book of printed maps and was looking at it when I was attacked." I shook my head slowly. "I'm sorry to say, I didn't have time to study the map well and can only remember the written directions, 'two rights, a left, and two rights.'"

Amelia stretched her arms over her head. "Okay, let's get this treasure hunt started. It's getting late and I've got a big

229

presentation to a commercial developer tomorrow morning." She smiled. "I need my beauty rest."

Ricky gave her a side hug. "You always look great, Amelia."

Amelia smiled at him gratefully then took the headlamp that Syd handed her. "Probably not with this on," she quipped.

Ricky laughed as he slid his own headlamp on. "Nobody can pull this look off, though I have a silver lame jacket which would reflect the light nicely…"

I punched him in the arm and he feigned as if it hurt. "Damn, girl! You haven't even been to the gym in two weeks."

I grinned wickedly. "I'm naturally strong." This was refuted a moment later when I tried to flex my arms, accidentally brushed against my head, and cried out in pain. I pulled out my container of painkillers and a bottle of water and quickly took two capsules.

"Karma's a bitch," I heard Ricky murmur as he led the way into the cave.

Chapter Thirty-Five

Syd sent a quick text to Ty so that he couldn't say that we weren't keeping him informed. I'm sure he was not going to be pleased that we were about to start exploring the caves, but at least we would be together. It wasn't our fault that he was stuck at a traffic accident.

We started out in high spirits which quickly burned out as tedium set in. After a half-hour, we realized that we had only explored about one hundred yards of one of the main tunnels and the side tunnels off of it. We would be here for days if we didn't split up.

Syd and I were the only two who were armed, so I took Amelia and Ricky went with Syd. The directions of two rights, a left, and two more rights off of the main tunnel were turning out to be remarkably ambiguous. Regrettably, I didn't remember which main tunnel or how far down the main tunnel we would have to travel to locate the correct first turn.

There were three main tunnels so we decided that Syd and Ricky took the one on the left and Amelia and I took the one on the right. If we didn't find anything in an hour, we would come back and check the third tunnel. Most of the tunnels went straight for a distance to a dead end and could be quickly eliminated. Some had two rights but no left – well, imagine the possibilities.

We were definitely covering ground more quickly now that we had split up. We had brought walkie-talkies with us but were having some difficulties communicating due to being underground and surrounded by rocks. We had also brought chalk so that we could mark each side tunnel we were currently exploring with a checkmark. When we exited each tunnel, we put an "X" through it so that nobody would waste their time looking in that tunnel again.

An hour later, Amelia and I were beat. We were taking a break on a large rock two right turns and a left turn down a side tunnel that abruptly ended when we heard voices. At first, Amelia thought it was Syd and Ricky, but the voices were too deep to be either of them and I shushed Amelia. The voices seemed to be coming closer and we looked around for a place to hide. There was nowhere to go so we crouched behind the large rock and turned off our flashlights and headlamps.

The sound of the footsteps came even closer and I realized they were approaching us down the side tunnel in which we were currently hiding. They seemed to be right at the mouth of our left turn and their voices drifted down to us.

"Do you really think Kenji will be able to help us?" The voice sounded slightly familiar, but it definitely wasn't Louis. I expected Louis' voice to be the next that I heard, but I was shaken when I heard the reply and that wasn't him either. Could I have gotten everything wrong? Maybe Louis had nothing to do with this at all and he was just occasionally creepy.

"Kenji knows a lot of people in Japan, dude. He'll definitely hook us up."

"How are we…"

The voices trailed away and I could no longer make out the words. I waited two minutes to be sure that the men weren't still nearby. Both Amelia and I were panting heavily. I turned on my headlamp and saw that Amelia's face was as white as a ghost. I'm sure mine was the same. I know that I was carrying a gun, however, nobody ever wants to get into a shoot-out situation, especially in darkened tunnels and caves. If the thought appeals to you, you shouldn't have a gun in the first place.

"Who were they?" whispered Amelia.

I shook my head. "I have absolutely no idea. Their voices sounded a little familiar, like maybe I've heard them speaking somewhere around town, but they are obviously not anyone I know well."

"Where do you think they went?"

I shook my head again. "I can't imagine." I thought for a moment. "This was the first left turn after the second right turn and there was nowhere else to go."

"Do you think we should leave?"

I nodded. "Yeah, let's get the hell out of here before they come back."

Amelia looked relieved, but still extremely frightened. We both stood up from our crouched positions behind the large rock and I knocked over my water bottle. The sound seemed to reverberate forever in the closed confines of the tunnels and I held my breath. We both stood stock still for the longest minute of my life and then we slowly released our breath. I pulled my backpack on and Amelia turned on her headlamp as we readied to get out quickly and find a safe place to hide. Preferably in a large group of people.

I took the first step and heard a scraping noise that caused icy fingertips to run up and down my spine. We both dove behind the rock again, turning off our headlamps just as we heard the male voices again.

"What was that noise?" the first guy asked.

"How am I supposed to know? I was with you, dude," the second guy responded. "Let's just take this painting over to Kenji's place and we can FaceTime with his connection. Show him that we actually have the goods in our possession."

Light from one of their flashlights flashed into our tunnel and I willed myself and Amelia not to move. The lights swept over the tunnel walls all around us. I was starting to sweat from the strain of keeping still.

"There's nobody there," the first guy said.

"It was probably just a bat," the second guy chimed in.

"Ewww! I hate bats," the first guy complained.

"Don't worry about the bats. Soon, we'll be richer than we ever dreamed and done with scrabbling for tourist dollars from stupid tourists. Man, if one more fat old lady comes on to me on our tours, I'll probably barf."

Amelia and I both realized who they were at the same time. I quietly clapped my hand over her mouth to stop her from reacting because they were so close. A flashlight beam tripped over the stones around the area we were hiding in one more time.

"I won't miss these damn caves, that's for sure," the first guy said. "Bats or no bats, I never want to see the inside of another cave unless it's that Great Blue Hole in Belize."

The second guy chuckled. "You're the only person I know who would rather deal with a shark than a bat."

We heard the sound of hands clapping together and I assumed they high-fived. Then, their laughter faded as they walked away from us toward the main tunnel, dragging something behind them.

I must not have moved for five minutes. Amelia finally pulled my hand off her mouth and we slowly stood up. My body ached from all the brutality I had put it through recently. My head pounded with a headache that I'm sure Amelia could hear. We were both breathing shallowly, afraid that they would come back.

Amelia was still wide-eyed when she said indignantly, "Can you believe those two idiots, Danny and Robbie, killed Pierre and May? I knew they weren't bright, but I didn't think they were actually criminals."

"I know. I never knew how they were even able to run a semi-successful tour business at the height of tourist season. They'd book clients for a harbor tour on their boat and then cancel last minute to surf *in Harmony*. The one place north of Boston with no reefs and barely any surfable swells." Something didn't seem right to me though. "It doesn't add up though. How would they have known about Pierre and his stolen art?"

Amelia shrugged. "I don't know." She paused for a moment. "Wait! I heard they wanted to launch a cave tour business, starting near where you and the interns ended up. Maybe they stumbled across it?"

It was now my turn to shrug. "Your guess is as good as mine." I took a long drink of water from my water bottle. "I know that I want to check out that tunnel before we turned left. They disappeared somewhere..."

Amelia looked around fearfully. "Are you sure they're gone? I don't have a weapon to defend myself."

"It's been quiet for nearly ten minutes now. If they were coming back, they would have been here by now."

To be sure, before we turned on our headlamps and flashlights, we peeked around the corner to see if we could detect any movement. When we were fairly certain that the tunnel was empty, we clicked on the lights and walked a short way down the tunnel.

Amelia stood in the middle of the tunnel. "There's nothing here except that big rock. Where could they have disappeared to?"

I walked up to the rock and shined my flashlight at the front and sides. I tried unsuccessfully to move it, but it wouldn't budge. Finally, I walked to the side and started laughing.

"What's so funny?" Amelia demanded, joining me at the side of the rock. She saw what I had just figured out – the rock was not attached to the tunnel wall on all sides. On the far side, so that you wouldn't see it when walking past, the rock had about an eighteen-inch wide gap that ran along the wall about five feet to what looked like an opening in the rock wall.

"Should we investigate?" asked Amelia, stepping back a little fearfully.

"How can we not?" I asked. I had to remove my backpack and turn sideways to inch down the gap. I heard Amelia sigh as she removed her backpack, too, and started following me.

After we had inched our way down behind the rock, I saw something that didn't look quite right. When I shined my light on it, it was difficult to see anything. Finally, I could make out a door that had been installed to close off an opening in the wall. It was painted the same color as the rocks and was very hard to see. I reached for the handle, fully expecting the door to be locked. I was surprised when it opened easily at my touch. I guess that the door was so well-hidden that Pierre didn't think he needed to lock it.

I took a tentative step forward and heard Amelia take a deep breath in anticipation. She followed me so closely, she was practically attached. As we stepped into the chamber, I was still shocked even though I had expected to find the Gardner paintings.

Amelia tugged on my sweatshirt and pointed at a light switch on the wall of the chamber. I reached over and flipped the switch on and the room became bathed with diffused light. Amelia and I were stunned into silence as we gaped at the magnificent room. I don't know how Pierre had managed to construct this room, but it must have taken him a long time. The stone walls were covered up with the same type of white walls that Syd had in her gallery. The paintings were hung throughout the room with gallery lighting as well. There was a club chair in the center of the room from which you could see all the paintings if you were seated there. No offense to Syd, but Pierre could have consulted on her gallery design. It was that nice.

I became aware of a low hum coming from a recess in the back wall. I went to investigate and found a smaller room with a small generator and dehumidifier. I stopped cold as my eyes became adjusted to the low light levels in the back room. The generator and dehumidifier were not all that was in the room. Louis lay dead in a pool of his own blood with his eyes wide open, staring at nothing. It looked like there was a fishing spear protruding from his chest!

Chapter Thirty-Six

"What's in he...oof!" I stopped so abruptly that Amelia walked into me. "What are you...?" she trailed off as she spotted the dead body on the floor in front of us. "Damn it," Amelia stomped her foot. "I knew that we would find a dead body if I was with you. You're always finding dead bodies."

I let my breath out slowly. To be fair, since we had become reacquainted at the reunion, she wasn't wrong. I held up my hands in a defensive posture. "I know it seems that way, but this is a relatively new occurrence for me. I'm hoping to kick the habit."

Amelia sighed as I stooped down in a futile attempt to check for a sign of life. No luck. Louis was dead. I stayed crouched down, trying to think how Louis' death fit into my theory of events. My mind was working all the pieces of the puzzle like a kaleidoscope. I was sure that Louis had killed Pierre and May. It couldn't have been those two idiots.

Don't get me wrong. Danny and Robbie's names often appeared in the police blotter of the Harmony Post, but it was usually for drunk and disorderly or public intoxication. Multiple misdemeanors, for sure, but they never seemed like felons. As far as I knew, they had never committed a violent crime against anyone.

Echoing my thoughts, Amelia murmured, "What does this mean? Louis didn't kill Pierre and May? Your theory made so much sense."

"Oh no, he killed those two," I heard a deep voice say before I was, once again, hit over the head. I crashed to the floor and my last coherent memory was seeing Amelia fall beside me, a look of astonishment on her face.

I struggled to wake up. My headache before was incomparable to the headache I now felt. I had double-, or maybe it was triple-vision. My stitches must also have released as I felt blood trickling from the old wound and a large bump developing on my forehead from where it hit the tunnel floor after I was knocked out – again.

Making it even more difficult to focus, I was unable to move my arms or legs and I was seated in a very uncomfortable position. I slowly opened my eyes but wished I had kept them closed. Amelia and I had been dragged back into the main display room. Our arms and legs were bound tightly with bungee cords and we were gagged with cleaning rags that had been in the back room. The stench of the chemicals was almost more overpowering than I could bear. I felt the blood flowing freely now from my scalp wound and I felt nauseated and in danger of passing out again. Something told me I had to keep my wits about me, so I tried really hard to concentrate.

I could hear Amelia crying softly next to me. I leaned into her to try to provide comfort, but she wouldn't look at me.

"You had to stick your nose into places it didn't belong," sneered Danny from across the room. My vision was still bleary, but I dragged my eyes up to where I estimated his voice was coming from. He wasn't a bad-looking guy – blonde hair, blue eyes, deep, year-round tan – but the look of hatred on his face made him the

240

ugliest person I had seen in a long time. "We weren't hurting anyone and here…"

"Well, maybe just Lu-iss," snickered Robbie. Robbie was a little bit chunky with dark hair and no front teeth. The missing teeth caused a bit of a lisp, but he didn't care. He was a hard-drinking, lazy jerk. I had babysat him as a kid and he seemed to be the same mean-spirited jerk he always had been.

"Right," Danny agreed. "Just Lu-iss." I noticed that he and Robbie both pronounced Louis' name as "Lu-iss" when it was supposed to be pronounced the French way, like "Lu-ee." I'm sure that probably pissed Louis off. When he was alive. Then Danny looked at me and Amelia. "Until now. Now, we're gonna need to do something with you two."

Amelia began to whimper quietly beside me. I refused to be scared, but I was getting angrier by the second. If I could just get my hands free, I could grab my gun and blast our way out of here. I tried to glance surreptitiously down at my ankle holster. Damn! It was empty. They must have found my gun.

Robbie began to cackle. "She must really think we're stupid." He hit Danny's arm. "Did you see? She just checked her ankle holster. Like we wouldn't look for that on an ex-pig."

Danny laughed along with Robbie, albeit a touch maniacally. "She won't have to think much longer about anything," he stared down at me threateningly.

I willed my eyes to start shooting lasers at the two of them, but science fiction eluded me and I sank back, helpless, against the

241

tunnel wall. Amelia was openly weeping and that was making it difficult for her to breathe with the gag in her mouth. She began gasping for air.

Robbie leaned down and removed her gag. "We don't want you to die, at least not before *we* decide how to kill you." Danny had picked up my gun and was playing at being a gangster, holding it sideways and striking poses. He truly looked like an idiot. Robbie was grinning and pretending to get shot. I closed my eyes and sighed. How did I end up with my fate in their hands? Could I be lucky enough that Danny might actually shoot Robbie?

Danny put the gun in the waistband of his pants and turned to Robbie. "We need to box the paintings up. There is way too much traffic down here and they'll end up getting found before we have a chance to fence them all."

"How much do you think we'll get for them all?" Robbie asked.

Danny thought for a moment. "I don't really know. I know they are each worth a few million – not that we'll get anywhere near that price at the black market, when we find it. When people get a look at them, there will be a bidding war." He nodded knowingly.

I looked at him in confusion. Did he really think that a black market for expensive art was like a flea market? It was my turn to nearly gag. Robbie shook his head and removed my gag then slapped me across the face. "Bitch! You got blood on my hand. I hope you don't got a disease or have anything catchy." He leaned down and wiped my blood on his pant leg.

I saw stars. Little ones. Big ones. Shooting stars. If I got through this, I planned on spending a week in bed. With good drugs. "Look, guys, there's no need to kill us. You're moving the paintings today anyway. Just leave us here. You'll have plenty of time to get away before anyone finds us."

Danny laughed again, much more cruelly. "Nobody is ever going to find you two bitches." He looked over at Robbie. "Should we tell them how smart we are, not that they'll be able to tell anyone?"

Robbie grinned and nodded his head. "Tell them. They'll ruin the day they thought we weren't smart."

Danny sighed, "Rue."

Robbie looked confused. "What?"

Danny shook his head. "Never mind." He looked around and took a deep breath. "Where to begin?"

Danny rubbed his hands together, relishing the story he was about to tell. "When we were down here earlier, we heard you two. We knew you were here but decided to trick you."

I rolled my eyes. "Please. You had no idea we were there. You thought you heard bats." I could tell I was getting to them. I wasn't sure if taunting them was the right thing to do though. I still couldn't think clearly. Based on Amelia's repeated elbow jabs, she didn't think I should taunt them. However, the more they talked, the longer we stayed alive. The longer we stayed alive, the better the chance that Syd and Ricky would follow our chalk markings and come find us. Syd was a crack shot and I'd put money on her any day.

"Shut up, bitch!" screamed Robbie. He backhanded me and my blood went flying across the room. He grabbed a rag and wiped my blood off of his hands, then dropped the rag on the floor.

I waited for a second for the pretty fireworks show in my head to stop. "What did you have to come back for, your phone or your keys?"

"My ke… Hey! We came back because we knew you were here." He was starting to believe his own lie.

Danny smiled. "We also overheard your friends in the far tunnel. They were starting to get worried about you two. The girly-man said they'd find you by following your chalk marks." He sneered. "So, we changed all your marks. They won't find you soon. Dead or alive!"

I gulped. We should have used something ultraviolet or invisible to the naked eye. That was a mistake I wouldn't make again – if we lived long enough to make another mistake.

I cleared my throat. "What did you mean when you said that 'he killed those two'?" I asked.

Danny chuckled. "You thought we killed that old dude and the Chinese girl. That was Lu-iss."

I felt slightly justified, but seeing as how they had obviously killed Louis, I didn't think it really helped me any.

Danny crouched down and looked at me. "Let me explain this to you because you obviously aren't very smart." He looked up at Robbie and shook his head. "She's not very smart, is she?"

Robbie shook his head emphatically. "She was a crappy babysitter, too. Always making me eat my veggies and do my homework. She was never any fun."

I remembered Robbie's idea of fun was to taunt their family dog and set ants on fire, so I paid no mind to his assessment of me.

"Okay, Lu-iss found us right after he started working at Milano's." I tried to keep a straight face as he pronounced it "My-Lano's." We met at The Stone Castle Tavern just outside of town." Danny started preening. "He seen our advertisements for cave tours and said he had a job for us that would really pay off if we were successful." He looked at Robbie again and winked. "He thought we were stupid, too. I guess we showed him who was stupid."

He looked toward the back room where Louis' dead body was laid out. He snorted and a snot bubble formed on his left nostril. He absent-mindedly wiped it away with the back of his hand. Ewww! "Anyway," he continued, "he asked me and Robbie how well we knew the tunnels. Lu-iss had seen the old dude go into the tunnels for hours and had figured that Pierre was hiding what Lu-iss wanted in there." He turned to Robbie and they fist-bumped with pride. "Well, Robbie and me have been playing in those tunnels our whole lives. We know the best hiding places and small rooms that most people never see." He looked around the art-filled chamber.

"We never found this place before, though. That old dude did a good job of keeping it covered all those years."

He jumped up and stretched. "Anyway, Lu-iss just told us we needed to find Pierre's hidden room. He said he would make it worthy awhile." I shuddered inside as his constant mis-use of the English language. "He never told us what was in the room. This room. Robbie and me started tracking the old dude whenever he came into the tunnels. We're sneaky and quiet. Sometimes he came for wine and he would be in and out quickly. Sometimes, it was for hours and we'd lose him until he left."

Robbie smirked. "He almost caught us a few times, too, but we were smarter than him."

Danny smirked, "Well, I don't like to brag, but okay, we were smarter than him. Way smarter." He looked around. "Where was I? Oh, yeah. We couldn't keep following the old dude without getting caught, so, Lu-iss had us go with him to the old dude's house one night. The old dude invited Lu-iss in for a glass of wine, like they were friends or something." He shook his head. "*He* was an idiot. We waited outside in the bushes and Lu-iss left the door unlocked. They started arguing and Louis pushed him. The old dude fell over and hit his head, but he was fine. Well, mostly fine. He was a little confused."

Danny began pacing. "Then, Lu-iss gave us the signal." He pushed his thumb against his nose. Clearly, they all lived in a delusional, fictionalized world. "We came in and dragged the old dude upstairs to the bathroom. Robbie and I held him down in the tub while Lu-iss just kept asking him, over and over, where the loot was hidden. It got boring."

He looked behind him curiously as if he had heard a noise and then looked at Robbie who just shrugged and then he continued. He was proud of himself and Robbie. "Robbie and I might have hit him a few times to, you know, encourage him, but the old dude would not tell Lu-iss where he hid those paintings." He shrugged. "That's when Robbie and me figured out that the old dude had paintings hidden in the tunnels." He shook his head sadly as if that fact is what bothered him most. "Lu-iss finally went nuts. His face got all red and at first, we thought he was going to have a heart attack. He walked in small circles around the bathroom and then pulled out a weird-looking pair of scissors from his back pocket." He looked deep in thought for a moment. "I think he took them from a bunch of tools the old guy had downstairs."

"Pierre's antique vineyard tools," I muttered, sitting up straight. I had only glanced at them when I went to dinner at his house, but I seemed to recall a pair of antique pruning shears in his collection. I don't know why knowing the weapon that killed Pierre was so important to me. I was starting to believe I wouldn't ever be able to tell anyone.

Robbie slapped me across the face again. "Shut up, bitch! Danny's talking." He leaned in and I could smell his sour breath. "The only reason you're not dead yet is because we need to stay clean to pack up the pictures." He turned and looked reverently at Danny. I glanced at Amelia and saw that she had conflicting emotions of disgust and intrigue flickering across her face. I have to admit, if my life wasn't on the line right now, this would be an interesting story. I feigned obedience, looked down, and leaned back against the wall. I noticed that more of my blood had flown around the room and was splattered on the floor. Robbie held his hand out to Danny in a "please continue" motion.

Danny cleared his throat. "As I was saying before I was so rudely interrupted," both men snickered at this, "Lu-iss lost it. He started stabbing at the old dude, even after it was clear he was dead. Stabbing, over and over and over." He held his hands up, defensively. "Me and Robbie didn't kill the old dude. We got the hell out of there as fast as Robbie's stubby little legs could move."

"Hey!" Robbie looked indignant. "Stop making fun of my height!"

"Sorry, dude," Danny held his hands up in a placating gesture. "I was just trying to explain how fast we were moving."

Robbie still looked disgruntled. Apparently, height was a sore topic for him.

Danny smirked. "As we left, we heard the water turn on." He chortled. "I guess he wanted to make it look like an accident in the bath." He continued laughing. "We just left."

I stopped. "Wait! Didn't you search the house?"

Danny and Robbie shook their heads. "Nope. Lu-iss must have done that after he finished with the old dude."

I thought of the mess he had made in Pierre's house and the irony of then helping us clean the mess and pack Pierre's possessions. I thought it was especially funny that he was the one who made a disparaging comment about the actual Monet we had found and thrown in the trash. Life is funny sometimes.

Chapter Thirty-Seven

Amelia had stopped crying and I wasn't sure if that was a good or bad sign. She was probably dehydrated. Robbie had been intermittently putting large boxes together and listening to Danny's story reverently. I winced as he pulled the paintings off of the wall and haphazardly packed them into the boxes. I had watched Syd pack paintings for buyers enough times to know that these would hardly be protected in transit. My heart ached for the potential loss of priceless art being carelessly thrown about by these buffoons.

Danny smirked at us. "That's enough for story time. We'll deal with you two after we pack these boxes." He strolled over and started helping Robbie pack up the rest of the art. I could see that my blood had splattered on a few of the boxes and hoped it had not landed on any of the paintings.

I watched them pack the final box and I grew more despondent. I hadn't figured out a way to escape. I don't know if it was the loss of blood or the knowledge that our friends would probably not find us in time, but my despair was making me woozy. I tried to shift my position because my arms were beginning to lose all feeling from being tied behind my back for so long. My right forearm brushed against something hard in my waistband. My knife! I had completely forgotten all about my Ka-Bar that I kept tucked into my pants. I couldn't believe they hadn't found it when they tied us up.

I turned slowly to face Amelia. She looked at me and her face mirrored the despair I had felt. Something about the renewed hope in my eyes must have tipped her off and she looked at me curiously. I mouthed "knife" at her and began working my hands clumsily behind my back. It finally popped free and clattered onto the cement floor.

Danny looked up from taping the boxes closed and Amelia began coughing to deflect his curiosity. He shook his head at us and kept working. I sighed in relief. I nodded at Amelia to cough again and opened the knife as quietly as possible. When it was finally open, I began sawing at the bungee cords that restrained my hands. It felt like it took forever, but I was finally free. I had to get Amelia free before we could try anything. I certainly wasn't going to be very effective with the blood loss, concussion and dehydration-induced, confusion.

Fortunately, Danny and Robbie were engrossed in a discussion about one of the paintings, *The Concert*, by Johannes Vermeer. They were crudely evaluating whether they would date either of the two women in the painting. I passed the knife to Amelia and she began working on her own bindings. When we were both free, I still had not devised a plan and my despair and fatigue were beginning to overtake my rational thought.

As Robbie taped up the final box, I was formulating and discarding increasingly more desperate plans. None of them seemed like they would be successful. Again, I thought I heard a sound in the corridor, but I wasn't sure. Danny made his way back to us.

"Now, what should I do with the two of you?" he pondered cruelly. He had my gun in his right hand and was tapping it against

251

his left hand. I was worried that he would set it off accidentally and damage the paintings or, more importantly, kill one of us.

"Wait!" Amelia cried. "Why did May have to die?" Her voice was raspy.

Danny looked at her, momentarily confused. "The Chinese girl?" he finally asked dumbly.

Amelia shook her head. "Yes. She didn't have anything to do with any of this."

Danny laughed mirthlessly. "That's just what we asked Lu-iss. Lu-iss didn't tell us about his father or the paintings, just that we were still looking for a hidden room." He cleared his throat. "Lu-iss told us that the Chinese girl had separated from her friend and was heading back to the vineyard. She must have gotten lost because she stumbled upon Lu-iss coming out of this tunnel. He didn't have an explanation as to why he was there without his partner and didn't want her to figure out later what he was doing there, so he killed her." He shrugged as if this made all the sense in the world. "We helped moved the body so nobody would find the room, but we didn't kill her."

The casual way he recounted the tale was bone-chilling. My brain was operating on fumes but something didn't make sense. "I thought you hadn't found the room yet?" I inquired casually.

Danny looked at me sharply and made a face. "Damn! I didn't mean to say that." He crouched down and looked me straight in the face. It was all I could do to not take my newly freed hands and throat punch him. He sighed loudly. "Yeah, me and Robbie found this room about a month ago. We don't know much about art and we weren't sure if Lu-iss was going to split the loot fairly or mess with us like the old dude messed with his father. He was shifty." Danny said this as if cheating them out of money was more important than killing Pierre and May.

Amelia spoke up again, "When did you figure out what was in this room?"

Robbie spat on the ground which made me shudder in revulsion. "There you bitches go, thinking we are ignorant."

Danny stood up and held his hand out to Robbie. "It's okay." He looked back at Amelia. "We didn't know anything about these paintings at first, but we did some *re*-search and figured out they were stolen thirty years ago from that Gardener Museum in Boston. I know they're worth a lot of money."

I winced at his mispronunciation but wanted to keep him talking. I had definitely heard another soft sound in the tunnel outside the room and was now certain that help was on the way. "Louis said he was going to split the money with you. Didn't you trust him?"

Danny laughed maniacally. "Yeah, trust a guy who had just murdered two people? Who's the idiot now?" He shook his head. "To make it seem we hadn't found the room, we kept asking him what was in there that he wanted us to find and how much he would pay us. He said that it was only sentimental family property and had more of a personal value but he thought we would each get about ten thousand dollars." He looked at me, outraged. "These paintings are worth millions and he was going to pay us only" he counted on his fingers, "twenty thousand dollars?"

Robbie shook his head sadly and parroted, "Twenty thousand dollars," like that wasn't more money than either had ever earned in their whole lives.

Danny nodded at him in agreement. "Right? Well, we weren't going to stand for that. We planned to box these paintings up and move them out before telling him we found the room." He smiled at Robbie. "We had a good laugh over that, right Robbie?"

Robbie nodded. "Yup, a good laugh."

I jumped in. "So, what happened? Louis found the room before you could move the paintings?"

Robbie hung his head sheepishly. "Yeah. Jerk."

Danny looked at him sharply. "The night that Lu-iss bashed you over the head at the old dude's house, Robbie and I were out pre-celebrating our wealth. The next day, we couldn't find Lu-iss and heard about you getting attacked. We knew he must have found a clue to finding the room. By the time we got here, he was already inside, sitting in the chair, enjoying the whiskey the old dude had left here."

He sighed. "As soon as we walked in, he knew we had already found this room and didn't tell him. He was pretty angry at us."

Robbie nodded. "Yeah, really angry."

"He screamed that we would never see a dime from the paintings after we obviously were planning to double-cross him."

Danny looked at Robbie. "We couldn't have that. We're not stupid. We already decided what we were going to do with our money."

Robbie looked around proudly. "We were going to buy a bar. That way, we'd have all the free booze we wanted."

Danny shrugged. "He had to go."

Robbie grinned, "He had to go."

Danny smiled slyly, "We strangled him with those bungee cords you are tied up with. But you'll find out about that soon enough."

Robbie repeated, "Soon enough."

I closed my eyes so as not to betray how stupid their plan had been and how scared I was. Suddenly, all hell broke loose. Syd and Ricky rushed into the room. Syd had her gun pointed at Danny and Ricky was brandishing a large rock in his right hand.

Syd yelled, "That's enough out of you two. Hands up!"

Danny ignored her and lunged for my gun which he had left lying on the table. Syd took quick aim and shot him in the leg. Danny fell to the ground, howling in pain, which infuriated Robbie. He seized the gun and turned toward Syd and Ricky as Amelia and I clambered to our feet as quickly as possible. Ricky was trying to aim the rock at Robbie and Syd was adjusting her aim when we heard a deep voice bellow, "Stop where you are! This is the police!"

I spun around and saw Ty, Marco, and Chance standing in the doorway. My befuddled mind wondered how they had squeezed down the narrow entranceway so quietly, but I was very happy to see them. Robbie looked at the trio and started raising the gun toward them. Ty thundered, "Police! Drop your weapon!"

Robbie's upward arc never faltered. That's when I noticed that Chance and Marco were also armed. They didn't hesitate and the three of them all shot Robbie. He dropped to the ground like a sack of potatoes, the light quickly fading from his eyes.

Everything suddenly imploded in my head. The attack, the head wound, the search in the tunnels, being held captive and threatened with death, and the rescue. Maybe it was just the blood loss. The darkness began to close in and I felt myself falling. I think I heard Syd screaming, "Kat!" as I lost consciousness, but I can't be sure.

Chapter Thirty-Eight

I woke up in the hospital. Again. Chance was right. This was becoming a habit. One that I desperately needed to break! I opened my eyes to see Syd and Ricky hovering over me, just slightly too close. As soon as I opened my eyes, tears of relief pooled in Syd's eyes and spilled down her cheeks, dripping onto my johnnie. She wiped them away with the back of her hand and leaned in to give me a hug. She brushed against my head and I wondered curiously why I didn't feel any pain.

I raised my hand to my head and realized I was attached to an I/V bag which probably was administering some powerful drugs. My hand brushed against something soft and fluffy that appeared to be wrapped around my head.

"That's just gauze, to protect *all* your head wounds," Syd said softly.

Ricky squeezed my hand. "It's a good thing you have a hard, stubborn head, Kat, or this could be your funeral."

"Shh, Ricky, we can yell at her later," Syd said firmly.

I smiled weakly and heard a noise from behind Ricky.

"Is she finally awake?" a very cranky-sounding Amelia demanded. She was sitting on a chair near the window.

"How are you, Amelia?" is what I tried to say. My throat and mouth were so dry, though, it sounded like "ow u, mela?"

"Drama queen," Amelia retorted. "A hard stubborn head is right." Her tone softened. "Lucky for me that you have so much crisis training, though, and were able to keep a clear head. I really thought we were done for." She stood up and joined Ricky by my side. She leaned in and squeezed the arm without the I/V. "Seriously, Kat. Thank you. Again. You're always helping me get out of hot water." She winked at me. "Well, after you help me get into hot water, that is."

Syd leaned in with a sippy cup of water. I sucked greedily at the straw and immediately felt a lot better. I cleared my throat and coughed a few times then drank some more water. "You'd do the same for me, Amelia," I croaked out, though less hoarsely this time.

I looked up at Syd. "How did you find us? Danny said they changed our chalk markings...?"

Syd snorted. "Those idiots used a differently-colored chalk than yours. It was easy to see that someone was trying to trick us so we ignored the wrong-colored chalk and followed your trail. Easy peasy."

Ricky cleared his throat, pointing his finger at himself. "Who noticed the different colors on the chalk markings, Syd? You forgot to say that it was me."

Syd put on her long-suffering expression. "I didn't forget. It just wasn't relevant to the story."

Ricky harumphed. "It would have been relevant if it was you that discovered that the chalk markings were different colors."

I squeezed both of their hands. "Thank you both for coming to my, or rather our, rescue. I wouldn't be lying here in this bed if it weren't for you two." I thought for a moment. "Wait! That didn't come out right." My head was beginning to hurt. "You know what I mean."

Ricky looked appeased. "We do. There's nobody I would rather rescue, Kat, than you and Amelia. Again."

Amelia sighed. "I think I need to retire from the 'needing to get rescued' club."

"Ditto!" I echoed.

"I cannot emphasize how much I agree with that statement," a loud voice boomed from the doorway. I looked over and saw Ty standing menacingly, trying to stare me down. I guess I must have looked really pathetic because his stern countenance soon melted and he smiled wryly at me as he approached my bed. "We are going to have a serious talk as soon as they release you from this hospital bed. I told you not to get involved," he said sternly.

"I know, and I tried really hard not to," I said weakly.

"Really hard? Doubtful," he shook his head disbelievingly.

"Well, maybe not really hard, but I was kind of involved and I had been personally attacked…"

"We're not going to argue now." He glanced quickly at Syd. "Syd would kill *me* later and I want to barbecue tonight." He grinned. "We are going to talk later though." He smiled quickly at Amelia. "I got most of the story from Amelia but I might want you to fill in some blanks."

Suddenly, I was overcome with fatigue. I felt myself drifting off to sleep when a thought popped into my head. "What about the paintings?" I inquired dreamily.

Syd smiled. "They are unbelievable! The Gardner Museum is ecstatic about their recovery and is sending someone tomorrow to pick them up. Right now, they're in my gallery vault under the careful supervision of at least three armed guards. The state police are also stationed outside the gallery. They're safe. There's a reward..."

That was the last I heard for a while.

Chapter Thirty-Nine

I woke up to Marco fidgeting in the chair next to the bed. He picked up his phone, flipped through some emails, then put the phone down for ten seconds. He then repeated the whole process twenty seconds later. I watched him for about a minute before I burst out laughing, though I felt my headache returning with a vengeance.

He jolted upright and looked at me suspiciously. "How long have you been awake?"

"Long enough," I joked. "Thanks for coming. Have you been here long?"

"Not really," he said. "Hospitals just make me nervous."

"And fidgety," I added.

He grinned. "And fidgety." He looked around and then looked at me with genuine concern in his eyes. "How are you feeling? How's your head?" Before I could answer, he continued, "Why would you do something so stupid? We're really going to have a serious talk about responsibility when you are feeling better," he said earnestly.

"Get in line," I cracked and he looked at me suspiciously.

"What do you mean by that?"

"Ty also wants to talk to me about being irresponsible when I'm 'feeling better'," I snapped.

Marco held his hands up to pacify me. "Let's change the subject." He looked around. "How long are they keeping you?"

"Let's back up," I said, sorry that I snapped at him. I then counted off my replies on my fingers. "I'm okay, but I think that's mainly due to the drugs they're pumping into me. My head is sore and I suspect I'll have a headache for a few days, at least." I held the third finger up. "I obviously didn't think I was being stupid and thought I had the whole thing figured out and would only possibly have to deal with Louis. And finally," I popped my fourth finger up, "I'm getting out tomorrow morning."

Marco grinned and jumped up. "Great! You'll be able to help with the harvest. I've decided we're going to harvest the grapes tomorrow."

"I don't think she will be in any state to harvest grapes tomorrow, Marco," a concerned voice said from the doorway.

Marco and I both nearly got whiplash as we turned our heads quickly toward the door. Chance casually leaned against the wall, looking tired and incredibly sexy. Maybe it was the drugs I was taking. Maybe not.

"I didn't mean that she would be out in the fields. I'm not that inconsiderate." He looked at me and winked. "Not all the time, at least."

Chance sauntered in and sat in a chair on the other side of my bed, making it awkward for me to watch both of them at once. "Just what are your intentions for Kat then, Marco?"

Marco gaped at Chance and narrowed his eyes. "What do you mean, my intentions?" He looked down toward the ground and muttered, "I could ask you the same thing."

Chance looked at him sharply. "What was that?"

Marco sighed. "Nothing. Sorry, I think we're all a bit on edge after last night." He stood up. "Kat works for me. Based on how she feels, and only if she's up to it, I'd like her to manage the workers, assign them to different fields and make sure there are runners to bring out water. All from a comfortably chair inside the tasting room. Nothing too strenuous." He then looked directly at Chance, "If that meets with your approval, of course."

Chance tried to smile but it got lost in his fatigue. "I'm sorry. Kat makes her own decisions, as she always proves to us. I'm just tired and testy and," he looked searchingly into my eyes, "I have been worried sick all day. I wish someone had called me to tell me how you were doing."

My ire melted away. "I'm so sorry, Chance. I woke for a little while earlier when Syd, Ricky, and Amelia were here, but then I fell back asleep. I just woke up about five minutes ago." I held up two fingers. "I promise that someone will call you the next time I'm in the hospital with updates."

Marco and Chance looked at each other and echoed, "The next time…"

I hurriedly tried to make it sound better. "I mean, if I ever happen to be in the hospital again, even for a hangnail, I will make sure that Syd and/or Ricky phone you both with updates on my physical health." I realized I couldn't make it sound better, so I stopped speaking.

Marco and Chance both shook their heads and Marco stood up. "I need to go see how the interns are doing. Those who are left, that is. They're pre-pruning the vineyard to be ready for tomorrow." He got to the door and turned around. "I'll talk to you after you are released tomorrow morning. If you're up to an inside job supervising people and trucks coming and going, I'd love to have you. If not, I totally understand."

"Wait!" I cried. "I'm not getting out until tomorrow morning. I wouldn't be able to be there until nearly noon."

Marco sighed dramatically. "I thought you knew. We're one of those *avant-garde* vineyards that harvest their grapes by the light of the moon. You'll have all day to rest up." He snapped his fingers. "I won't be available to give you a ride home though, so see if you can make other arrangements." He winked at me and nodded at Chance who had his back to Marco. He then smiled and called out, "Later, Wolf."

Chance chuckled as Marco walked out the door. "Sometimes, he can be insufferable though his heart is in the right place. I see why you're such good friends with him."

I took a deep breath. "Chance, you know that's all we are, right? Marco is my boss and my friend. He just likes to joke around and harmlessly – maybe inappropriately – flirt. If I told him that it made me uncomfortable or asked him to stop, he would stop immediately." I looked up at him. "Or, if it makes you uncomfortable…?"

Chance looked deep into my eyes. "Just friends?" he murmured. "You looked so...so..." he shrugged, "more-than-chummy the other night at my opening."

I reached for his hand which was on the side of my leg. "Definitely just friends. We talked about it at your opening when I pretty much flat out asked him what his intentions were."

Chance looked at me, surprised. "You asked him?"

I nodded. "Yes. I was fed up with his weirdly flirty one moment then all business the next moment attitude." I thought back to our conversation. "He said that he just considered me a good friend and that he was getting over a serious relationship that recently ended." I squeezed his hand. "Truly, we're just good friends."

Chance looked at my hand. "How come you've never asked me how I feel about you, Kat?"

I whispered, "Because before you kissed me, I was terrified the answer would also be 'just friends,' too."

Chance leaned in and placed his other hand on top of our joined hands. He had a twinkle in his eye as he whispered, "And *after* our kiss?"

I blushed fifty shades of crimson and stammered, "That made it a lot more clear, Chance." I paused. "Until it wasn't."

He looked abashed. "I'm sorry I haven't been more clear with you, Kat. It's just that I wasn't sure where you and Marco stood and I didn't want to get in the way."

"Well, now you know and now we've kis..."

The door burst open and Syd and Ricky came in noisily with balloons and a bag of food.

"Hey, Chance!" Ricky called out. "Thanks for the backup last night." He looked at Chance slyly. "Though I think Syd and I had it covered."

Chance chuckled and straightened up, but not before Syd noticed our entangled hands and her eyes bulged. "Yes, I agree. That rock could have done some serious damage against the bullets Robbie was about to shoot at you."

Ricky bristled. "I can take care of myself, Mr. Wolf."

Chance smiled, stood up, and gave him a half-hug. "I know, Ricky. I'm just teasing you." He looked at Syd. "Plus, you had Syd Randall at your side. Who could beat the two of you together?"

Syd punched his arm lightly. "Don't let my husband hear you say that. He's been upset with me all day for going into those tunnels. He's not sure whether to be angry or proud that I carried my pistol."

A thought popped into my head. "Why *did* Ty bring you and Marco, Chance? Where were his officers?"

"They were all tied up at that huge traffic accident. I think there were two or three fatalities and Life Flight had to be called in to transport the victims to Boston Medical." He grinned. "I could tell that he didn't really want to ask us for help, but he also didn't think it was smart to go in there by himself. He knew that Marco and I know how to handle guns. We used to go shooting together back in high school. He also knew that I would do anything to protect you." He stammered, "I mean, that we would do anything to protect the four of you."

He looked at me with a bit of worry in his eyes. "Ty only had your text messages as to where and when you went into the tunnels. Then, when he had a free moment and couldn't get ahold of either of you, he panicked, a little, but don't tell him I said that. I guess the tunnel walls must have blocked the calls and the texts." He smoothed my hair back avoiding my stitches and large lumps. "I was worried, too."

I felt the blush creeping back as Syd and Ricky tried not to snicker like schoolchildren.

Syd looked sheepish. "Well, the calls did come through but I decided not to answer them. I didn't want him to ask me to leave and then not do what he asked." She wrung her hands. "I was stupid. I should have taken his calls." She looked at Chance uncomfortably. "Thank you for your help. We were in over our heads."

"Don't ever tell Ty that you didn't take his calls that night, Syd," Chance suggested. "I think that would just make him even more angry." He looked at her pointedly. "Justifiably so, considering the circumstances."

Syd nodded in agreement and looked remorseful.

Chance stretched and rotated his torso to work the kinks out. "I'm sorry to leave so soon, Kat, but Two Cups has been swamped since we opened and I promised my sister that I'd be back to close so she can have a night off. I think we're going to have to hire a manager to help out so we don't get overwhelmed."

I felt bad that he had been called away last night to help Ty rescue us. I grabbed his hand and squeezed it tightly. "I'm sorry I've taken up so much of your time, Chance. I truly appreciate everything you've done for me the past few days."

Chance smiled sweetly at me. "No worries, Kat. I'll be there for you whenever you need me." He leaned over the bed and kissed me gently, then whispered meaningfully, "And, we *will* continue our earlier conversation the next time we're alone." He stood up and grinned. "Do you need a ride home tomorrow? I can be here by ten."

I felt my face blushing from the warmth of his mouth on mine. I was momentarily speechless, a rare occurrence in my world. "I, uhm, think…"

"That would be great, Chance," Syd answered for me. "I have the transport from the Isabella Stewart Gardner Museum coming first thing in the morning. We need to pack the artwork properly for transport back to Boston." She looked at me with a twinkle in her eye. "The museum people are so incredibly excited, Kat. They already started making plans for a grand exhibition in the next few months and they've made me promise that we will all be there. The recovery has been all over the news, even though the details are still sketchy."

"What about the *Musée Marmottan*?" I inquired. "They can't be too happy to acknowledge that they've been hanging a fake Monet since the paintings were returned."

"They're still skeptical that we have an original Monet. They would like to have an art expert authenticate the piece. Whatever." She shrugged. "We know that we have the real painting."

Chance grinned. "Now, you're famous, too, or infamous in some circles." His eyes twinkled in mirth. He waved good-bye and called out, over his shoulder, "I'll be here tomorrow at ten, Kat. Call me if you need me earlier."

"Thanks," I yelled to his retreating back.

We spent the rest of the evening, flipping through the television channels and watching all the coverage of the art recovery that we could find. Fortunately, our names had not yet been publicized and I was certain that Ty was trying as hard as he could to keep us anonymous. It was a thoroughly relaxing and mindless way to spend my – hopefully – last night at the hospital.

Chapter Forty

The next morning was sunny and warm. A perfect autumn day. I was looking forward to going home and laying in my hammock all day until I had to go to the vineyard for the harvest. I was also looking forward to the harvest, but I had never worked on one before so I was a bit nervous about what I would be expected to do. I had originally planned on being out in the fields but that couldn't happen with the concussion and head wounds.

I was also a bit giddy, looking forward to Chance coming to pick me up. I suppose I can be forgiven the disappointment that coursed through my body when Ricky strolled through the door with a wheelchair at ten a.m., announcing "Your chariot awaits!"

I instantly regretted the look of chagrin that passed over my face as I saw that I had upset Ricky. I stood up slowly – after all, I was still recovering from a rough couple of days – and gave him a big hug. "Thank you for coming to get me," I tried to sound enthusiastic but I know I was failing miserably. "I'm sorry that my face made me look unhappy or ungrateful." I looked down. "I just thought that Chance was picking me up."

Ricky seemed somewhat appeased. "I understand how you feel, Kat. I saw Vlad at the Pelican Beach Bar with another guy last night. I really thought that *we* had connected."

I gave him a tighter squeeze. "I'm sorry. That sucks."

He hugged me back, careful of all my bruising and abrasions. "This will make you feel better. Chance did want to pick you up today but his sister woke up with a migraine and he didn't feel like he could ask her to work through it. He did say that he would see you at the vineyard tonight at six o'clock."

"Thanks, Ricky," I felt my mood instantly lighten. Chance didn't blow me off. He was being responsible for his new business. "Let's get out of here. I want a big, juicy burger and a chocolate shake."

Ricky helped me into the wheelchair. "Okay, but let's split an order of fries. I'm cutting back on carbs this week."

That made me laugh until my stitches hurt and then I groaned through my laughter. Ricky was legendary with his fad diets, as if he had a spare ounce to lose. He tried to drag Syd and me onto his diet cycle, but I was never willing to give up the real food that I love to eat.

We went through a drive-thru on the way back to my house and sat on the patio, enjoying the weather, our food, and the company, in no particular order. I finally shooed him away at one o'clock so that I could take a good long nap. Ricky promised to be back at five to help me wash my hair – I wasn't up to that yet and we hugged goodbye.

I really was fortunate to have such great friends.

Chapter Forty-One

We arrived at the vineyard a little early and found about one hundred people milling around in the parking lot. Marco had said some people from Harmony usually showed up to help with the harvest in return for a free bottle of wine, but I didn't realize there would be so many.

I climbed out of Ricky's Escalade to a round of applause from the crowd. I guess they were happy that Harmony would be associated with clearing up one of the biggest art mysteries of all time and could move on from the reunion massacre association. I felt myself tearing up at this outpouring of community support. Ricky grinned and ushered me into the tasting room.

Marco came over and gave me a big hug. Justina was right behind him with her own hug, though she looked at me crossly. "Why don't you ever invite me on your adventures?" she demanded.

I laughed and shrugged. "I thought it would just be a boring walk through the tunnels. I never expected such," I searched for the word, "excitement."

Justina grinned and shook her head. "Your life is never boring, Kat."

Marco stood on a chair and addressed the vineyard staff. "We have a great turnout for the harvest tonight so I need all of you to act as supervisors for the volunteers. You know the vineyard and the grapes and what needs to be done." He pointed at me. "Kat will be here, assigning the volunteers to specific areas and I'll be outside, giving the volunteers the tools that they need." He pointed to his mother – who was a very active sixty-year-old – and ten-year-old niece Charisma, "My mother and niece will be riding around on a golf cart with coolers of water and snacks for anyone who needs to take a break. They will also be able to transport anyone who needs a longer break down to the tasting room or even the medical tent, if necessary."

He looked around with a big grin on his face. I could tell that he was thrilled that so many people from the community had shown up to help. "Any questions?" he asked. Nobody raised their hands. "Okay! Let's try and get this done in one night!"

He jumped down from the chair and came over to make sure I was set up and knew my duties. I had maps, blank nametags labeled with grape varieties, and some sign-up sheets so we could track who had come to help. Marco jogged outside and addressed the crowd through a bullhorn, saying much the same thing he had just said to us. The crowd roared when he finished. It was great to see everyone so excited. The air was bristling with anticipation.

Marco then opened the tasting room doors and let the crowd in. They lined up in front of my table and we began the process of signing in volunteers and assigning them to teams for each of the grape varieties. The interns and the rest of the staff stood outside to shepherd the volunteers to their designated areas.

As the night wore on, the excitement never ebbed. People would come in for a bathroom break or to sit for a few minutes, but they were always eager to get back to the grapes. Chance was there, but I didn't get much of an opportunity to speak with him. He ended up working with Jayson and the cabernet sauvignon grapes, along with Syd and Ricky.

After all the volunteers were sorted out and assigned, I went out and waited for the trucks to come in. Some of the volunteers would be sorting the grapes when the trucks brought them down to make sure no bad or broken grapes would be processed.

I have to hand it to Marco. The process really ran smoothly. I guess years of harvesting ensured this one ran like a well-oiled machine.

As dawn broke, the volunteers started trickling down from the vineyard. Everyone looked exhausted, but nobody was complaining. Instead of the traditional after-harvest dinner feast, Marco provided a breakfast feast that was overflowing with food. Chance provided four different types of coffee and an assortment of teas and hot chocolate from Two Cups. Sunny provided delectable, fresh-baked pastries, and Mindy – despite her black heart – provided hot dishes like Belgian waffles with fresh fruit, three types of quiche, and brioche French toast, accompanied by sides of hash browns and locally-sourced bacon and sausage. Cal Jr. had his juice bar staff on hand to blend fresh-squeezed juices and smoothies. For those who felt like indulging, Marco supplied some Milano sparkling wine for a variety of Bellinis. It was all very scrumptious.

By the time I was done eating, I could barely move. Mindy and I may detest each other, but I do have to (begrudgingly) admit that she cooks well. Syd, Ricky, Amelia, and I must have told the story of how we recovered the artwork at least ten times each. It still hadn't registered with me that we had solved one of the biggest art crimes in history.

People started trickling away to either go home and nap or start their day. Marco had given the vineyard staff the rest of the morning and early afternoon off and asked if we could be back by three o'clock to continue sorting the grapes. Then, the magic would happen.

Marco pulled me aside to see how I was doing. I assured him that I was tired, but I would be fine after a quick nap. He gave me a long hug and thanked me for working so hard, especially after everything I had just gone through.

"I thoroughly enjoyed myself, Marco. I never knew there were so many moving parts and pieces in a wine harvest." I looked over toward the fermenting and bottling room. "I can't wait to see the rest of the magic."

Marco also looked a little tired already as he tried to prep me for the coming days. "I know you're recovering, but don't plan on much sleep over the next week or so. After we finish sorting the grapes later and removing all the stems, they'll get crushed to release the must. Then, the must will be moved into the fermentation tanks and we'll add yeast. Then, we wait."

"That's when the *real* magic happens," I laughed.

He hugged me again and then went to help Max. Our four remaining interns insisted that they didn't need to rest and were going to start sorting now. I remember feeling invincible when I was young, too.

Ricky called my name and I turned toward his voice. He was speaking with Amelia and I saw Chance behind them. Chance had an unreadable look on his face, but it certainly wasn't pleasure. I started walking toward Ricky slowly, my eyes on Chance the whole time. He made eye contact with me and purposefully turned away and walked out the door. I kept a stiff upper lip, but a feeling of loss was washing over my entire being. I must have hidden it well because neither Amelia nor Ricky mentioned anything to me.

Ricky gave me a ride home and promised to come back later to help with my hair. I climbed into bed and set the alarm, feeling empty and alone.

Chapter Forty-Two

I slept for a few hours and Ricky came by to help me get ready. The stitches were starting to itch and throb and I had some bruising on my face from where Robbie had repeatedly slapped me. Fortunately, my sometime-drag queen best friend knew a lot about makeup.

I made it through the rest of the day on auto-pilot. I knew I shouldn't let Chance's actions affect me so much, but it had been a long, rough week.

I was home by eleven and slept fitfully all night long.

I woke up the next day with a feeling of determination. I'd be damned if I was going to let a guy – even an incredible guy like Chance – ruin a time in my life when I should be fairly euphoric. I loved my job and the people I worked with every day. I had great friends whom I would do anything for and knew that I could count on them wholeheartedly as well. We had just solved a decades-long art mystery and recovered some rather valuable artwork. Amelia and I could have been killed! All is good. No. All is great!

I went into town for coffee before going to work. Usually, I would stop at Sunny's for some of her freshly-roasted coffee and a *pain au chocolat*. Not today. Today, I was going to take charge of my personal life. I had already called the therapist that Syd had recommended and made an appointment for the next day. I had come around to agreeing that I did need some help coping with all the trauma I had experienced in the past year – from being attacked by the meth addict to being forced into early retirement due to disability, to everything that happened at the reunion. Let's face it, I thought ruefully. I still hadn't even dealt with the death of my mother. She hadn't been a great mother, but she was my mother and there were still feelings of loss.

So, as part of my new-found desire to move forward with my life and take responsibility for my decisions and actions, I was going to speak with Chance. No more of this hemming and hawing and kissing... Well, maybe more kissing. That kiss had been kind of incredible.

I walked into Two Cups with more courage than I was feeling. Fortunately, I had chosen a moment when there was a lull in the morning rush. The benefits of working at a vineyard meant that my day didn't usually start until ten o'clock or later, well after most people had started their days.

Chance looked up as I walked in and we locked eyes. He watched me as I approached the counter and gestured to Hope, his sister, that he would wait on me. "Hey, Kat," he said softly. "What can I get you today?"

I tamped down the sudden anger that blossomed in my chest. "I'd like a large hazelnut coffee with cream, no sugar, please."

He smiled weakly. "Sure." He turned to start prepping my coffee.

I continued, "And a few minutes of your time, if you don't mind."

He jerked involuntarily and then his shoulders sagged. He looked around the coffee shop but there was only me and one other customer, so he couldn't say he was too busy. He nodded and repeated, "Sure." He sighed. "Why don't you have a seat and I'll bring your coffee over."

I nodded and sat at a table far enough away for privacy from the other customer. He brought me a coffee and a coffee roll and brought a glass of orange juice for himself. He lowered himself slowly into the chair opposite me. "What's up, Kat?" He tried to sound upbeat but I could tell that it was an effort.

I stared at him for a few seconds. "Seriously? What the hell, Chance. We're both too old to play games. We've been playing this flirty friend game since the reunion. I finally thought we got past that when you," I paused and took a deep breath, "kissed me at your opening…"

"You kissed me, too, Kat." He interjected quickly.

"Yes, yes, I did. I thought that meant something. I thought that meant we would be moving forward. We even talked about things at the hospital." I looked at him in confusion. "I don't understand your behavior yesterday at the vineyard. I thought we had sorted stuff out…?"

He made no response. Just stared into his orange juice.

"Chance," I continued, "I just need…" I searched for the right words, "I need to know where I stand with you." I threw my hands up in agitation, but that hurt my aching body a little and I winced.

Chance sighed. "You're right, Kat." He took a moment to compose himself. "I'm sorry that I've been so...that I've sent some, a lot, of mixed signals."

"That's a good start," I said hotly.

He grinned and lit up my world and then it faded quickly. "This is going to sound lame, Kat, and I want to apologize for that in advance." My heart began sinking fast. "It really is just a matter of timing." He scrubbed his face with his hands and let out an agitated moan. "This is so hard to say!"

"It's not easy to hear either," I quipped. Humor was always my strongest defense.

He searched my eyes. "There's just so much going on right now, Kat. The business isn't even a week old and I'm a lot more overwhelmed than I thought I would be. Who knew that a career as a lawyer didn't really prepare me to run a coffee and wine bar?" he muttered with a shrug. "I don't want to fail my sister or myself or any of the staff." He looked around appraisingly. "I'm proud of what we turned this place into." He looked embarrassed. "I'm sorry. I know it was your mother's bar, but it was not in good shape."

I held up my hands. "No worries, on that count at least. I know it was a dump and I think you and your sister did an incredible job. This place is a hundred times better than when it was my mother's bar."

"I could be a little more sensitive, though," he explained. He let out a big sigh. "It's not just me being overwhelmed though. I'm also feeling a bit lost now that I'm not practicing law. I'm sure you can understand that feeling."

I skewered him with a piercing stare. "I was forced to retire on disability because a meth addict stabbed me ten times, taking away my livelihood. You chose to leave the practice of law and open a restaurant. Not exactly comparable."

He at least had the grace to look abashed. "You're right. The two instances are not the same, but they are both transitions and very confusing. We both spent a lot of time building our careers and then to no longer do it. It's just weird. I think you can agree with that?" he asked hopefully.

I nodded in agreement, afraid of what might pop out if I opened my mouth.

"You have a lot going on in your life, too. Your new career and a lot of friends and, well, a boss who doesn't understand boundaries…" He held up his hands. "Sorry, again. I never realized how jealous I was of Marco and that's my issue." He shook his head. "It's just not a good time, Kat, for either of us. Maybe in a few months…"

"A few months…" I echoed, my heart breaking into about a million pieces. I knew what that meant. Soon, I'd see him around town with one of those glittery young women from his opening on his arm.

He apparently thought I was agreeing with him. "Yes, a few months. I'll be more settled in a routine with this place and you'll be more settled in your career, too. I'm sure I'll be ready to start dating by then."

I pushed my chair back abruptly and stood up. "Fine," I muttered through gritted teeth. "I'll see you in a few months." I turned and started striding quickly toward the door. I had to get out of there before I gave into my tears.

He caught up with me before I reached the front door and grabbed my arm. "Kat, I still want to be friends." I cringed. "I don't want that to end. I just don't have the fortitude to start a new relationship with all the other pressures right now." His voice was plaintive and I could hear that he was emotional, too. I couldn't look at him though. He couldn't see the tears that threatened to spill from my eyes. I will not cry in front of Chance Wolf. I will not cry *over* Chance Wolf, I repeated to myself in a trance-like mantra.

"Fine, we're friends," I grumbled. "See you around." I pushed open the door and walked down the block to my car. I may have heard him call my name, or it may have been my wishful thinking.

Chapter Forty-Three

It's not easy to be both brave and indignant when you are upset, but I think I pulled it off alright as I walked down the street. Things were a bit different though when I got to my car. My whole body began shaking and the tears that had threatened a few minutes ago began cascading from my eyes. I swiped angrily at them, smearing all of Ricky's carefully-placed makeup.

"Damn him!" I screamed in a primal rage inside my car. The sound must have traveled, even with the windows rolled up. I guess cars are not soundproof. People on the sidewalk looked at me with concern. I waved an "I'm okay" gesture and started the car, swiping angrily at my eyes once again.

I drove straight to Syd's gallery. I knew she was closed today and would be painting in the back. I pulled into her small parking lot at the back of the building and noticed Ricky's car was parked there too. I banged at the door and realized I was still shaking with anger, hurt, mortification, and, if I had to be honest with myself, a bit of abandonment.

Ricky opened the door in full-on drag, took one look at me, and enveloped me in a bear hug. After that long, and much-needed, hug, Ricky grabbed my hand and pulled me back to Syd's studio. Syd yelled down the hall on her way back from the kitchen, "What's with all that racket?" She came into the room and stopped abruptly when she saw me. She crossed the room and also hugged me tightly.

Syd waved her hand at Ricky in a gesture that could only mean "get some wine" and he stalked out of there in his four-inch stilettos. Even in my enraged mind, I registered that Ricky was walking around in drag on a Wednesday morning. He usually saved that for Friday nights and a cute little bar called Heaven.

We sat around and drank wine. I told them everything about Chance. They were righteously angry on my behalf and vowed to shun him. I loved having best friends.

Ricky then shared his story. After the harvest, Ricky had rested up and went out later that night. He had called Vlad in a moment of loneliness and was supposed to meet him at Heaven. When he got to the bar, Vlad was with a bodybuilder named Bruce. Apparently, the two were making out like there was no tomorrow. When Vlad finally came up for air, he saw Ricky across the bar. He strolled over to Ricky and said, "I hope you're not upset. I'm just not that into Asian guys."

Ricky was indignant. "Like he was everything I wanted in a guy. Not! There's no need to be insulting though."

Syd and I agreed with him and we poured more wine. Fortunately, I had had the foresight to call Marco and beg off work for the day. Sometimes, a head wound could be beneficial. Almost never, but I would take advantage just this once.

I was sure I shouldn't be drinking with the painkillers and I certainly shouldn't be driving. Within a few hours, I was mostly incoherent. Ty had stopped by to pick up Syd. He looked at the three of us, mostly intoxicated and inarticulate, and shepherded us into his car. I'm sure I rambled on about what a great guy he was and how

284

lucky Syd was to have him, but I'm not sure he understood my incoherent testament to him.

Way too early the next morning, I opened my front door to Ricky. I was glad he looked as bad as I felt, though I know I looked worse. I had chanced a look in the mirror this morning when I was brushing my teeth.

The bruises on my face had taken on a greenish color hue and the abrasions on my head both itched and throbbed. Some of the throbbing was probably due to the copious amount of alcohol I had consumed the day before. Ricky winced when he saw me. "Ouch," is all he said.

We stumbled through my getting ready. I had decided to just pull my hair into a ponytail. I could cover the stitches with a hat. As we prepared to walk out the door, my phone rang. It was Syd.

I answered the call and put her on speakerphone. "Go for Kat and Ricky," I grumbled. I needed more coffee and a huge cinnamon roll. Fortunately, Sunny's shop had both of those things.

"I'm glad I got you both together," Syd gushed. "Oh my God, you're never going to believe this!" she cried.

"Slow down, Syd, and lower your voice a decibel please," I scowled as her voice pierced my skull. "What's up?"

Syd was practically hyperventilating on the other end. "Hold on, let me get Amelia on the line, too." There was some fumbling and a few clicks and then I heard Syd's voice again. "Okay, are you all sitting down?"

Even Ricky had grown impatient at this point. "Spit it out, Syd. We need to get to work." This was kind of funny as Ricky owned the company and Marco was remarkably tolerant of my tardiness.

"Okay, never mind. I won't tell you about how I just got off the phone with the people from the Isabella Stewart Gardner Museum. Or that they told me that the four of us are entitled to the reward for the missing artwork."

"That's great," I heard Amelia say.

"Yeah, cool," said Ricky.

"Great? Cool? You guys are more than a little underwhelmed," she huffed in indignation.

"Perhaps we would be more whelmed," I looked at Ricky as if to ask him if that was a word, "if we knew how much the reward was," I said, trying to sound reasonable and not grumpy and hungover.

"Oh, right," Syd giggled. "Ten million dollars."

The silence on the phone was deafening.

"Hello?" Syd called. "Are you guys still there?"

Ricky and I had nearly collapsed onto my sofa after her revelation. I can only surmise that Amelia did the same.

"That is a terrible joke to play on us, Syd," Amelia said finally.

"It's not a joke, Amelia. The reward is being offered by the museum. They wanted to verify with me who deserves a share."

Ricky was sitting next to me with his mouth hanging open. I reached over and popped it closed which brought him to his senses. He was already fairly wealthy because of his video game business, but who wouldn't be excited about a large reward?

"Okay, then," Amelia was trying to sound reasonable. "I-I...I don't know what to say."

Syd laughed. "Don't say anything yet. Especially not to anyone else. Let's meet up this evening though and talk some things out."

"Sounds great," I finally found my voice.

"Do you think you'll be ready for wine by then?" Syd teased.

Ricky and I looked at each other, the color returning to our faces.

"Absolutely!" we both sang out.

Epilogue

I don't remember what happened at work that day or what I actually did. I do remember a feeling of euphoria and hope. I met with the psychiatrist and that turned out to be another good thing for me. She didn't think I was broken but did agree that I had gone through a lot of stress and hardship over the past year. She thought she could help me cope a little better and I think that I tended to agree with her.

That night, Amelia, Syd, Ricky, and I met up and discussed what our options were and what we each might do with the money. Nobody made any firm decisions that night, but I was confident that this next phase would be wonderful as long as I could face it with my friends.

Check back with Kat and her friends in the next book to find out how they each spend their share of the reward money.

Wines featured in this book:

- 50 by 50 of Carneros Rosé of Pinot Noir

- 50 by 50 brand Sonoma Coast Pinot Noir

- Bodega Norton Reserve Cabernet Sauvignon, Argentina

- Baron Philippe de Rothschild Escudo Rojo Cabernet Sauvignon, Chile

- Rust en Vrede Stellenbosch Cabernet Sauvignon, South Africa

- Marques de Grinon Dominio de Valdepusa Cabernet Sauvignon, Spain

- Vina Robles Estate Cabernet Sauvignon, New Zealand

About the Author:

Thank you for reading *Vineyards Can Be Murder*. Please join Kat and all her friends in the next installment of *The Wine Tasting Mystery Series*, due in Autumn 2021.

Tammy Wunsch currently resides in the Quiet Corner of Connecticut though she has also called both New York City and Los Angeles home. Formally educated in business, she has worked in a variety of industries and is both entrepreneurial and adventurous by nature. She is passionate about animals and loves to travel, cook, kayak, and read.

Where can you see everything that Tammy writes?

1. Download a **FREE** copy of *The Holidays in Harmony*, at TammyWunsch.com and peruse her author library and portfolio.

2. Visit HowDoIMoveTo.com for a series of podcasts, YouTube videos and country guides where Tammy discusses the factors that retirees, future expatriates, and digital nomads need to consider before moving abroad.

3. Stay in touch. I love to read comments, suggestions, and don't forget to leave a review!

Made in the USA
Las Vegas, NV
06 September 2021

29734076R00173